Praise for *Where All Light Tends to Go*

"Joy's debut is about hope as much as it is fate . . . [it] is harrowing. Joy's voice is authentic, his prose sparse, his eye for detail minute. Everything works in this novel to push the reader closer and closer to the cliff's edge, hoping against hope that what won't be required is to jump off." —*Mountain Times*

"Joy works with the materials many call the stuff of 'country noir.' The result calls to mind the work of powerful writers such as Ron Rash, Daniel Woodrell, Mark Powell, and Cormac McCarthy. . . . Joy has crafted a piece of masterful fiction. His sense of pace, his ability to catch the reader off guard with explosive and often upsetting incidents, his way with the shape of a chapter—all herald a major young writer." —*Still: The Journal*

"[A] story written in lyrical prose with an eye to critical detail and minute descriptions of people and place."

—Champaign *News-Gazette*

"Readers of Southern grit lit in the tradition of Daniel Woodrell and Harry Crews will enjoy this fast-paced début thriller. Fans of Ron Rash's novels will appreciate the intricate plot and Joy's establishment of a strong sense of place in his depiction of rural Appalachia." —*Library Journal* (starred review)

"A perceptive look at rural young love in a dead-end town, embedded in an account of a brutal family crime business . . . while the prose does often touch on lyricism, the writing and plot remain fairly direct, with the forward motion of a good three-act thriller."

—*National Post* (Canada)

Where All Light Tends to Go

Also by David Joy

NONFICTION

Growing Gills: A Fly Fisherman's Journey

Where All Light Tends to Go

DAVID JOY

G. P. PUTNAM'S SONS | *New York*

PUTNAM

G. P. PUTNAM'S SONS
Publishers Since 1838
An imprint of Penguin Random House LLC
375 Hudson Street
New York, New York 10014

Copyright © 2015 by David Joy

The Library of Congress has catalogued the G. P. Putnam's Sons hardcover edition as follows:

Joy, David, date.
Where all light tends to go / David Joy.
p.   cm.
ISBN 978-0-399-17277-9
1. Fathers and sons—Fiction.   2. Drug dealers—Fiction.   3. North Carolina—Fiction.
4. Appalachian Mountains—Fiction.   I. Title.
PS3610.O947W54   2015   2014023349
813'.6—dc23

First G. P. Putnam's Sons hardcover edition / March 2015
First G. P. Putnam's Sons trade paperback edition / February 2016
G. P. Putnam's Sons trade paperback ISBN: 978-0-425-27979-3

Printed in the United States of America
1   3   5   7   9   10   8   6   4   2

BOOK DESIGN BY NICOLE LAROCHE

For those with whom I share my morning coffee:
Rudy, Cecil, and Clyde

Only now is the child finally divested of all that he has been. His origins are become remote as is his destiny and not again in all the world's turning will there be terrains so wild and barbarous to try whether the stuff of creation may be shaped to man's will or whether his own heart is not another kind of clay.

—CORMAC MCCARTHY, *Blood Meridian*

Where All Light Tends to Go

1.

I hid the pickup behind a tangled row of pampas grass that had
needed burning a good year or so before. The law never liked
for folks to climb the water tower, but I hadn't ever cared much
for the law. I was a McNeely and, in this part of Appalachia, that
meant something. Outlawing was just as much a matter of blood
as hair color and height. Besides, the water tower was the best
place to see graduation caps thrown high when seniors wearing
black robes and tearful smiles headed out of Walter Middleton
School one last time.

Rungs once painted white were chipped and rusted and slumped
in the middle from years of being climbed by wide-eyed kids looking to paint their names on the town. Those things that seemed

as if they'd last forever never did. I didn't even make it out of tenth grade, and maybe that's why I hadn't felt the need to scale that tower with britches weighed down by spray-paint cans. There was no need to cement my name. A name like Jacob McNeely raised eyebrows and questions. In a town this small, all eyes were prying eyes. I couldn't show my face, didn't want the problems and rumors that being down there would bring, but I had to see her leave.

The grate platform circling the water tank had lost all but a few screws and curled up at the edges like a twice-read book. Every step I took shifted metal, but it was a place I'd stood before, a place I'd navigated on every drug I'd ever taken. With only a buzz from my morning smoke lingering, there wasn't need for worries. I sat beneath green letters dripping a nearly illegible "FUCK U" across the front side of the tank, pulled a soft pack of Winstons from the pocket of my jeans, lit the last cigarette I had, and waited.

The school I'd spent the majority of my life in seemed smaller now, though looking back it had never been big enough. I grew up twenty miles south of Sylva, a town that really wasn't much of a town at all but the closest thing to one in Jackson County. If you were passing through, you'd miss Sylva if you blinked, and the place where I was from you could overlook with your eyes peeled. Being a small, mountain community that far away, we only had one school. So that meant that kids who grew up in this county would walk into Walter Middleton at five years old and wouldn't leave until graduation thirteen years down the road. Growing up in it, I never found it strange to share the halls with teens when I was a kid and kids when I was a teen, but looking down on it now, two years after leaving for good, the whole thing was alien.

The white dome roofing the gym looked like a bad egg bobbing in boiling water, the courtyard was lined in uneven passes from a lawnmower, and a painting of the school mascot, centered in the parking lot, looked more like a chupacabra than any bobcat I'd ever seen. To be honest, there wasn't too much worth remembering from my time there, but still it had accounted for ten of my eighteen years. Surprisingly, though, that wasn't disappointing. What was disappointing about that school, my life, and this whole fucking place was that I'd let it beat me. I'd let what I was born into control what I'd become. Mama snorted crystal, Daddy sold it to her, and I'd never had the balls to leave. That was my life in a nutshell. I took a drag from my last cigarette and hocked a thick wad of spit over the railing.

I was watching a wake of buzzards whirl down behind a mountain when the side door cracked against the gymnasium brick. One kid tore out in front of the crowd, and even before he jumped onto the hood of his car, I knew him. Blane Cowen was the type to drink a beer and scream wasted. I'd tested him once back in middle school, brought him up here on the water tower to smoke a joint, and when his legs got wobbly and vertigo set in he decided awfully fast he didn't want to play friends anymore. In a school filled with kids who swiped prescription drugs from their parents' medicine cabinets, Blane was the village idiot. But despite all that, I kind of felt sorry for the bastard, standing there, arms raised in the air as he dented in the hood of a beat-up Civic, no one in his class paying him a lick of attention while he howled.

The parking lot that had seemed so desolate just a minute before was crawling now as friends hugged, told promises they'd never be able to keep, and ran off to parents who had no clue of who their children had become. I knew it because I'd grown up with them, all of them, and all of us knew things about one

another that we'd never share. Most of us knew things that we
didn't even want to confess to ourselves, so we took those secrets
with us like condoms, stuffed in wallets, that would never be
used. I wanted to be down there with them, if not as a classmate,
then at least as a friend, but none of them needed my baggage.

Not until she took off her cap did I recognize her in the crowd.
Maggie Jennings stood there and pulled her hair out of a bun,
shook blond curls down across her shoulders, and kicked high
heels from her feet. The front of her graduation gown was un-
zipped, and a white sundress held tight to her body. I could almost
make out her laugh in the clamor as her boyfriend, Avery Hooper,
picked her up from behind and spun her around wildly. Maggie's
mother hunched with her hands covering her face as if to conceal
tears, and Maggie's father put his arm around his wife's waist and
drew her close. A person who didn't know any better would have
thought them the perfect American family. Live the lie and they'll
believe the lie, but I knew different.

I'd known Maggie my whole life. The house she grew up in
was two beats of a wing as the crow flies from my front porch, so
there hadn't been many days of my childhood spent without her
by my side. About the first memory I can recall is being five or six
with pants rolled up, the two of us digging in the creek for spring
lizards. We were tighter than a burl, as Daddy'd say. In a way, I
guess, Maggie and me raised each other.

Back before her father *found Jesus*, he'd run off on a two- or
three-week drunk with no one seeing hide nor hair of him till it
was over. Her mother worked two jobs to keep food on the table,
but that meant there wasn't a soul watching when Maggie and I'd
head into the woods, me talking her into all sorts of shit that most
kids wouldn't have dreamed. I guess we were twelve or so when

her father got *saved* and moved the family off The Creek. Folks said he poured enough white liquor in the West Fork of the Tuckasegee to slosh every speckled trout from Nimblewill to Fontana, but I never figured him much for saving. A drunk's a drunk just like an addict's an addict, and there ain't a God you can pray to who can change a damn bit of it.

But Maggie was different. Even early on I remember being amazed by her. She'd always been something slippery that I never could seem to grasp, something buried deep in her that never let anything outside of herself decide what she would become. I'd always loved that about her. I'd always loved her.

We were in middle school when the tomboy I grew up with started filling out. Having been best friends, when I asked Maggie out in eighth grade, it seemed like that shit they write in movies. We were together for three years, a lifetime it had felt like. What meant the most to me was that Maggie knew where I'd come from, knew what I was being groomed into, and still believed I could make it out. I'd thought my life was chosen, that I didn't really have a say in the matter, but Maggie dreamed for me. She told me I could be anything I wanted, go any place that looked worth going, and there were times I almost believed her. Folks like me were tied to this place, but Maggie held no restraints. She was out of here from the moment she set her eyes on the distance. If I ever did have a dream, it was that she might take me with her. But dreams were silly for folks like me. There always comes a time when you have to wake up.

I was proud that she was headed to a place I could never go, and I pulled my cell phone out of my pocket to text her, "Congrats."

When Avery let go, Maggie jumped into her father's arms, bent her legs behind her with bare feet pointed into the sky. Her father buried his head into his daughter's hair, pretended for a split second that he'd had something to do with how she turned out, then placed her on the ground for her mother to kiss. Maggie stood there for a moment, rocked back and forth before she turned away. She glanced behind her to say something as she ran off to Avery's truck, but her parents had said their good-byes. In a way, I think they knew she was already gone. They knew it just as much as I did. A girl like that couldn't stay. Not forever, and certainly not for long.

2.

Jack pines crowded the property in all but a tiny sliver carved out a long time ago to make room for a house. The old pine plank cabin Mama lived in had always sat at an angle just right enough to hold off folding in a strong wind. The house was truly unfit for any sort of long-term living, but she'd been there most of my life. Boards once pitched dark had lightened with years and rotted with rainwater that held this place damp year-round. Transparent plastic I'd put over the windows to keep her from freezing a few winters back hung loose and torn from the frames, the plastic now opaque and dotted with mildew.

I wasn't old enough to remember the day Daddy sent her there. The way he told it, she was stealing crank and spent most of her time climbing around the peter tree. So he sent her to this place. Loved her too much to give her nothing, but giving her anything at all squared things so he'd never have to love her again.

I don't recall going over there much when I was a kid. I don't remember seeing her but once or twice a year when those I'm-going-to-set-this-right moods hit her. It was always just me and Daddy, but I was older now, old enough to take the good and the bad for what it was worth and never any more. Besides, I just needed a place to kill a few hours and a safe spot to dodge the law while I got stoned.

The front screen door was propped open with a tin bucket half filled with blackened sand and smashed-out cigarette butts, and I could see straight through the house. I heard her before I saw her: yelling profanities, breathing heavy, snorting and sniffing. From the sounds of her, a line of dope had just lit her afire, and, while it may have seemed wild to anyone on the outside, I knew I was lucky to catch her at the beginning rather than the end.

She rammed her shoulder hard against the doorway into the kitchen as I came into the house. Her eyes wide, she seemed to look right through me. Her jaw racked and her teeth chomped on some imaginary thing she could never get chewed enough to swallow. When her eyes pulled back and settled onto me, she went to scratching her arms. "Where the hell did you come from?" She meant that question wholeheartedly, as if maybe I'd just man-ifested out of an Appalachian summer.

"Just pulled up. Needed a place to hide out for a bit."

"Well, you're just in time."

"Just in time for what?"

"Just in time to help me find that goddamn lightbulb." Her

head yanked to the side, and she scurried into the back of the house, but I didn't follow.

I plopped down on a ratty couch within falling distance from the front door, foam pushing through tears in the cushions. I reached into my pocket and took out what was left of a sack of weed, just shake now, but still enough to roll a pin. There was a half-empty pack of JOB rolling papers propped against a tarnished brass lamp on the side table. I pulled a paper from the sleeve, creased a fold in the 1.5, and dumped in buds that had been ground to powder. I was already twisting it tight and licking it sealed when Mama stumbled back into the front room.

"Jacob! Jacob, you not going to help me look?"

"Look for what?"

"The goddamn lightbulb, I done told you I need the goddamn lightbulb."

I lounged back on the couch, struck a lighter to the end of the joint, pulled hard, and offered it toward her for a drag.

"Have you lost your ever-fucking mind, Jacob? You know I don't smoke that shit and you can't smoke it in here, you got to go outside if you're going to be smoking that shit 'cause the last thing I need is the goddamn law."

My mother was the definition of rode hard and put up wet. Her eyes were bulbous, her face sunken in, just a thin layer of skin stretched tight over bones. Hair that was thick and brown in old pictures strung greasy down her neck now. She was nothing like those pictures anymore, though she was exactly how I'd always remembered. She was absolutely pitiful. Before I could even respond, she was off again hunting that lightbulb, and I just loafed there and toked till a run crept down the seam of the joint.

Licking a little spit onto the tip of my finger, I dabbed the fire, kept it burning even, and hit it again.

I slid my cell phone out of my pocket and checked to see if Maggie had written me back. She hadn't. I knew she'd respond eventually because she always did, just never right away. Maggie hadn't cut me out entirely, but there seemed to be few words left between us, or words too heavy for either of us to say. She loved me too much to let me go and I loved her too much to drag her down. That type of love doesn't work. I recognized it before she did, I guess, so instead of hurting her for a lifetime, I broke her heart right then and there, and now she was gone. Probably in another world, I thought, and leaned back into the couch smoking on that joint to find a universe of my own.

I could hear Mama in the back cussing, drawers being ripped off rails and slamming against the floor, and only when there was nothing else to throw did she return. "Jacob, what the fuck did you do with that goddamn lightbulb?"

I laughed and coughed and spit on words that couldn't make it out of my mouth quick enough to stop me from choking. "I didn't do anything with a lightbulb." She had me gassed, but there was always uneasiness in laughing at my mother. Even while I was laughing, there was an uncomfortable feeling that settled in the pit of my stomach. She'd given birth to me. She was blood. Those types of things are deserving of love, and I did love her. Since I was a kid, I'd carried those few moments when she came around sober like treasure. I'd always hoped she'd become a real mother. But with time, I realized that someone can't give what they don't have. She was what she was, an addict, and there was nothing that could be said or done to change her. Death was her only savior.

Staring intensely, her eyelids seeming to roll back even further on eyes the size of taw marbles, she swept her hair back against her neck, trotted over to the couch, and cannonballed down beside me. "Give me a hit off that shit."

"You didn't even want me to smoke inside, and now you want to hit it?" I leaned away from her and took a few quick drags off the roach that was already burning my fingertips.

Her jaw still racked like she was trying to saw logs with dull teeth, and that serious look never left her face. "What the fuck do you mean, I didn't want you smoking inside?"

"That's what you said. You just told me I had to smoke outside."

"I didn't ever say that shit." She scooted closer. "Give it here."

I bent forward, rested my elbows on my knees, and held the roach out to her. Mama picked it from my fingers like some cranked-out chimp culling fleas, and I stood up from the couch to let her lay with it. She sucked back on what little bit of paper was left to burn, and all of a sudden that son of a bitch shot into her throat, and she went to choking till I was sure her eyeballs were going to pop out of her head. I couldn't stop laughing and fell into the doorframe on my way to the bathroom while she coughed and gagged and tried her damnedest to curse me without enough air to start a blow-and-go.

There were tears streaming from my eyes by the time I made it in front of the bathroom mirror. I pulled a bottle of eyedrops out of my pocket, tilted my head back, squeezed a bead into each eye, and stared at my reflection. Seeing a smile spread across my face lumped that uneasy feeling into my throat. I shouldn't have found how bad-off she was funny, but with a lifetime of disappointment, it was the only way to handle it. Smiles outweighed tears. Laughter outweighed pain.

I turned on the faucet and wiped a palm full of water across my

face. Daddy needed to see me in an hour, and he never liked han-
dling business when I was stoned. My green eyes began to clear,
and I brushed my thick brown hair with my wet hand. Daddy
never cared that I smoked. He didn't care that I popped pills. He
drank and smoked and was known to eat a few painkillers when
the mood hit him. The only drug off-limits was crank, and seeing
what it'd done to my own mother, I'd never wanted anything to
do with it anyways. But the line of work my father ran demanded
a clear head, so I had to appear collected.

When I headed into the main room, Mama was in the kitchen,
one foot standing in the seat of a dining room chair, the other foot
propped up onto the back. She leaned out over the table to get her
hands on the lightbulb, her head constantly shaking hair away as
she twisted the bulb free. Her shirt lifted up and her belly hung
out: loose skin, no meat, and stretch marks still visible after all
these years from where she'd carried me. Just when I was about to
speak, the chair rocked and she slapped down out of the air onto
the floor. Her head smacked the laminate tile hard, but it didn't
faze her. She popped up to her knees and scanned the room, her
jaw still chewing, and I didn't say a word. I left her there on the
floor like a bad joke, a bad joke that's really not funny at all, but
that a man is forced to chuckle through until the awkwardness
fades.

3.

The Walkers belted out long, jowl-stiffening howls as I pulled up the drive. It had never seemed to matter much that I'd been the one to fill their feed bowls each morning. Those dogs still snarled and bit at the tires every time I drove up to the house. Everyone in the country knew Daddy had the meanest line of hounds to ever run bear or hog in these parts. He'd had offers from far-off places like Maine and Wisconsin to have his hounds stud, but that never interested him.

Dogs were tied strategically across the property so that anyone making their way onto McNeely land would have to know a dance consisting of precisely thirty-four two-steps, fourteen ball changes, and a chassé to get anywhere near the door without being mauled. In the old days, Daddy used it as a tactic to ensure that only the customers in the know ever made it up to the window for late-night sales. Nothing ever really moved through the house anymore, and hadn't in years. The business was too big for that nowadays, but I guess he kept the hounds out of habit more than anything.

I'd been around crank my whole life, so it had never been a drug, only money. When I was young, Daddy would put it to me like we were carrying on a family tradition, a matter of course that started with moonshine runs in chopped cars to make enough bread to survive the winter. It didn't seem so bad when he put it like that. Outlawing was just a way of earning a buck. By the time I was nine or ten, Daddy had me helping him break down big bags of crystal into grams, never anything smaller, and I got a cut just like most kids got allowance. That's what he told me anyways, though he kept the money for "safekeeping," and merely upped the number in a little notebook for the day I'd cash out. Birthdays brought on new responsibilities, and by the time I'd hit tenth grade, I was staying up half the night working for him. I went to school to keep child services off his back, but slept through every hour right up until the day I turned sixteen, walked out of Walter Middleton, and never looked back.

From the porch, I could hear Conway Twitty's "I'd Love to Lay You Down" and the drone of some mechanical buzzing that sounded like a bug zapper. I walked into the house, and a cloud of cigarette smoke hung in the room around my waist. Daddy was bent over a folding chair with his back exposed and some long-haired Hispanic man was digging into Daddy's skin with a tattoo gun. Neither of them looked up. The only one who did was a skinny blonde Daddy had been seeing, who glanced me over before focusing back on the tattoo.

I didn't speak but walked over to the coffee table and grabbed someone's pack of Winstons. I flipped a cigarette into my lips and fell back onto the sofa beside the blonde. From where I sat, I could see that the Hispanic was halfway through spelling out that skinny blonde's name in cursive between Daddy's shoulder blades. He was covered in tattoos for the most part, and in the patchwork of my father, nearly all of them had started off as a woman's name at one point or another, only to be covered by something more permanent down the road.

"What in the fuck are you putting her name on your back for?" I leaned into the sofa and lit the cigarette with my eyes still stoned and half closed.

"Shut the fuck up, Jacob!" Josephine hollered, but none of the others even looked up.

The tattoo gun shut off, the Hispanic man patted my father on the shoulder, and Daddy straightened up and reached for his cigarettes. The Hispanic had snubbed her name short at Jose, and I started to laugh, the joint from earlier still heightening humor. "Who the hell is José?"

"It says Josie, dipshit, that's your daddy's nickname for me, but what do you know? Ain't like you can spell. You never even finished school."

Daddy cut eyes at her to shut her mouth, and she knew to shut it fast. It was a mouth he'd paid for after all, so I reckon it gave him that right. Her teeth were damn near rotted out the first time she came around, but Daddy said he saw something in her, put fifteen thousand dollars' worth of work into those gums just to have her smiling with teeth like corn pearls.

"From over here that looks like J-O-S-E, and far as I know, that spells José." I glanced at the Hispanic and his stare widened. Part of him looked like he was about to laugh, but then there was this fear I could see way back in him like he just might piss himself.

"J-O-S-E?" Daddy turned around to look the Hispanic man square. That fear I'd seen suddenly shot up to the front of the Hispanic man's eyes.

"Son of a bitch, that dumb fucking spic left out the *i*," Josephine squealed. She was boiling now, her face getting flushed as she stood up with legs that ran from ankles to heaven in short shorts, and a tank top that she was all but pouring out of. For a split second, I thought I saw what Daddy had seen in her, but then she opened that mouth again. "Charlie, you better not let him do this to me! You better not let some spic ruin what we have."

The Hispanic man watched her with eyes spread, and I knew if I handed him a knife at that moment, he'd stab that old loudmouth bitch till there wasn't any sound left to be made but gurgling.

Daddy stayed calm like he always did, and there was something a bit more frightening about a man that could stay at ease while doing the sorts of things he was known to do. He never raised his voice and never raised his hand, just turned to the Hispanic man and asked him if he could fix it.

"Hell no, he can't fix it!" Josephine squealed. She started to open her mouth again, but Daddy duct-taped her lips closed with nothing more than a glance.

"The two of y'all just get the fuck outside, so I can have a talk with Jacob." Daddy rose and carefully rolled his T-shirt down over his back. "You're going to fix this when I'm done talking to the boy."

The Hispanic man stood first, laying the tattoo gun down on a side table before sidling toward the door. Josephine, on the other hand, stuck around for a minute, rose and hung around my father's neck like a yanked-loose necktie with corn pearl teeth strung at the knot. She kissed him on his neck, and he paid her little mind. Josephine strutted toward the door and glared at me as if I was responsible for the misspelling of her name. I smirked, and it ate her up.

Daddy walked over to the record player—even now in 2009 "nothing sounded as good as vinyl"—and cranked the knob on the speaker dial till Twitty filled the room. He always turned the music loud when it was time to talk business so as no one outside of the conversation could catch a word without ears pressed close to our lips. He dragged the folding chair in front of me and straddled the chair backward.

Even to me Daddy had that look about him like he'd seen and done things that glazed over any bit of light that had ever been in his eyes. All that was left was what folks from war called that "thousand-yard stare," and though he was my father and hadn't ever done me wrong in any sort of way deserving of my cower, I was always a little fearful when he spoke.

He lit a fresh cigarette with the one still burning and leaned close so that I was certain to hear him. Dark hair was slicked and parted across his brow, and divots from teenage acne freckled the flanks of his face. His nose had a bit of a crooked hook to it, but it was the acne scars that drew a man's eyes, the way his face seemed pitted. "You're going to go to the camp tonight." Afternoon beers swerved along his words. "You're going to make sure it happens just like I need it to happen."

I knew what he was talking about, so I just nodded. I reckon in the old days when Daddy first started the business, he didn't have any choice but to dirty his own hands, but that time had long since passed. The story had started when he made some small-time connection with a mid-level crystal dealer from somewhere over in Tennessee, back when it was one-percenters responsible for most of the trade. Back then they'd run an ounce or two across state lines in the crankcases of their motorcycles. For a long time Daddy stayed pretty low on the ladder, but connections came about and he latched on. Now he no longer touched anything that came or left Jackson County. He just directed traffic with low-spoken conversations in music-filled rooms. Methamphetamine was a living, breathing body in Appalachia. The dope came from Mexico, but Daddy was the heart of the body here, pumping the blood through every vein in the region. Though it all started here, by the time that crystal made it into the hands of local crankers, it had been passed all over the mountains a dozen or more times to lap back.

What this problem boiled down to, though, was the way that Daddy handled the money. Once it went from being just enough to get by on to big money, he'd had to come up with a way to make all those dollars look legal to prying eyes. That's how he came up with the idea for McNeely's Auto Repair. In a tight-knit scheme where every service offered cost four or five times that of any normal mechanic, Daddy laundered the money into something legal. Every dollar that came back to him had a receipt. Everyone who brought in a car to be serviced was on the payroll, and the majority of cars being worked on had been purchased at one time or another by my father. They paid him in his own money.

When legitimate folks brought in a car, they left outraged at

estimates. When some rookie deputy got the gall to try and figure out what was going on, he got the same price gouge as anyone else. A few of those deputies even forked it over to try and get
close, but nothing ever came of it. Some of those bulls were on
the payroll too, and the folks on the payroll were tight-lipped.
They just brought in the cars and paid to have them serviced, and
in return Daddy kept food on their tables when winters killed
everything from field grass to dreams. The one thing he'd never
done was allowed anyone cranked-out to get near the business.
That was up until now, and now that one person was threatening
it all.

"You understand what I'm asking, Jacob?"

I nodded.

"This ain't something you can just nod about, goddamn it. I
need to hear you fucking tell me that you understand what I need
done."

"You want me to head out to the camp with the boys and take
care of Ro—"

Daddy slapped me hard against the side of the head. "Don't say
his fucking name! Don't you ever say his fucking name! You don't
know his name, you understand?"

"I understand."

"Good."

That was all that was said about it and that's the way it had
always been. Daddy only said enough to ensure that what needed
to be done got done, because any added details might lead to confusion. There was no room for confusion in a business like this.

Daddy hoisted himself from the chair and wandered to the front
door. He opened the door, stretched his arms wide, and yawned
as he headed onto the porch. The Walkers were still howling,

noisy even over the blare of "She Thinks I Still Care" from the speakers. Though the sun would still be shining for another hour or so in the flat land, here on The Creek it was already casting an orange haze through the open doorway as sunlight melted behind the mountains. I took the pack of smokes from the coffee table and lit another. The three of them stayed out on the porch, Daddy silencing the other two so the Hispanic and Josephine didn't start cutting each other. I just let the record play.

4.

The camp sat way back in a dark, damp holler between Walnut Creek and Ellijay. Though a full moon had kept the road nearly lit enough to ride without headlights for most of the drive, soon as the pavement ended and dusty gravel swept into the mountains, there wasn't an ounce of moonlight that made it through the trees. The old logging roads saw little upkeep anymore, and it wasn't a place many ventured without a good four-wheel-drive and a chainsaw.

I'd been there hundreds of times through the years, and in the days before rich folks went to preserving this and preserving that, Daddy and I would spend many a night at the camp during open seasons for hog and bear. That's really all the camp was good for, keeping folks dry and from freezing when the weather snuck in, but it was hardly good enough for that anymore. The shack was dilapidated and caving, just skeletal remains of curved gray planks and rusted tin.

I could tell the boys were already inside. A rectangle of thin light around the door and a few sparse beams shooting through holes in the roof were all that shone in the darkness. I made my way down to the camp on a path cut through laurels. The sound of a small stream bubbled up from behind the shack, but I could hear them talking inside.

Robbie Douglas was cinched down with wire thin as guitar strings binding his arms and legs to a metal folding chair. Blood ran from his forearms where the wire had sliced clean when he, at one point or another, tried to yank free. He was sitting there calm as a beat dog now, his shirt off and bare chest riddled with burns where the boys had pressed their cigarette butts. Despite his body giving out on him, Robbie's mouth was in a constant struggle to detach itself from his jaw. Bug-eyed and vicious, his stare took on a wildness I'd only ever seen in a coon's eyes after a night spent in a trap.

"Where the hell have you been?" Jeremy spoke first. It was just him and his brother, Gerald, there in the room with Robbie. The brothers spent their days working for Daddy at the shop. Both of them were certified mechanics to make the whole deal look pretty official. Really, though, there'd never been much of anything official about Jeremy Cabe aside from a few mug shots. He was a skinny little cuss with cold blue eyes, a mustache that never seemed to grow ripe sprigging over his lips. Those wiry, wide-eyed types often proved the most dangerous men, and that's what it was about Jeremy Cabe that made me uneasy. He always had a glint in his eye like if you didn't believe what he was saying he'd prove it right that fucking second.

"Tree must've fallen after you came through. I had to saw my way in here," I said.

"This son of a bitch gave us a hell of a time! Spit all over my work shirt and scratched the hell out of Gerald's eye!" Jeremy looked down at his navy blue work shirt and rubbed at a smeared white splotch that looked like a cum stain above his name patch.

I could barely distinguish Gerald's face as he stood in the far corner of the room behind the chair. A small lantern was set on a makeshift table beside Jeremy and a 315,000-candela spotlight was propped on the floor and angled directly into Robbie's eyes. Gerald stood in a shadow cast by Robbie, but I could still make out a dark red line running sharply from the corner of his eye down into his beard. He was the type of man that wouldn't say boo to a goose, and other than those blue eyes, the brothers looked absolutely nothing alike. Gerald was as big around as a forked hemlock and always wore a set of suspenders clamped to his britches with a T-shirt just short enough to allow his belly to fold over his belt buckle. He kept a tangled mat of hair stuffed under a Joy Dog Food trucker cap, and had a grisly beard wiring from his face. But as intimidating as he was, it was Jeremy you had to keep an eye on.

"Calm the fuck down, Jeremy. Looks like y'all handled yourselves just fine without too much blood to show for it."

"Calm down hell! If it wasn't for your daddy, we'd have this son of a bitch buried down deep in an old asbestos mine or somewhere! I be damned if anybody's going to be calm!"

"Judging by the cigarette butts on the floor and these burns all up and down his chest, I'd say you're about even." I tried to sound tough and calm, and as the words came out of my mouth, I thought I'd done a pretty damn good job. Daddy wanted me to be a man and it was things like this that made you one. Truth was I hadn't ever taken part in anything like this. Truth was, shit like this didn't come up too often. For the most part business was smooth, and folks had enough respect or fear or whatever you call it for Daddy to never let it come to this. I was scared shitless. "Has he said anything yet?"

"He's said a whole lot of shit, but that's it, just a bunch of bullshit. Ain't said a fucking useful word."

Gerald still hadn't spoken, but walked over and stood directly behind Robbie. Gerald's belly was almost close enough to rest on top of Robbie's head.

"I've already told y'all I ain't got nothing to say, I ain't said nothing to nobody and that's it, that's all there is to it." Robbie spoke fast and it was hard to unravel the words with his jaw racking in that way as he chewed on the same invisible thing that kept Mama's teeth sawing.

"If you haven't said anything to anyone, then that's good," I said. "That's good, Robbie. But the problem is we heard a little different. Problem is that person you talked to is someone my father has known for a long, long time."

Robbie had gone under the radar for months. He didn't come around too often and maybe that's why none of us knew how hard that crystal had him. If Daddy'd known, it wouldn't have come to this. But Daddy hadn't known, and it took Robbie getting the deputies called on him while he tried to steal a stereo and television from his own folks before Daddy found out. Robbie hadn't ever been deep. He'd never made runs, never even seen the dope the Mexicans were bringing in nowadays. He'd been on the payroll for a long time, though, driving in different rigs for high-price oil changes and such, and he had a pretty good idea of how it all worked. When the deputies had taken him in, it was a bull on the payroll, a "family friend" as Daddy called them, who conducted the interview. Without even a line of questioning building up to it, Robbie went to spilling beans that shouldn't be spilled.

He'd been up for nearly a week at that point and was starting to come down. That coming down was always the hardest, it seemed, and when the hole got deep, folks lashed for any rope they could find to drag themselves out. That's what separated the crankers from any other type of drug addict I'd ever been around. Folks on pills or cocaine or methadone or any other kind of dope could hold it together when they were in that hole. I'd done everything under the sun and never had any mind to start snitching. Crank, on the other hand, seemed to bring on a certain paranoia. After a week or so running that high, no dreams to let you regain any sort of grasp that you ever had, the mind starts going places that minds oughtn't go. After that, those lips'll say just about anything to get back some sort of clarity. That's why Robbie was here. That's why this had to be done. If he told one, he'd tell them all, and there wasn't any way of knowing who those others might be. Some dogs had to be put to sleep.

"What in the fuck are you talking about, Jacob, you know me and I've known you for a long time now, hell, your daddy has known me for a long time, and I ain't ever been nothing but good to none of y'all, and now you're going to treat me like this, saying I said something to somebody, and I ain't said nothing." All of that rambling left him out of breath, but Robbie sat still from the waist down. It was his neck and head that were in a constant wrestling match, his head wanting to spin off like a top.

"You said something all right." I knelt down and tilted the spotlight out of his eyes and beamed it onto his chest so that he could look me square while I approached. His scruffy, thin face jittered, but those big dark eyes that were popping hung on to me as I spoke. "It's not a question of whether or not you said *something*. We know you said *something*. What we need to know is who all you said it to."

I don't know if it was me moving closer or Robbie finally being able to see something other than white light that triggered it, but at that moment he convulsed every which way with those wires cutting into him like razor blades. "I ain't said nothing!" he screamed over and over, the blood pooling on the floor now as the wires cut deeper and the blood ran down and dripped from his elbows and fingertips.

Out of the corner of my eye, I saw Jeremy rush forward and Gerald start back-stepping fast, and before I knew what the hell was happening, Jeremy had splashed something all over Robbie's face and the screams electrified the room. It was like Jeremy had just run a high-voltage line into that little old shack and all of a sudden everything was bright. Robbie was screaming till the veins bulged out of his neck, and after four or five of those screams that bellowed till there was no air left for fuel, the skin on his face started whitening and peeling off like wetted tissue. I was a hunk of granite during all of that commotion. I couldn't have moved to step away from the gallows. But Gerald moseyed casually across the room and grabbed a tin pail from the corner. There was no hurry in his step while he strolled, nor when he dumped what must've been water overtop Robbie's head.

"*What the fuck was that?*"

"Wasn't saying nothing," Jeremy said. He had a wild look about him, like a kid that had just slapped a frog against the concrete. "Had to kick it up."

"No, I mean what the fuck was that? What the fuck was that you threw on him?"

"Acid, man. Sulfuric acid a buddy of mine swiped from the paper plant over there in Canton." Jeremy let into a loud whooping holler that rose above the screams for a second or two, and then he started laughing like he'd just witnessed the funniest thing he'd ever seen. His brother never said a word, nor did his facial expression change. I could feel my face turn. I could feel it still souring as the smell swept over me.

"Well, who the fuck told you to do that? Who the fuck told you to bring that in here in the first place?" I was looking dead at Jeremy now, but he still had that smirk on his face. He had a leather work glove over the hand he'd thrown it with, and even that was starting to burn as a few drops of acid crept along the side of the pint jar he'd used to contain it. "Did my daddy tell you to bring that shit? Did my daddy ask you to handle it?"

I could see that the mention of my father and what he might do for something like this forced Jeremy's hand.

"Sorry, man. It's just, it's just he wasn't saying a goddamn thing. Bullshit. Bullshit was all he'd said and that ain't going to cut it." The funny smirk on Jeremy's face turned sinister. "Your daddy asked us to get to the bottom of it, and he ain't saying shit."

Robbie Douglas was still screaming, and if his eyes had held any tears to cry, they would have poured, but the skin was peeling where those eyes used to sit. He was still shaking hard in that chair, those wires still cutting, and none of us said a word until his body gave out and all that was left was heavy lifting and falling in his chest.

"Now, Robbie, you know me as good as anyone and you know it's not like me to sit and let this happen." I put aside the toughness and went back to what I knew. "You need to tell me who else you talked to so that I can make it stop."

"I done told you, I ain't said nothing to nobody, no time, and it wouldn't matter if I had 'cause y'all are going to kill me one way or another, and I know it, and I'd rather it happen now, right now, right this fucking second."

Jeremy ran forward again and splashed another jar full of acid against Robbie's face before I ever knew it was coming, and that meanness, the sheer meanness of what Jeremy did, seemed to spark a trail of gasoline straight to his brother. Gerald pulled out a curved skinning knife with a gut hook angled back from the end of the blade. There was a dangerous look in his eyes, a vicious calmness as if he knew he would not only keep pace with his brother's actions, but also try to top him. He loped forward and yanked that knife back hard just above Robbie's collarbone. The screaming let loose again, and I pulled a revolver Daddy had given me in case things went awry from the back of my jeans and pointed dead between Jeremy's eyes.

"I told you it wasn't your place!" I tried to yell over the screams, but my voice seemed muted, like my lips opened and closed but no sound came out. "I told you Daddy sent me to handle this!"

Jeremy didn't say a word. He just stared down the dark hole of that barrel and kept his mouth shut, but out of the corner of my eye, I caught Gerald easing out from behind Robbie, face peeling, blood dumping out of his shoulder, and screaming. I mean screaming. I turned the gun on Gerald and backed myself into the closest corner I could find to where I could see both Cabe brothers at once. Gerald knelt down and wiped his blade against Robbie's pants leg, and sheathed the knife to his hip.

"Ain't no need for us turning on one another!" Jeremy hollered. "Nothing good's going to come of it!" And as Jeremy spoke that second sentence, the screaming stopped and all of a sudden his words were loud and clear.

The three of us looked over at Robbie, his head fallen down to his chest, and that heavy rising and falling going slack. His breathing shallowed over the next few minutes, and none of us said a word. One last big wheezy huff and then all of a sudden he was as still as water freezing. Silent.

THE LOGGING ROAD ended at the start of a creek bed where the first bits of water seeped from bedrock. There was a sparse clearing in the trees, and the moon filtered through to set the small stream flickering with light.

"There's a bluff on over that hill, but we'll have to drag him to there," Jeremy said.

The brothers had wrapped the body in a tarp, loaded it into the bed of my pickup, and tailed close behind up the logging road until there was no place left to drive. Daddy'd always said that at the end of the long, cold day the only thing that mattered was who you could really trust. I knew I couldn't trust either of those Cabe brothers as far as I could throw them, so I crammed that snub nose down the back of my britches and stepped out into the night.

"Probably best if we just use that tarp for the dragging. There's a decent game trail for most of it," Jeremy said.

I didn't say a word. I wasn't supposed to be around for this part. The way Daddy'd planned was for me to get Robbie to tell who he'd talked to, and then I'd leave the Cabe brothers to handle the end part, but we were all in it together now. There wasn't any way out of that darkness but forward.

Gerald yanked the tarp out of the truck bed like some drunken magician trying to pull a tablecloth from under a coffin, and Robbie's body folded and fell to the ground. Those burns on his face proved sticky and held on to the blue tarp in places, and I had to look away to keep from getting sick. He was the first dead person I'd ever seen outside of the niceties of mortician makeup and dimly lit funeral parlors. Even at that moment, I understood that what was taking place was the type of thing that would never leave a man, the type of thing to shake him from dream for the rest of his life.

Jeremy leaned down and wrapped the body up in a cocoon with the tarp, and I was glad that I didn't have to see it any longer. We trudged off into those woods with Jeremy clearing a path, Gerald doing most of the dragging, and me kicking the tarp free every time it hung on a root or rock.

"I don't know about you boys, but I got me a date with Jack and Ginger when all this is said and done," Jeremy said as he brushed back a laurel tangle to let Gerald pass. "Yep, I can hear that whiskey and ginger ale calling to me right this second. How about you? Got any plans?"

I found it strange that he could talk so casually amidst the horror, but like it or not, we were partners right then and partners had to amuse each other to make the time pass. "Thought I might slide by a party on the way to the house."

"A party? Well hell, Jacob, why ain't you tell us you knew of a party? We might all pack up and go. Ride together, you know, make one hell of an entrance. Those folks won't think they ever knew what a party was before we got there and I pop into that motherfucker like *tah-dah* with my pecker out." Jeremy jumped and turned to look at us. He dry-humped the air with a shit-eating grin spread wide enough for rotten teeth to catch moonlight.

"Ain't much of a party. Just a bunch of high school kids."

"Sixteen'll get you twenty, Jacob. Reckon I'll stick with Jack and Ginger."

The woods were loud with nighttime sounds in the distance, but it was quiet where we walked. The silence rode with us. Gerald let out a grunt as we got to a steep embankment on the hillside and we all pitched in to drag the body to the crest. The bluff wasn't so much a sheer rock face as a steep decline riddled with boulders that hadn't been moved since water set them there thousands of years before. I stood back while the Cabe brothers grabbed the tarp by the ends and started swinging. When the body swayed high, Jeremy let loose of his end and Robbie's body rolled limp, limbs flailing, down the hill till it caught on a big, round stone. Gerald folded the tarp up as if it was something worth keeping, and I stared down at the place where the first man I'd ever seen die fit around the boulder like a tongue and groove. The Cabe brothers started making their way toward the trucks. "Later, Jacob," Jeremy hollered. But I just stood there for a while and stared at it. I figured if it was going to hang with me for a while, I might as well get the details right.

5.

Cars parked crooked on every square inch of grass and had started bleeding out onto the side of the highway by the time I got there. The whole place looked like a Scrabble board, with all those blocks spelling words like "underage" and "drunk tank." Though the law would have to show at some point or another, the deputies were usually civil about giving kids a good start on a night they'd never remember. Besides that, I kind of hoped those squad cars would pull up any minute and get a damn fine look at my face. That would have to be as strong an alibi as any.

I was already half lit off a bottle of Dr. McGillicuddy's that Daddy wouldn't miss from the liquor cabinet, seeing as it was still months from cold season. Between those menthol schnapps and a half a roach I'd found in the truck ashtray, I was well on my way when I dropped a white Xanax bar onto my tongue and swallowed.

There were kids spilling out into the yard, most of them too drunk to stand upright as they made out with friends they'd grown up with and confessed love that would fizzle by dawn. I hoped she was there. I hoped that somewhere in the crowd Maggie was there and that she'd be happy to see me. I couldn't have cared less about the rest of the faces. It didn't matter if any of those old chums were alive or thrown out on some bluff for the buzzards to pick apart.

The inside of the house was ransacked and any dignity that had ever resided there had called it a night. Charlie Mitchell's parents would undoubtedly wring his big-ass Adam's apple plumb flat whenever they came home, and maybe that's why he was running around picking up empties and filling black trash bags with the clock just a hair past one. That poor boy was sweating, beads forming under that bright red hair just as fast as he could wipe. He did a double take when he caught me standing in the doorway. His eyes swelled for a second as if I'd just dropped a shit on a night that was already piled high and steaming.

I scanned the room filled with faces that I'd known all my life, but it was different now. When I was sleeping in the back of the classroom and even a few months after I'd dropped out, those kids had looked at me like some sort of hero, like I was doing things and going places that they'd always dreamt about but never had the guts to say aloud. Not anymore. Now they recognized me for what I am, I guess. Trash. Trash that wouldn't have known a fucking thing about them if it weren't for Facebook.

Blane Cowen was the first to speak to me. He came stumbling

up on gimp legs and that top half of him circling around just a few degrees short of full orbit. His curled mess of hair was coming off his head in every which way and he blinked slow, made it look like he was drunker than Cooter Brown and barely able to talk when he said hello.

"What's up, Jacob?" Blane dragged out my name as if it were hieroglyphs.

"Not shit. What about you?"

"I'm fucked-up, man! Drinking. Smoking. I'm fucked-up!"

I laughed a little bit. Playing along with that kid's game was almost enough to make me forget where I'd just come from for a minute or two. "I hear you, buddy."

"All right, man." Blane seemed to sense that the type of attention he warranted wasn't anything I could give. "Well, it was good seeing you, man! Hit me up sometime. We'll go burn one."

I didn't respond but watched Blane stumble away till he got in the center of the room. That was the place he'd always wanted to be, right there in the center of things. Only no one was watching. He turned his head every which way and with eyes held half closed, he waited to catch anyone looking. When a couple folks got to noticing, Blane fell stiff as a board face-first into the couch. The ones who were watching snickered, and old Blane started grunting and mumbling things that didn't make a lick of sense. He was destined for Hollywood.

I made my way through a crowded hall where rap music blasted family pictures into angles on the walls. Most of the kids didn't even notice me passing, but the ones who did lifted Dixie cups filled with warm beer to their lips so that they wouldn't have to speak. I don't know what it was about being gone for two years, not spending every waking hour next to those sons of bitches, but they looked at me nowadays like saying hello would throw their whole universe off-kilter.

Along an island bar in the kitchen the popular guys were throwing beer pong, while the girls with crushes stood near wondering if any of those boys were lit enough to consider putting their panties on the ceiling fan. What they didn't know was that those types of guys were too worried about impressing one another to concentrate on important shit like pussy. Those guys were too busy chugging beers and trying to memorize rap lyrics to pay attention to what girl had that fuck-me look in her eyes. Still, I knew if Maggie was at the house, she'd be somewhere close by. The guys splashing Ping-Pong balls into Dixie cups of suds had ridden Avery Hooper's coattails to get to that table, and I was certain she was there somewhere with him.

Smoke hung heavy on the far side of the room and the brass chandelier overhead set the smoke aglow around a small table. I could see Avery sitting with his back to the window. He said something I was too far away to hear and I caught a glimpse of Maggie. She rocked back in the chair beside him, her head tilted with blond curls trailing, and laughed. Though she smiled as if she were having a good time, it was obvious she didn't belong. Most of us born here would die here, never having seen anything further away than Pigeon Forge, but not her. When we were nine or ten years old and first learning cursive, she spent hours upon hours memorizing every curve of her name. "All famous people have to sign autographs," she'd said. I couldn't even remember the twists and turns of x's and z's. Lot of folks set their eyes on the distance at one point or another, but in time those eyes drew back. Maggie's never had. The biggest difference between her and other dreamers was that she was determined enough and smart enough to will it into existence. It had always been obvious Maggie was only passing through.

Part of me was hesitant to even walk over, but the other ninety-eight percent had Xanax pumping any anxiety that ever existed into oblivion. Avery Hooper was the type of guy that every time he looked at you, you just wanted to haul off and hit him in the fucking mouth. He'd grown his hair long, and tufts of that brown hair rolled out over his ears and curled back toward the ceiling. A tight string of thick wooden beads, one of those necklaces from shit-town novelty shops in shit-town places like Gatlinburg, was fitted around his neck. It was that college look, that I-smoke-weed-and-kick-Hacky-Sacks kind of look, that was spread all over that son of a bitch, and I hated him for it.

I shuffled past the pong game and past the line of girls who had just enough baby fat left to make them vulnerable. When I got to the table, she saw me. Maggie looked up with those silvery blue eyes, and where I'd hoped to find welcome, I thought I spotted some sort of fear. She glanced down at the table and then up to me with eyes getting wider. There was a plate there, one of those floral-pattern plates that parents keep well into silver anniversaries, on the table. And there was powder on that plate, chunky powder flickering like glass shards and cut into lines in that yellow light. I looked at her again and saw a straw in the hand she used to push her hair back behind her ears. Then there was this rage that started building inside of me. There was this anger that washed all of the haze left from reefer and alcohol and ladder bars out of me and left nothing more than a need to break every last bone in that motherfucker's body. Right then, there wasn't a thought that could've calmed any of it down, and so I went with it.

"You snort any of that shit?" I looked Maggie dead in her eyes, and I could see she was scared.

"Who the fuck are you talking to? Ain't none of your goddamn business, Jake!"

My eyes flicked over to that mouth that shouldn't have been talking but was, that mouth that just might shoot me over the edge. Avery's eyes were lit up like firecrackers and his jaw had been put into motion. "Did you give her that shit?"

"Fuck you, Jake. I suggest you go find some other place to be a fucking hero, because nobody wants you here. There ain't a goddamn soul that wants anything to do with your sorry ass, especially not Maggie."

I could hear the music playing, but all the noise of folks talking and hollering had shut quiet. I could feel their eyes pressing into the back of my skull, and those eyes went to pressing so hard until they were pushing me forward. Before I knew it, I was moving too fast to stop and I was into him.

That first punch sent a red mist hanging on air and the blood started pouring and I could see it in his eyes, I could see it in there even as I was hitting him, that he'd never been in a fight and wanted it to end. But that next fist came and split his head against the window, and glass went haywire, and I kept forward. My hands were on him now, and I had him out of his chair and onto the floor and I was braining him, his skull just cracking as it bounced off the tile into another line of knuckles.

It was when his eyes started fading and that wide-eyed rabid look had turned stupefied there on the floor that I got my wits about me. Something came over me, something screaming that anything more would kill him, and it held my fist still as the moon there above him. I stood up, and I could feel those eyes pressing into the back of me, but it was a different kind of pressing now, a feeling like those eyes belonged to kids who weren't ready to see something like this.

When I got up, I looked at Maggie. I looked at that plate and the place she'd set the straw. I looked at that shit she'd been just seconds away from snorting up her nose, just seconds away from a glue trap that would've held her to this place and this life just like me. She was staring at my hands, skin torn, blood of him and me spread across those flattened knuckles. And she just kept staring at my hands while that pile of shit gasped and puddled on the floor.

6.

My eyes opened that next morning into a blurry, brown shadow that slowly came into focus as a pair of leather boots with mud caked to the soles. My mind started running that what-the-fuck-happened checklist, but number one checked out: those were my boots. Hardwood floors, dirty as hell from men too lazy to push a broom, was my second clue that it was all right: I was home. I pushed myself up from the floor with arms that felt loopy, and I could see that I was in my bedroom. I just hadn't made it quite to the bed.

That was every night I'd ever spent mixing alcohol and Xaney bars wrapped up in a nice, neat little package. Nights that began sharp always had this scary tendency to go black in a hurry. I'd start off having a good time, and next thing you know, I'd wake up to nothing but stories from friends to shed light on what I'd done.

Unfortunately, I'd taken that pill just a little too late in the night. Should've started earlier, I guess. I could still see Robbie Douglas's body wrapped crooked as hell around that rock. It played backward from there and it was clearer than the room I was standing in. I could see his distorted face peeking out of that tarp as Gerald was dragging. I could see his chest go from still to raising and lowering, raising and lowering. I could hear that screaming and I could see his face peeling, and before that, before that, I could see just him, Robbie Douglas, sitting there on a week-long binge with unblinking eyes and a chomping jaw as those wires cut into his arms. That was what pushed me to the bathroom and threw my head into the toilet, and that was what spilt over into the bowl. It was the fact that he was real. It was the fact that he was real and alive and breathing and had parents that buried my head just inches from where vomit filmed on that little pond of toilet water.

"Jacob! Jacob!" Daddy was hollering, and I could feel him pushing on the door where my feet were wedged. "Jacob, what the fuck's the matter with you?" The sound of his voice made me heave harder and Daddy banged that door open till I was sure every toe I had was severed clean off. He was laughing now as he stood over me. "Well, goddamn, boy. Look at you." He was chortling something horrible at me. "Must've been one hell of a night. Yes, sir, I don't think I've had a night that put me in a place like this in a coon's age."

If he was talking about the puking, I'd seen him do it a week or two before. If he was talking about what had pushed me into that bowl, I'd heard the stories.

"Get the fuck up now, and be a goddamn man. I got something that'll take the hurt out of you." I pushed off of the toilet with hands still bloodied and scabbed, but just couldn't find enough strength to get off the floor. "Goddamn, Jacob! Quit being a fucking pussy about it and get up!" Daddy leaned down and braced his arms under mine. He hoisted me up without even a grunt.

I stood there for a minute with my head hung low, my whole body limp as rope. I looked my hands over and hobbled to the sink to wash off what I could from the night before.

"Bloodied the hell out of those knuckles. Who'd you hit?"

"Avery Hooper." I turned on the faucet and scrubbed hard at my knuckles till water stained dark red spiraled down the drain.

"Avery Hooper? That's old Thomas Hooper's boy, ain't it?"

"I think that's his uncle." My eyes were focused on that spiraling, the sink seeming to swallow the only thing I cared to remember.

"Yeah, I think you're right. That's Thomas's brother Aiden's kid, ain't it? Boy, I used to hate that son of a bitch when we were growing up. Tied that cocksucker to a tombstone one night at Cub Scouts and left him there. We could hear him just screaming down there when we were sitting around the campfire. They kept asking what that racket was, but I told them I didn't hear a thing. I'd had half a mind to slit his fucking throat." Daddy started laughing again and stared into the mirror till our eyes met.

"Well, his son ain't much better."

"Looks like it. Looks like there might be a little of that McNeely blood in you after all."

That's what I was scared of. I cupped a handful of water to wash my face and let some of that handful into my mouth to wet my tongue. My whole mouth was dry as talc, and I just kept filling my hands as fast as the faucet could pour to get some sort of dampness back into my mouth.

"Sounded like you were in here dying. Should've known you were just being a pussy." Daddy stared at me like he couldn't believe we were kin, like I was the biggest disappointment he'd ever had. "Well, whenever you're finished, come in the kitchen and I'll mix you up something to get those hairs standing again."

From the way he carried himself, I knew old Josephine had given in pretty easy at some point after the tattoo was covered. As he walked out of the room, I could see that the name had been buried beneath flowers like the Mexicans draw inside of skulls, and there up above it was Josie spelled just right, with an *i*.

THE SMELL of bacon and eggs still held in the kitchen, but it was obvious the cast iron had cooled hours before. It wasn't that appetizing kind of smell when everything is still sizzling in the pan, but rather that sweaty-feet kind of must that comes on later.

"Well, Jesus Christ, look who decided to get up."

The sun shone bright through the blinds so that even those slivers of sunlight lit the room to something unbearable. "What time is it?"

"What time is it, he asks. Care to venture a guess?"

"No."

"Well, it's a quarter past four. You've been in there hugged up to the toilet all goddamn day." Daddy sat on the couch with his bare feet propped up on the coffee table. He didn't have a shirt on, and his tattoos darkened the places that never saw sun. He stood up and situated a loose-fitting pair of sweatpants on his waist before coming over to the kitchen and grabbing a coffee mug from the cabinet. "Just go sit your sissy ass over there." Daddy started to mix some concoction into the mug, but I didn't stick around to catch the ingredients. I stumbled toward the couch and took a liking to the place he'd sat. When he came over, he put the mug down in front of me, some acrid-smelling shit steaming over the rim. Daddy sat beside me and kicked his feet back to the coffee table. He started flipping channels just fast enough for eyes to catch a glimpse of what was showing. "Drink up. That shit's a goddamn McNeely cure-all."

I grabbed the coffee mug and took my first sip hesitantly. The taste sent my mouth to spitting and Daddy laughed as the mist glittered the air. "What the fuck is that?"

"Black coffee, a little dash of bourbon, and two Goody's powders."

"Tastes like shit."

"Ain't supposed to taste good. Just quit being a pussy about it and drink it."

I took the next gulp in one big swallow, and though my face locked sideways like I was sucking something sour, by the time that medicine had hit my gut, I could feel the heaviness shedding.

"Tell me about last night."

"Ain't nothing to talk about."

"Don't go giving me that shit. Now, tell me about your night."

"None of it worked out like you wanted it—"

"Goddamn, you're loose-lipped! I ain't even talking about that! The boys came by late last night on a tear and told me all about it.

Those are tales that only need to be told one good time. It's better like that. Better to just let sleeping dogs lie, like they say. That's the only way to let a fuckup like that come somewhere close to forgetting."

"Then what the fuck are you asking about?"

"I'm asking about your night. Trying to have a little friendly conversation with my son, if that's all right with you. So what the fuck kept you out all night and had you plowing my forsythias all to shit?"

"I ran over the bushes?"

"Did you run over the bushes? You come piling up that driveway on a goddamn tear. I was grabbing for britches and a gun just as fast as I could till I seen it was you through the window."

"Don't remember that."

"Bet you don't."

I grabbed the coffee mug and gulped down as much as I could stand. "Went to a party that they were throwing for graduation."

"They graduate yesterday? I didn't know that."

"Yeah, they graduated yesterday and last night they were partying a little bit over there in Foxfire, over at Charlie Mitchell's house. I don't really think they wanted me there, and I don't really know why I went. But one thing led to another, and I left Avery Hooper spread out on the floor."

"Shit doesn't just unfold like that, now. Would be out of your character to just walk in and go to hitting somebody. Wouldn't put it past me, but you avoided that kind of meanness somehow or another. No, I reckon something had to have happened for you to just haul off and hit somebody."

"Maggie Jennings."

"And there it is, a goddamn woman."

"She ain't just some woman, first of all, and you know that."

"Well, I know a lot of things. I know you two were tighter than a burl growing up. I know you two were together a good while and, hell, you might've even popped her cherry. But I know that a woman's just a woman, and there's no changing that. If they didn't have pussies, the dumpsters would be full of them."

"How about you stop right—"

"I know anything that can bleed a week straight every month and survive is the devil's doing." Daddy guffawed.

"*Shut the fuck up!* It ain't like that. It ain't ever been like that. And it ain't like none of that trash you keep piled up around here." I was sitting forward on the couch now and my knuckles were pressing those scabs wide open. "You can say whatever the hell you want about whoever the hell you want to, but you keep her fucking name out of it."

Daddy resituated himself on the couch into a little lazier position than he'd held. He smirked knowing how riled I'd become, knowing that there wasn't a chance in hell I'd hit him. I think he pushed me like that just to see if he could drag what genes he'd given out of me to inspect. "Guess my boy's in love."

I knew he'd said it just to get my blood boiling, but that didn't really matter. There wasn't any woman fit for talking like that as far as I was concerned, not even Josephine, but certainly not a girl like Maggie, certainly not someone so innocent.

"Well, are you going to tell the goddamn story or not?"

"She was there with Avery, and he was fixing to make her do something she didn't need to be doing, so I hit him."

"What was he fixing to make her do?"

"That ain't important."

"Of course it's fucking important. Stories hinge on shit like this. So, tell me." Daddy looked at me with a lowered brow that cast a heavy ledge over his eyes.

"He was cranked out of his brain and was about to try and put that shit up *her* nose. You happy?"

"Matter of fact, I am. Matter of fact, that makes me awfully fucking happy." Daddy scooted toward me, slapped me in the back of the head, then palmed my crown and rattled my skull. He settled his bare arm around my neck and that warmness in him felt as close to anything fatherly as I'd felt in a long time. "Awfully fucking happy," he said.

7.

The sun had dropped low until the reflection in clouds sent purples, blues, and pinks prisming through the blinds. I hadn't moved from the couch and had nodded off for a minute or two before the Walkers began to bark. I stood and walked into the kitchen to peer through the blinds onto the yard.

Maggie Jennings was carefully dancing that thirty-four two-steps, fourteen ball changes, and chassé through the maze of angry hounds. It was a dance she'd learned long ago, and while they say you never forget how to ride a bike, there are certain things that you hold an equal mastery over, certain things that scare you into remembering.

My mind raced as I hurtled over a pile of dirty laundry into the back bedroom and tried to find something to throw on over gym shorts. There was still vomit wiped across my chest, and my mouth still held the taste. Slinging the dresser drawers in a frenzy, I saw nothing but cedar boards. All of the clothes waited on Daddy or me or Josephine, if we were lucky, to run a load. With no time, I ran back into the living room and yanked a wrinkled T-shirt and the pair of sweatpants Daddy slept in from the pile.

I'd just made it to the couch and was trying my damnedest to make it seem like I wasn't expecting her, when she peered in through the glass and pecked a few times with her fingernail.

"Come in!" I tried to act like I didn't care if it was her or Jesus, like there weren't any feelings there.

She opened the door and stepped inside onto a rug meant for stomping mud from boots. She wore tight jeans that seemed fitted to her legs, leather beach sandals showing off lime-green-painted toenails. A loose-fitting tank top, pieced lace the color of coral, draped her torso. The neck was cut low and showed the tan of her chest, the slight shadows of collarbones. She stayed put there on the rug, didn't come any further, like that little rectangle was an island or something and all that hardwood an ocean that neither of us could swim across to get to each other.

"Where's your dad?"

"He's gone."

Maggie held a look in her eyes that spoke volumes, but her mouth didn't mutter a thing. There seemed to be words racing around inside of her, turning a tornado about her brain, but the wall she'd built, the wall I poured the footing for, wouldn't let a damn bit of it out.

"What you doing on The Creek, Mags?"

"We have to talk." Her blond curls were balled up on the back of her head and there was something in that hair that had it smelling like honeysuckle. I could smell it from where I sat, such smells having a tendency to carry further in a house that reeked of men.

"What in the world do we have to talk about?"

"There are just some things that I need to say to you, Jacob."

I scooted to the far side of the couch and cleared a spot for her. She looked down on that rug for a minute as if the moment her feet went any further she'd be leaving a place she could never get back to, but she braved it, came over, and sat beside me.

"What is it, Maggie?"

"I need a minute."

"I'm not worth more than a handful of texts for damn near two years, and you come over here saying you have something to say but ain't ready to say it?" I'd always given it to her straight and I think that was one of the things she always liked about me. Growing up in a house where nearly everything was a lie, Maggie respected the fact that I never lied to her.

"I just want my thoughts to be clear. I don't want to say anything that I don't mean. I think a lot of times in the past we've said things to each other without thinking them through, hurtful things, and I don't want to do that. I don't want to say anything without knowing for certain it's what needs to be said. But part of it is that after last night, I just wanted to be sure you were all right."

"Well, I'm fine."

"Your hands aren't." Maggie glared at my knuckles, the place where skin was still rolled back and dried tough as calluses. The cuts were that yellowish brown of scabbed skin and had started crusting over. It stung a little bit, but I wouldn't tell her.

"My hands are fine."

"You didn't have to do that. I can take care of myself, Jacob. It's not like when we were kids."

"No, it's sure not like when we were kids."

"It's not like when we were together either."

"No, it's not like when we were together."

"So long as you know that." Maggie shuffled on the couch as if she were about to stand and leave.

"You came all the way over here just to tell me that?"

"That's what I said, isn't it? I just want you to know that I can take care of myself."

Her answer was direct and I sat there for a second unsure how to take it. "He had it coming, Mags. I mean I hate you were sitting there, and I wish you hadn't have seen it, but he had it coming and has had it coming most of his life."

Maggie didn't say anything for a long time. She sat there with her eyes fixed on my hands. I didn't say anything either but watched commercials flick by on the muted television set. Finally, I turned and looked at her. Those silver eyes were set awfully hard on my hands, and I could see that all that strength I'd admired for so long was there, but fear was fencing all of that possibility deep inside.

"He'll forgive you, Mags. I reckon if there's any sense in him at all, he'll forgive you."

"It's not me he'd have to forgive, asshole." A wide smile spread across her face and those teeth were just about as pretty as anything I'd ever seen, a whole lot more than fifteen thousand dollars' worth. Dimples pressed into the corners of her smile, and raised cheeks squinted her eyes. She was far too gorgeous to be sitting next to me on that ratty couch. This house, this town, and everything about this place were beneath her and always had been. I was beneath her as well, but she'd never seemed to notice, or at least not to care. "You hit him. I was just sitting there."

"Like I said, he had it coming."

"You're right about that, Jacob. Matter of fact, you're right about a whole lot of things that people never seem to give you credit for."

"What the hell does that mean?"

"Nothing." For the first time since she'd come into the house, Maggie looked me square. Her eyes dilated like she'd just eaten one hell of a pill, but I knew she hadn't. "Turns out, he and I just weren't cut out for each other."

"Well, no shit, Mags. I could've told you that a long time ago." I was damn near jittery in hopes that she'd come to rekindle what we'd had. I wanted to kiss her. I wanted to tuck her hair behind her ears and hold her while I kissed her. But I tried to summon what little bit of Daddy's calm held in my veins so as not to let it show. In all honesty, it was ridiculous to think a girl like that would want anything to do with me, especially after I'd already broken her heart. "What makes you say that?"

"A whole lot of things, Jacob, a whole lot of things that have been building up for a long time. It wasn't just you hitting him."

"What the hell did you ever see in him anyways?"

"I don't know, Jacob. When you left, he was there. I guess that's part of it. And part of it is that I always thought he had potential to be something. I always thought he had something to offer the world if he'd ever get his shit together."

"Yeah, it looked like he really had his shit together. Looked like that son of a bitch is really headed somewhere from what I seen."

"I know, Jacob. I just thought—"

"That kind of thinking ain't worth a damn, Mags. That type of

thinking will have you waiting around a lifetime for something
that's never going to happen. God knows you're too smart for
that."

Maggie didn't answer. I know that she knew I was right, deep
down she knew that, but those types of things are hard to admit
to ourselves.

"You didn't do any of that shit, did you?"

"No. But he was trying awfully hard to get me to, and to be
honest, I was just about ready to do whatever it took to shut him
up. I just wanted to shut all of them up. They're always giving me
a hard time, like I'm a goody-goody or something."

"You kind of are."

"What?"

"You are a goody-goody, Mags, but that's not a bad thing. It's
not like any of these assholes are headed anywhere."

"I'm not any different, Jacob."

"That's bullshit."

"Why?"

"Since the moment I set eyes on you, I knew you were headed
somewhere. I haven't ever known where, but I knew you weren't
going to be here forever."

"No one is, Jacob."

"Every goddamn one of us aside from you is going to be here
forever. You point your finger to one person who left out of here
and made something, just one person."

"Jennifer Brinkley."

"Jennifer Brinkley? Fuck, Mags, she's working at a strip club
in Greenville! That place isn't two steps better than hocking
jewelry."

"Well, how would you know that?" Maggie cut eyes at me as if to jokingly disapprove.

"I don't, Mags. But regardless, that isn't what I'd call getting out. There's going to come a time when the only thing she's got going for her ain't worth a damn thing to anybody. Then where you think Jennifer Brinkley's going to be? She's going to be right back up here on this mountain, or laid up with some old boy in a single-wide in South Carolina and that's not any better. It's hot as fuck down there. She'll be lucky to have air-conditioning."

"And what about me, Jacob?"

"What about you?"

"You still haven't said how I'm any different."

"Different than Jennifer Brinkley?"

"Different than everyone else."

"Because you're getting out of here, Maggie. You're going to head off to college and make something out of yourself, and what you're going to become won't have a reason in the world to ever come back here."

Maggie looked angry, as if there was suddenly something eating her alive inside. Moments passed between us then, silent moments that neither of us knew how to break. She seemed to be thinking long and hard about something that she wouldn't let out. She was staring at the floor when she finally spoke.

"I was just about ready to do whatever it took to shut them up before you got there."

"Well, then I'm glad I got there." I looked at her, and though we hadn't been together in two years, I felt just as protective over her now as ever. She had places to go and would become something incredible, and I knew it. Even if she couldn't be mine and even if

I couldn't go with her, I would go against an army with a hand-gun to make sure her road was paved. "That shit's not like other drugs, Mags. I mean, it's not like smoking weed or eating a couple of pills. Just look at my fucking family. That shit's—"

"I know, Jacob. You don't have to tell me. I know." Maggie reached out and grabbed hold of my hands. She held underneath my palms and stroked her thumbs across my knuckles just barely light enough for me to feel. She was holding my hands and look-ing long and hard at the lines her thumbs ran, and I thought I saw tears rising from just above where those bottom eyelashes turned down. I'd never understood what she saw in me. Even when I was younger I knew that a girl like that kicking around with a guy like me couldn't last, but she never seemed to notice the lines that had been drawn. I think she'd always thought of me as something worth saving, and when you find something that you truly believe you can save, it's awfully hard to let that kind of shit go. That's the only reason I'd ever been able to come up with for why she cared.

She leaned in and looked about as far into me as anyone ever had, like she was going to carry those silver-dollar eyes of hers somewhere deep inside of me and find something to buy and like she was going to bring that thing back out to hold it for keeps. I was going to let her if she wanted to and I thought she was going to kiss me and I just held there not saying a word. Instead she placed my hands onto my lap and stood up from the couch. That gleaming in her eyes started to rise again, and rather than fight it, she headed for the door. Maggie didn't say another word, but in a way, those eyes had said more than words ever could. She left me sitting there to wonder what those things unspoken might have meant. She left me wondering if I'd been forgiven.

8.

The loud shrill of a chair scooting across the kitchen floor and the gradual increase in volume on the scanner woke me up from a dream that had me pitching a tent and humping a pillow. I started to just get up and close the door, but I needed a drink of water.

There were no lights on in the kitchen, but my eyes were settled to the dark and I could make out a shadow hunkered over the table with its head held sideways toward the speaker. I opened the refrigerator and grabbed a carton of orange juice that Josephine liked to mix with vodka and peach schnapps. The refrigerator light flicked on and off, and scintillated a broken view of my father at the table.

"Where are they?"

"Shut the fuck up." Daddy's head stayed tilted, his ear chewing on every morsel that came out of the scanner, and he looked right at me with eyes that settled on some far-off place through me, through the refrigerator, outside.

I shut the refrigerator door and took the carton of orange juice with me to the sink, turned on a small tube light so that I could see Daddy sitting there. I took the chair across from him, drank a long swig, and turned my head opposite of his so that I could focus all of the sound into one side like him.

"Charlie-Two, County. I'm going to need you to send another unit this way."

"Ten-four, Charlie-Two. Can you offer any update on the nature?"

"Subject has been unresponsive to voice commands, County, and has a knife."

"Charlie-Two, are you able to see the subject from your location?"

"Ten-four, County. Subject is moving from the porch into the house and I'm waiting for backup."

"Ten-four, Charlie-Two. There's a unit headed your way."

There was a long pause of silence with only a few blips of static making their way over the airwaves, and Daddy leaned back in his chair.

"Where are they?"

"At your fucking crazy-ass mama's house."

"What for?"

"Ain't real clear, but the way it sounded at first was like she called the goddamn law on herself. Said she'd reported somebody outside of her house."

"Reckon anybody was?"

"Hell no, Jacob. That shit's got her all goony. Ain't nobody after her. Nobody would want her sorry ass. You know that."

It took the other deputy a good fifteen or twenty minutes to make it up the mountain, with only one officer usually working this territory per shift. David-One checked on scene and Daddy and I listened for a long while to snippets of a story that never revealed enough to paint any sort of real picture. When it was all said and done, it was Charlie-Two who had more than he could stand and drew his Taser to probe about fifty thousand volts through her. Any bit of fight she'd had must've left awfully fast after that, because the weapon was secured and before too long they were checking en route.

"Charlie-Two, County. We're going to have the subject in custody on a 10-73 and will be coming down the mountain."

"Ten-four, Charlie-Two."

I WAS ALMOST dozed off again when Daddy screamed.

"Goddamn it, they're coming up here now! That fucking bitch, that dumb fucking bitch!"

His bare feet nearly stomped holes in the hardwood as he made his way from his room to mine. The lights came on and I was blinded for a second or two, that brightness just eating at my eyes before it settled.

"Get the fuck up! Come on!" Daddy was at the edge of my bed and slapped my feet beneath the covers. "Jacob, the goddamn law is coming up here and you need to get up quick. Get anything you got put up. Bud, pills, I don't give a shit, just hide it."

I didn't have anything more than stems and a little bit of shake, and that Xanax bar I'd taken had emptied the bottle. As far as real dope, there wasn't anything in the house that needed hiding any-more, but that type of GO-GO-GO at the first sign of blue lights and badges was something ingrained in Daddy long ago. It had kept him out of trouble many times, so he made it a command-ment.

I don't really know why I went with him. I guess in case he needed help with an alibi or something, but by the time I'd put on a pair of shorts and slid untied boots over my feet, Daddy was in the kitchen peering out of the window to where headlights lit the side field yellow.

"Thought I'd go with you."

"What for? Use your fucking head." Daddy thumped against my forehead with his fist like he was knocking on a door. "You know as well as I do they're looking for me."

"Thought you might want somebody to back up your story."

"Well, I'll be a son of a bitch if that ain't a good idea, Jacob. Damn good idea." Daddy shut the blinds and I followed him to the front door. "Get all your shit put up?"

"It's up."

The moon lit the yard a funny kind of blue, even the trails cut by the running of hounds that usually showed red in sunlight had a robin-egg kind of color about them. It was early summer on The Creek, but the night air still held a chill. The hounds barked like they always did and Daddy led the way to the headlights. He was the only person I knew that never had to memorize that dance to escape snarls and teeth. As Daddy walked, the hounds parted like Moses had thrown his hands over them, and even the meanest one, Kayla, cowered back as far as the lead would let her. I fol-lowed him closely, and the dogs paid me little mind.

The bull was already out of the SUV and leaned up against

the front driver-side fender. His body cast a wide shadow in the moonlight. Neither of us could tell who it was, and neither of us spoke, but the fact that he wasn't driving the standard black-and-white pinned him for ranked. Then, as we got within talking distance, the bull flicked a Zippo down his britches leg and held the flame close to his face to light a smoke. It was Lieutenant Rogers, the friend of the family, as Daddy said.

Rogers was a thick brute, even thicker now that he spent most of his time behind a desk. He didn't wear the tan button-down shirt and creased slacks that deputies wore. He fastened his badge to his belt alongside his cuffs and gun. After years of night shifts and a résumé filled with what went for big busts in a place like Jackson County, Rogers had worked his way up to comfortable polo shirts and loose-fitting cargo pants. Those years on the road had taken his hair, and the years behind the desk had added a bit more pooch around the middle, but he was still strong. Toughness never wore out of men born with it.

"Hell fire, Jessup, you piling up in here like that at this hour had me all sketched out."

"Shit, Charlie, I don't reckon I've ever seen you on edge." Lieutenant Rogers held the cigarette between his teeth, rocked his gun, cuffs, and magazines on his belt, and leaned back about as far as he could without falling onto the hood of the Expedition.

"What the fuck brings you up here?"

"That's the thing, Charlie. Had a call over at your old lady's house earlier in the evening. She was strung out all to hell and called the law up there. Said you were outside of her house wanting to kill her. Said you'd been peeking through the windows all night. Now, you and I both know that's a bunch of bullshit, but the thing is it was one of those new boys who got the call. Thing is she told him a lot of details as they were riding down the mountain and your name got mentioned an awful lot. I told them she was out of her fucking mind, but to keep them little peckerheads happy, I said I'd come up here personally and see if your story checked out."

"I appreciate that, Jessup. I really do. Pays to have friends, don't it?"

"Friends, hell. Just business, Charlie." Rogers squinted his eyes as smoke rose over his face, and took another long drag from his cigarette.

"So what in the fuck did you ride all the way up here for? You afraid of telephones?"

"Well, I guess because I thought you ought to know that the little lady was throwing your name around."

"I can't have that." Daddy pulled a pack of cigarettes from his side pocket and lit a smoke.

"No, you can't have that."

I stood there in silence and tried my damnedest to stay just a sliver more than a shadow.

"Well, Jessup, as you can see, me and the boy are right here safe and sound. Not a whole lot more that I can tell you other than that."

"Just so I got something to tell them boys to let them sleep a little easier, were y'all here all evening?"

"I'll do you one better. I'll give you the whole goddamn day." Daddy folded his arms across his chest, making his muscles defined in moonlight. "Woke up this morning and cooked myself some bacon and eggs. Then I did my best to get this pussy-ass boy of mine feeling better after he let his body get a little in front of his head last night. After that I headed over to Josephine's this afternoon to get my pecker wet. And then I guess me and the boy fried up some cube steak and hit the hay."

"So when's the last time you saw Laura?"

"You mean the bitch?"

"Yeah, I guess."

"I've just been calling her the bitch for so long I'd almost forgotten she had a real God-given name." Daddy smirked, and the way he talked about her, the way he always talked about her, got me riled. But I never had the gall to say anything about it. "Aw, she came over wanting to borrow some money about two or three months back, but other than that, I don't have shit to do with her."

"So neither one of you has had any type of contact with her?"

"No."

I don't know if it was my way of speaking up after holding back for all those years, or if I'd just grown tired of listening to those two ramble on, but I stepped out of Daddy's shadow for the first time in my life and looked Lieutenant Rogers dead where that cigarette kept his face aglow. "I saw her yesterday."

Daddy turned with eyes that looked as if they'd just been hit with a drip torch. We never mentioned her, and if her name ever got brought up, he dogged her and expected me to keep quiet. "The fuck you did."

I tried to look at Daddy, but the way he stared turned me coward. "I went by there yesterday."

It was eating at him that after all these years I'd went to see her the day before. His fists clenched and his jaw pulsed. I thought he was going to hit me.

"Say you saw her yesterday, son?" Rogers asked.

"Yes."

"And was she on the dope then?"

"She was just getting started, I reckon."

Rogers straightened himself off of the Expedition and folded his arms just like my father. "Now I know the two of you are well aware of what type of life she's come to lead, and I know the two of you was around to witness it. But I'm going to tell you that the place she's at right this second is a place that very few ever get to. There are folks going on weeklong vacations with dope crammed plumb up into their brains, and those folks start seeing shit and talking to things that just ain't there. That comes with the territory. But where she's at, where she's at after all these years, is a place long gone from ever getting back from."

"The boy here's just too fucking stupid, Jessup." Daddy still had that meanness lighting him afire, and I kept my mouth shut and didn't look at him.

"We took her tonight and didn't charge her. We committed her, you see, and they'll keep her in there for a week or two if the beds are empty, but probably less, and then she'll be right back there doing it all again. I'm saying this more for you, boy, than anything else." Rogers pulled the cigarette from between his teeth and fixed his eyes onto me. "Don't go latching your feet into stirrups on a horse that's run lame. It ain't going to get you anywhere."

It wasn't like he was telling me something I hadn't known my whole life, but at the same time I appreciated the fact that he'd said it. Rogers was tough as piss oak, but he had a heart. I reckon if my daddy had ever been much of a father, that would have been the type of thing he would have carried, some blend of toughness and compassion. But if he had it at all it was something I'd seldom witnessed.

"Thing is, son, a woman like that is just waiting around to die," Lieutenant Rogers finally said.

Rogers was trying hard to offer some sort of insight into a reality that he knew led to hurt. But I'd known it since I was a kid. That was my reality: the hurt, the shame, and everything else entailed. So, waiting around to die was something I'd known for a long time, and it wasn't the dying part that ate at me. It was the waiting.

9.

I was standing on the inside of a glass door, one of those sliding glass doors folks use to separate kitchens from patios for easy access to grilled hot dogs when the house is full for summer barbecues. It was nighttime, pitch-black inside, and only a dimly lit blue shining on dewed grass before the darkness continued at the woods line. I don't know why I stood there, no recollection of a sound that may have woken me up and brought me to scan the yard. It wasn't my house, but that didn't seem strange, and I didn't question it. It all seemed natural. I knew I was at a house I'd gone to with Maggie and her family when I was little, her uncle's house in Ellijay.

All of a sudden, one of those motion-sensor lights, the kind I always thought Daddy should buy, lit up the yard with a jaundice yellow and out of the woods came this bloody, naked body walking like a string puppet. As it got into the light I could see the skin bubbled up in the few places it still held around the jaw, the rest of the face just indistinguishable meat. When I saw where the knife had stuck him, I knew it was Robbie Douglas, but not until then. The place that skinning knife had hooked into him was lapped over and seeping with a yellow almost the color of black-eyed Susan petals, even yellower in the light. He was moaning something heavy, but no words, and he just kept walking closer and walking closer and nothing I could do could move me from that glass door. As he climbed onto the patio, I could feel that snub nose tucked down the back of my britches, cold steel riding right beneath the waistline, but my arms couldn't move to grab it. My brain said go and my arms never moved. Wasn't a goddamn thing in the world that could bring those arms to life, and before I knew it he'd slid that door open and was on me.

That was the part that kept shaking me from dream. At that same place I woke up out of breath, heaving for air as if I'd just had the wind knocked out of me. My arms were crammed under my body and dead as nails, and I had to roll my whole torso toward the edge of the bed to get those arms dangling so the feeling would run back into them. I hadn't slept more than a few hours. When I closed my eyes that drippy face was taped up to the insides of my eyelids like a poster, and when that faded long enough to sink a bit deeper, that dream started playing again and before I knew it I was choking for air. With my fingers still prickly, I grabbed my cell phone and checked the time: 4:42 a.m. Scared of closing my eyes, truly scared of what would happen next if that dream played out any further, I just decided to get up.

There was a pretty blonde on the television trying her damned-est to sell some type of chopping gadget to housewives still awake after their husbands had pushed them past the point of sleep. The blonde cycled through a round of salsa just about as fast as she could pull onions, jalapeños, and tomatoes from the bag, and not long after she was hammering away at whole bulbs of garlic. That chopping gadget pulsed tomatoes way too thin for any sort of sandwich and I'd lost hope in it being of much use, but that pretty blonde kept my finger from surfing channels.

She had long curls tucked up behind her head and blue eyes. Light freckles dotted her cheeks just enough to be cute, and her teeth were set straight like someone had filed away at them and balanced bubbles in a level till it all lined up perfectly. It was that smile and how her hair wanted to just burst out and drape across her shoulders that made me realize how much she looked like Maggie.

I grabbed a cigarette from Daddy's pack on the coffee table and lit my first. My eyes were melting into the glow of the television, but I couldn't see what came next to the chopping block. My mind was someplace else, shooting back and forth between the way Maggie'd looked at my hands that night when Avery quit moving, and the way her lips had pursed just a little when she sat right beside where I was sitting now. I wondered if she'd wanted to kiss me, if somehow or another she had the feelings in her that were eating me alive, if maybe she'd forgiven me, if anything in the world could make a woman like that fall for something like me not once, but twice? There wasn't but one way to answer any of it, and so I made up my mind right then and there that just as soon as dawn broke over the jack pines I would settle it, put an end to the wondering.

———

THE TRAIL TURNED steep just a hundred yards from a kidney-shaped gravel parking lot. The Little Green lookout wasn't far, but from there, the trail cut switchbacks down angled grade and didn't flatten for a second until the valley. When I was younger and Daddy still took me to the woods to get away, he used to bring me down that trail to chase speckled trout with red wrigglers where the headwaters of the Tuckasegee was nothing more than a creek. He'd poach those specks by the dozen, sliding the six-to-eight-inch trout into the top of a milk jug until it was full and those fish were flapping against one another. He'd never cared much for game wardens, and considered all those newfangled laws an attack on a family that settled here before the first land grants were cut loose. We'd head home and Daddy would fry the trout whole, eat those specks, bones and all. I ate them too, but the memory that stuck out most was the way those fish smelled on my hands, that mossy kind of smell that was clean and dripping wet with something older than any of us, and the smile on my father's face. Those were the times when Daddy was most like a father, the times when he shared fragments of what truly made him happy. That was what stuck out in my mind as I sat down on the rock that morning and stared out at Little Green.

Maggie had started running during the middle school years after her family left The Creek. The Creek was a beautiful place, but it was lawless and always had been. The land was of little use for farming, so the folks who settled way back when were mostly drunkards and thieves. I was generations away from those earliest outlaws, but things like that have a way of staying in the blood. Maggie's father didn't carry those ties, but he fit right in. When

Maggie and I were kids and her father tied on weeklong drunks, he'd wander the road, stumbling tranquilized, speaking gibberish, wake up covered in dew when the booze wore off. Even the crankers took him for a joke and searched his pockets for any dollar left while he lay sprawled like a cadaver. It was when he *found Jesus* that he moved the family onto Breedlove Road. I guess he figured he could leave it behind.

With their house on Breedlove just up the gravel from Panthertown, Maggie took a liking to the trails that wove through that wilderness. For years now, she'd been coming here every morning when the sun rose, and would run from the parking lot to Schoolhouse Falls and back, no matter if it was drowning frogs or snowing over tire chains. I'd never cared much for running. I wasn't about to run unless something gave chase, more specifically something with teeth, something with a gun, or something with blue lights and a badge looking for someone to take down to Sylva mid-shift. Maggie ran from things all her own. She ran from circumstance. She ran from things that would never catch her. And somewhere down in that valley, Maggie was running right toward me without even knowing.

I'd stolen a soft pack of Winston straights from a carton Daddy kept in the freezer, and by the time I heard someone coming out of the valley, I'd already smoked that pack half flat. I heard her long before I saw her, tennis shoes crunching gravel, then her breathing as she blurred behind a laurel thicket. She saw me standing as she passed and threw on the brakes, her soles sliding to stop on loose gravel.

"Jacob," she said, huffing for breath and searching for words. Her hair was pulled back into a ponytail and a tight lilac-purple top stretched at her breasts while she panted. Black sweats followed the curves of her legs to just past the knees. "You scared the hell out of me."

I made my way through a thin line of brush and stood beside her on the path. "I didn't mean to scare you."

"No, not like that, Jacob. You just surprised me, that's all."

"I had to see you."

"I wish it weren't like this." Maggie looked herself over, eyed the places where she sweated as if she were embarrassed. She took a long swig of water from a sports bottle. She was still out of breath.

"You look beautiful."

"That's sweet. Maybe a little bit of a lie, but sweet."

"I've never lied to you."

Maggie's eyes were fixed on me. We didn't speak, and she didn't come any closer, but there was something brewing in that space between us. It was me who broke the silence.

"I have to ask you something."

"What is it?"

"I want to know if you've forgiven me."

"Forgiven you?"

"Yeah, Mags. That shit has haunted me since the minute we broke up, and I thought I was over it, and then you were graduating, and the thought of you leaving without me ever knowing for sure is fucked. It's just fucked."

"I don't understand."

"I know it doesn't make sense. I know it doesn't. I left you. I did it. I'm the one who fucked it all up. But the thing is it never felt right, and then you came to the house, and the way you were looking at me—"

"How was I looking at you?"

"Fuck, I don't know, Maggie. You were looking at me like you used to."

"I'm not trying to be difficult, Jacob. I just want to hear it."

"You looked like there were feelings still there."

Maggie stared at the ground as if looking at me any longer just might destroy her. She didn't say anything for a while, and I didn't know how to fill that silence. There was nothing I could say to fill that space. Then her head came up and her eyes were filled with a sadness and anger that I hadn't seen since the day I left her. When I walked out of high school, my life was decided, and with my life decided, keeping her any longer would have bound her just the same. I broke her heart in the parking lot and drove away with her crying her eyes out, left that school and her and any shot I'd ever had of making it off this mountain in one clean cut. That sadness and anger is what I'd spent the last two years trying my damnedest to forget. But there was something different about it this time. There was strength with it. There was something solid about her now, a confidence that seemed to guarantee that what I broke would never be broken again.

"I loved you, Jacob. I always loved you. From the time we were tiny. But you broke my heart. You left me and you broke my heart and I've done everything I can to get over it."

"I know I did. I know I did, and I'm sorry. I'm sorry, Maggie."

"I needed an apology a long time ago, Jacob. I needed you to be there. I needed you to be there until it quit hurting, and the fact that you weren't is what hurt most of all. The fact that you just upped and left. But if there's one thing you can do for me, it's tell me why you thought you had to do it? I've never been able to understand why you left."

"Because I loved you."

"I don't think you and I have the same meaning of that word."

"I loved you then and I love you now. I can't imagine ever not loving you."

"That doesn't make any sense."

I'd always known why I left her, but I'd never had to put it into words. I knew the words would be too hard to come by. I knew the words would have to be perfect. She deserved those kinds of words, but I didn't know if I'd ever had them inside of me. The only thing I could offer Maggie was honesty, brutal honesty. That was the one thing I'd always given her.

"I couldn't stand the thought of keeping you here. I couldn't stand the thought of it then and I can't stand the thought of it now. You're better than this place. You always have been. You've had your eyes set on someplace else since we were kids, but where you're different is that you've actually got something that can get you there. You're smart enough to do any fucking thing you ever wanted to do, and you're stubborn enough to make it happen. But I'm not, Maggie. I'm not getting out of here and I know that. I came to terms with what I was born into a long fucking time ago. I can't get out of that. So how in the fuck would that work? One way or another you were going to get hurt. I loved you too fucking much to drag it out."

"There's nothing keeping you here, Jacob."

"Bullshit."

"There's never been anything keeping you here but you."

"Bullshit, Mags."

"I mean that." Maggie moved closer and that closeness cut my words. She stood directly under me now, her head almost pressed into my chest, gorgeous blond curls wadded up close enough to nuzzle. "I wouldn't have fallen in love with you if it weren't true."

I wasn't quite sure what to say and so I said nothing. I just stood there staring into her eyes. And in that moment that passed between us, there was this energy in the air that seemed to cup the two of us like lightning bugs in closed hands. I felt numb. I felt weightless and numb, and it was the closest thing to perfection that I'd ever felt. And out of that feeling came words. And maybe they were the perfect words, or maybe just the closest thing to perfect words that I'd ever had, and so I spoke them.

That same look I'd seen appeared again. Those silver blues dilated like she was on some fine drug. She pushed up onto tiptoes, her head cocking sideways as she came, and before I knew it I could feel her lips pressed into mine and I struggled to catch up. I hooked hair that had fallen along her cheeks back behind her ears, and continued with my right hand down her arm till my fingers found their place along her ribs. I ran my left hand down her cheekbone and feathered my fingers under her chin to hold her there a second longer if I could. The numbness stayed with me. It was an old feeling that I had all but forgotten, a feeling that I never knew I'd missed until right then. She pulled back and smiled, and I was left there wide-eyed as a child when she ran away.

10.

The roach had no more than caught the wind when I saw that son of a bitch hiding out in the Jehovah's Witness parking lot at the three-lane. I'd scrounged up a skimpy pin joint by plucking what little bit of bud clung to stems picked clean at least twice by now and had brought it with me on the ride to smoke after seeing Maggie. I'd figured it for a disappointment-easing kind of smoke, but after what had just happened, I was riding high. It was a fucking celebration in the cab of my pickup, and now this son of a bitch was pulling out to cut the music at the first dance.

He rode along behind me a good six or seven car lengths back for the first half mile, gave me time to light another Winston and let the morning breeze soften the stench. I reckon it was about the time I held that cigarette out the window to let the wind carry ash that he sped up and put the Crown Vic right up against my tailgate. That's when the lights came and sirens blared, not one of those chirps like pull over and everything will be fine, but full fucking sirens. Though the first thought in a McNeely is always *Floor it*, I knew that my old beater might just give out coming through Glenville and there I'd be racking up charges. So instead, I slowed down, flicked the blinker, and pulled into a real estate office just Cashiers side of Bee Tree Road.

He stepped out in the same way all those bulls do, opening the door and leaving it wide as they resituate the weight on their belts. He rolled his neck around to push out cricks left from sitting in a cruiser too long, and he shut the door across his body with his left hand as his right flipped the snap on his holster and settled onto the grips.

I was eyeing him awfully hard in the side mirror as he came up to the truck. He sported the same high-and-tight haircut as all rookie deputies. They must have had a deal worked out with the barbers, something to give them all that same I-eat-shit-for-a-living hairstyle so that us lowlifes couldn't tell the difference from where one asshole started and another began, all of them just shitting on us from a conveyor. He was young—not so young as me, but in my dealings I'd come to recognize the just-out-of-basic look about a man with a badge. Those types all had the same attitude, something to prove, and this bull was no different. This bull was no friend of the family, and that being the case, I knew I was in for the whole play strictly by the books.

"License and registration." It was standard programmed protocol, but this one had to add his own twist. "Slowly."

I was already moving pretty *slowly*, but I let up even more as I reached toward the glove box. Papers were shuffled inside, and I was hoping there wasn't a bag or two stashed somewhere in a place I'd missed the night before when I'd gone scrounging for something to smoke. There weren't any bags, but no registration either, so I just pulled out my wallet and slid the license out from under clouded plastic.

"License and?" He looked at me like he wanted me to answer, but I didn't say a word. "License and?" He gave me one more shot. "Registration."

"Can't seem to find the registration. Truck's in my daddy's name."

"And who exactly might your daddy be?"

"Charles McNeely." I didn't want to say, knowing good and damn well where that name would get me, but then again *McNeely* was printed nice and clear on my license, as telling as DNA. I flat stunk with McNeely, and it wouldn't take some dickhead bull long to move into questioning. "Most folks know him as Charlie."

"I know all about old Charlie McNeely, and I'm quite sure this truck here is registered in his name. I'm quite sure you're his son. Thing is, I'm not really worried about that registration right now, you see? Thing is, you've got some bigger troubles."

"What's that?"

"Well, son, I'm getting the munchies just standing here." Truth was he'd never smoked a day in his life, but the way he said it put me into a snickering fit. The bull stepped back and slid his pistol up and down in its holster just enough for the slide to peek. "I'm going to need you to step out of the vehicle for me, all right, Jacob?"

"All ri—"

"Slowly." And there he went again, pushing that *slowly* on me like I was getting wide-eyed and hairy in the stall with a cowboy cinching tight on the nut rope. But just as he said, I rolled out of that truck *slowly*, extra slow just for him, my body spilling out like syrup.

The bull led me to the back of the truck and popped the tailgate with his left hand, that other hand never leaving the handle of his .40, and he asked me to stand there with my legs spread. He asked some bullshit line of questions the state had to be teaching at basic, something that must've passed for humor with lawmen. "Now, you don't have any hand grenades, missile launchers, AK-47s, anything like that stuffed down your pants, do you?"

Don't give the cocksucker an inch, I thought. "Might be a fucking Sherman tank there in the front if you want a feel."

The patting got harder, and he yanked out everything I had in my pockets and slung it into the bed of the pickup: wallet, a half-crushed pack of smokes, a lighter, my cell phone, and a bottle of Clear Eyes. He worked his way down my legs and started coming back up, running his fingers along the seams of my britches as though I may have hired a seamstress to sew a few condoms filled with black tar heroin into my jeans. Cars were passing with out-of-state tags and children on vacation pressed their noses against the windows like slobbering pigs to get a look at what life was really like in Jackson County.

"Mind if I search the vehicle, Jacob?"

I knew the line of questioning, and I knew the line of action. The McNeely in me said to tell him no, but even a McNeely understood that a no would mean a three-hour wait for the magistrate to sign off on a warrant before they'd search that son of a bitch anyhow. Either way I went about it, he was going to search that car, so I thought I'd save myself some time, especially since that roach I left up the highway was all I had till I could get a bag come afternoon. "Mind? Not a bit, sir. You just go on in there and snoop around till your heart's content."

"You've got quite the mouth on you, boy. You know that?"

I didn't say a word, just stared at him till he knew I could see right through that distilled toughness and point out the chicken-shit that lay thick, had always lain thick, in shitheads like him.

"Seeing as I'm alone, I'm going to put these cuffs on you and put you in the back of the car while I search, just to keep you from any funny business."

"Am I under arrest?"

"Not yet. Ain't found anything worth arresting you for just yet. I just need you to sit back there and hold tight. Understand?"

I didn't say a word when he cinched the cuffs down till my hands turned white. Nor did I say a goddamn word when he cupped the crown of my head to slide me in and rapped my fore-head against the doorjamb of his cruiser. No, I kept awfully quiet, awfully quiet until that door was shut and he was on his way back to my truck. *Cocksucker!* I screamed at the top of my lungs, and he turned around pissed for a second or two with my teeth just shining at him through the smudged separation glass.

I had to wriggle to get sitting upright, my legs cramped side-ways in a space not big enough for pygmies. The patrol car smelled sanitized, a chemical reek left behind from something used to scrub the blood and vomit of drunken folks who never went peacefully. From where I'd pulled over there was a perfect view of Lake Glenville, and with the sun just starting to boil mercury, the summer residents, country-club types, were headed out onto the lake in long cigarette boats and pontoons dragging tubes slathered with screaming children. The locals only ventured out onto the lake when the leaves changed and walleye pushed up to waterfalls and run-ins. There used to be loads of walleye and smallmouth in that lake until the state dumped a load of egg-sucking blueback herring in by accident. Just another reason to hate the law, I reckon.

Radio chatter told the tale of Adams and Bakers down the mountain running routine traffic on domestics and burglary alarms that never turned up key holders. I could see the bull rummaging through the cab of my pickup, and knowing that I didn't have a salt lick to lap on, I figured it was just a minute or two more before he'd stagger out disappointed. Just when I'd turned back from watching an Evinrude slice a clean wake across the middle of Lake Glenville, sure enough here that bull came, his head all but hanging. He opened the door and I smiled up at him knowing I'd beaten him, knowing that, friend of the family or not, the McNeelys had just taken another battle in a war that would last till the tombstones ran out.

"Find anything?"

"Just a pack of rolling papers crammed up under your seat. But I guess rolling papers don't count for much if there's nothing to roll, now does it?"

"I've been looking everywhere for those papers." I upped the sarcasm as the thrill of his defeat brought back the joy I'd held since Little Green. "Hope you left them on the seat for me?"

"Afraid not. Afraid I can't let you go knowing good and well a boy like you might get himself into trouble, now can I?"

I didn't answer, but stood up out of the car and turned fast, those cuffs warming in sunshine as I waited for him to cut me free. He unlocked the cuffs, those teeth let loose from biting, and I turned to him for salutations. "Reckon I'll be on my way."

"Just one more minute there, Jacob. You just go have a seat back in your pickup while I run your name." I started walking away, and he hit me with it again, a sucker punch to let me know there was not a white flag to be thrown and he was still in charge. "Slowly."

The cab of the pickup still smelled sweet as skunk piss, and it kind of brought my mood up even higher knowing that he knew what I knew and that there wasn't a damn thing in the world he could do about it. A day late and a dollar short didn't get you far in this business, and despite a few hiccups, that joint still had me feeling toasty. After a minute or two of thumbing through pages of CDs, I watched the bull make his way back up to the driver side, my wallet in one hand and his right hand still gripping that pistol.

"Spend much time in Foxfire?"

"Not really. Why?"

"Well, son, seems we've got a warrant out for you. Seems you mashed somebody up pretty good at a party there the other night and seems he's been laid up in the hospital ever since."

"I don't know what you're talking about." I knew who I'd mashed up, but I didn't know of any warrants out for my arrest. I figured that would be the type of thing they'd hunt a man down for, and being a McNeely, I wouldn't have been hard to find. But most of the lawmen were lazy. And in a place this small, the hunt between lawmen and outlaws was about like chasing rabbits: give it time and the quarry will always circle back, land in your lap if you wait long enough.

"The way those knuckles are healing, I'd say that you do." The bull shot that shit-eating grin at me, and he backed up from the truck. "I'm going to need you to step back out of the vehicle, Jacob."

It was right then that the McNeely blood screamed run, and it was right then the high that was left started turning to a headache. I knew that he had me. I knew that there was no use in running. So once again, I held back on instinct and did as I was told.

"Slowly."

11.

The concrete was painted a warm kind of gray, something not so depressing as snow clouds but more of a gray like an old woman's perm. It was a thick, shiny kind of paint like might've been used on a floor, and it reflected what little bit of light shone down from two fluorescent tubes flickering and dying. Sound came through the cuffing hole on the steel door and white light beamed through the thin rectangle of glass. Every once in a while footsteps tromped closer, voices grew louder, and I'd watch a bull or two slide by the door, their eyes cutting in at me as they passed.

While I'd let the tongue fly when I wasn't under arrest, the minute it was official, I zipped it. That deputy had gone to talking even more with the battle won, asking all sorts of questions about my family and about my father, but Daddy had taught me well. Talk shit when you're free. Shut up in the cuffs. Lawyer up first chance.

That was the call I'd made.

I'd never been to jail before, and that's why it took so long to get to the cell. That jail was the embodiment of, "When one door closes, another door opens," only there wasn't anything bright on the other side. When the bull had driven up, one fence opened, he pulled up to another fence, stopped, the fence behind closed, and the one in front opened. When we headed through the back door, we entered into a small room, and when the door behind closed, the one in front opened. The whole place seemed to work like that, until I got to booking and they fastened my cuffs with chains to a chest-high shelf in front of a window. The woman on the other side asked all sorts of questions about when I'd been born, what sorts of scars and tattoos I was marked with, any aliases I might have, or any gang affiliations. That's what had taken so damn long, and though I didn't like being there, I was looking forward to the fact that future visits, and I was certain there'd be future visits, would only require updating that file. Hell, by then I might have a good nickname.

They'd put me in a smaller cell after booking, one right beside the magistrate's office. I reckon they took the warrant into the office and had the magistrate recheck a bond amount he'd already signed off on when he issued the arrest. I'd been charged with assault and battery, and that old codger must've figured me for the running type, setting a secured bond for ten thousand dollars. When the bulls had explained the charges, I was awfully certain of the battery. I reckon I'd batteryed the ever-living hell out of that boy, but the assault, or "threatening of violence" as they put it, was a question I needed answered. I'd never said a word. Not one goddamned word. I'd moved straight into the batterying. Seeing as they said Avery was in the hospital with a shattered orbital, likely to need some reconstructing, I must've been a pretty good batteryer. And seeing as how that son of a bitch deserved every lick he took, I figured the fifteen percent needed to post out wasn't too high a tab: fifteen hundred dollars in crisp bills and I'd be lapping up supper on The Creek come dinnertime. Daddy might even spring for a steak dinner considering how proud he'd been.

I hadn't seen hide nor hair of Daddy, the lawyer, or any friends of the family for the duration of that first cell, and the bulls were about to escort me into a finer abode, so I could have neighbors and company and such, when I heard someone screaming. Two deputies were leading me down the hall, my arms stiff and cuffs cutting into my wrists.

"You two! Deputies! Stop right there! You just stop this goddamn instant!"

The three of us all turned together like a drum line, and once I got facing that way, I could see that little pudgy bastard shuffling down the hall, his bald head beaming reflective. Mr. Queen had been born with fourteen rattles and a button, just about the snakiest son of a bitch to ever come off of Caney Fork. The whole family of snakes had been denned up in that cut for generations and had a long history of clanking jars and copper worms, but I reckon he'd seen early on that the battle waged against lawmen was fought and won in courtrooms, in fancy suits and ties. Every bit of moonshine a McNeely ever swallowed had come from a Caney Fork Queen, so when things got big enough to need full-time representation, Daddy'd snatched him up. So far there hadn't been a friend of the family who spent more than a few days clinked up, and we had that vole-faced peckerwood to thank for it.

There was a bull close on his coattails and as Mr. Queen shuffled that bull reached out and grabbed ahold of Queen's sleeve.

"Unhand me, you maggot! This suit was tailored custom by Jos. A. Bank. Ever heard of him? Can you spell it?" Mr. Queen stopped pacing just long enough to yank his coat sleeve out of grubby hands and then on he came. "That boy you've got there, now you need to get those cuffs off of him this instant. His bond is posted and he's a free man till trial." Mr. Queen continued until he was standing directly in front of me. He scrunched his nose to lift glasses over squinted eyes, and he kept that scowl long enough to shoot both bulls an I'll-have-you-for-dinner-on-the-stand kind of look. "How are you, Jacob? I hope these gentlemen have treated you well."

Mr. Queen held out his hand to shake mine, but I was still hemmed up and could only offer a nod. "Been better."

"Well, say no more, son. Don't say one word, and we'll be taking you home for supper. How about that?"

"That'd suit me fine."

"Sure it would." Mr. Queen turned his stare back to the bulls. "Now, I want my client out of cuffs immediately."

The bulls looked at their ringleader standing behind my lawyer, and that older bull shook his head okay. That quick and the key clicked, the teeth were loosened, and I was rubbing the red bracelets left behind off my wrists. As quickly as I'd come, I was headed out in true McNeely fashion. Like I thought, I'd be home by supper.

MR. QUEEN AND I walked out of the front of the Jackson County Administration Building through doors that opened with a push rather than buzzing. It was almost night now, yellow fading into darkness over the peaks. He led me to a long, fat Lincoln trimmed in gold where most folks would've settled for chrome. While I'm certain it had cost him a pretty penny, I personally found the touch a tad gaudy. The look was a bit jarring to me, reminiscent of those thick gold earrings old women with blue hair wear in church, the kind that drag their earlobes down and make the piercing holes stretch long.

"Nice ride you got here, Mr. Queen."

"Irving."

"What was that?"

"I said call me Irving." Mr. Queen shot me a smile and scrunched his glasses back up over his eyes. He hit a switch on his key chain, the headlights blinked, and I could hear the latches flick up on the inside of the Lincoln.

The car smelled of stale cigar smoke with a hint of baby powder, an offensive odor that fit him well. Leather seats were stained with coffee spills and the passenger-side floorboard was littered with empty coffee cups and pints of whiskey. He had classed it up a bit on the inside with one of those air freshener trees hung on the vent.

"Think you might want to trash these liquor bottles?"

"For what purpose?"

"In case you were pulled over."

"Pulled over for what?"

"I don't know, just pulled over."

"Now, if you're going to start throwing around scenarios, you're going to have to be specific. Generalities won't get you far in this line of work."

I kicked my feet through the swamp of trash, and Mr. Queen headed down the hill out of the parking lot. "Let's just say you came up into a traffic stop. Let's just say the law had one of those roadblocks they like to set up so good, and—"

"I'm assuming this roadblock is perfectly legal? Not set up in a racially profiling manner, you know? Not set up on a road traveled primarily by migrant workers, is it?"

"Perfectly legal, and let's just say you pull on up there, and they get to seeing all these liquor bottles." I kicked my feet around until the hollow bottles clanked against one another. "Let's say they ain't too keen on a man in a fancy car with liquor bottles piled up in the floorboards."

"Ain't a damn thing illegal about being a good community steward, Jacob."

"Community steward?"

"Yes, a community steward. Litter cleanup is all. I just have a habit of keeping the highways clear of litter."

"And I reckon it's whiskey bottles making up the majority of litter on these highways."

"Well, of course it is. Folks guzzling RC Cola certainly don't throw bottles out of car windows. No, sir. It's the drunks you have to worry about." Mr. Queen pulled a mashed-out cigar from the ashtray and put the butt end between lips that wrapped around his face like kielbasas. He struck a match and nearly veered across the white line as we headed into town. He puffed hard to get that cigar going, his cheeks sucking and blowing till fat wads of smoke started pouring out of that old potbelly. As the fire crept, snubbed

leaves of tobacco peppered lit embers into his lap. "Goddamn it!
Goddamn it!" he screamed, and yanked the car onto the shoulder
as his right hand patted hard in his crotch. "Not the Jos. A. Bank's!
Not the goddamn Jos. A. Bank's!"

We rode through town in silence. I think I'd crossed him a
little when he damn near lit his junk afire and I laughed, but as we
passed the university, he finally continued the conversation.

"Remember what I was saying about trial?"

"No. Not exactly."

"Remember I was telling those deputies that you were a free
man till trial? Remember that?"

"I reckon so."

"Well, don't you worry about that, Jacob."

"What do you mean?"

"I mean there isn't going to be any trial."

"How's that?"

"Well, there was a reason I was the one that came to pick
you up this evening. You see, your father went to have a little talk
with Mr. Hooper and it seems they've come to an understanding.
Seems it couldn't have been you that did that to his son, seeing as
you were with your father at home on that night. I reckon the *vic-
tim* must've been mistaken."

"And it's all going to work out like that?"

"Why, yes, Jacob. I just need to have Mr. Hooper accompany
me to the district attorney's office, the district attorney and I go
way back, and Mr. Hooper will explain that this was all a big misunderstanding, you see. After that, free and clear."

"Free and clear, huh?"

"Free and clear."

We rode past the Moonshine Mini Mart, a cream-colored

building with a cobble foundation where bear hunters often stopped to shoot the shit. The parking lot was always filled with pickups covered in antennas, dog boxes filled with dead-tired hounds. Anyone with a lick of sense had known for a long time that the owners were running a shake-and-bake lab right beneath the register. It was bad, cheap yellow dope that only the lowest folks turned to when the money for McNeely quality ran out. I'd always been amazed at how none of the bulls stumbled onto the man running that operation. Every time he handed out change to deputies buying tins of tobacco, it was plain as day that his hands were eat up from burping bottles, the lithium strips just bubbling in the syrup beneath the register. How those bulls never caught a whiff of all those chemicals, I'll never know.

Mr. Queen shot a glance up Caney Fork Road, and to me, it seemed he was looking way back into the place he'd come from. He resituated himself against the leather seat and tugged on his Jos. A. Bank's lapels. There was pride in the way he jerked on that jacket. He'd come a long way, I reckon, a long way from that holler he'd slithered out of. But if it had been me, I'd have slithered a little further. If I were going to leave, it would be to a place where nobody knew me, a place where McNeely was just another name. Folks like us needed aliases.

12.

There was no hero's welcome. No rib eyes sizzling over charcoal briquettes. No cold beer in koozies. Instead I walked in like a discordant note on the Townes Van Zandt song spinning around the record player.

The Cabe brothers were sitting on the couch—the skinny one, Jeremy, pressing his hand nearly white against his forehead. Red oozed out from under Jeremy's hand like he'd smashed a tomato just above his eyes. The blood dripped down onto his baby-blue T-shirt and had dotted lines along the thighs of brown canvas britches. Gerald sat beside his brother with his arms folded and resting across his knees. He was hunched over, fat swallowing suspenders, and seemed to just kind of hover there with his stare fixed on the hardwood. My father was standing over them, his slender frame casting a shadow that neither Cabe brother could've crawled out from under. Daddy had his shirt off, white skin almost completely covered in ink, and as the screen door closed behind me, his eyes cut into me in a way I'd never seen in any man. That stare, that cold, rage-filled fucking stare, cowered a man's soul, and suddenly, all of the stories I'd ever heard about him were glaring down into a place inside of me that had never been touched.

"Goddamn it, Jacob! Of all the fucking days to get pinched! Of all the fucking days in your shitty-ass little life to get pinched, you go and do it on a day like this!" I just stood there frozen in headlights lit by rage and waited for him to tell me to move. "Sit the fuck down over there." Daddy motioned with a .45 auto, a Commander-sized 1911 he'd gotten for a short bag of dope when bags were still pushed through windowsills, but I still couldn't move. "Goddamn it, boy, I said sit the fuck down!"

Jeremy's knees were knocking and his eyes had grown two sizes too big for his head. "Do we really need to get the boy into—"

"Shut the fuck up!" Daddy backhanded the pistol across Jeremy's face and the front sight caught just beneath his eye, cutting a sliver that shone white for a second before filling red. Gerald's arms lifted from his knees and he looked like he might stand, but Daddy hammered the bottom of the magazine square into his nose and that knoll of flesh mashed flat. Under the bill of his Joy Dog Food trucker cap, Gerald's eyes watered and he squinted to hold it in, but there was nothing to stop the fountain that dumped out of both nostrils, ran over his lips and chin like a stream over stone, and dripped into a stain on his undershirt. The Cabe brothers' eyes were fixed on Daddy now, and it was a fear of what might happen when the trigger broke that held them there. I still hadn't moved. "Jacob, I've already told you with my mouth." He motioned with the pistol to the chair beside the couch. I scampered over to the chair and sat down, never taking my eyes off of Daddy or that gun. "What do you think happened, Jacob? Why do you think these two are piled up over there on the couch?"

"I don't know."

"You don't know?"

"No, sir. I don't reckon I do."

"You don't reckon you do." Daddy smirked and sort of chuckled under his breath. "You don't reckon you do. My own fucking flesh and blood, my own fucking son, and you don't reckon you do!" In an instant Daddy had slid the pistol into the back of his sweatpants and was straddling me. His hands settled around my neck and squeezed so hard that in the first seconds I knew I was dying. There was no gradual rise into choking. I knew he was going to kill me. I was drowning in his hands, and the lights in the room were changing. I tried to breathe but there was nothing. I searched as hard as I could for air and there was nothing, and I knew I wouldn't last a second more, and just before it all went black, Jeremy rose out of the corner of my eye.

Daddy was off me and had the gun back out in one clean motion, and he hammered the side of the pistol into Jeremy's face, sent his skinny frame flying and falling limp beside his brother. Gerald started to rise again and Daddy yanked the slide back, pulled the trigger just as the hammer set. *BOOM!*

The shot ripped apart music still blaring from speakers and my ears rang as I coughed for breath. My eyes jumped to where Gerald had sat, and as my vision cleared, I was sure I'd find a mess in that first moment of clarity. I was certain there would be an entry hole .45 inches wide in Gerald's forehead, a splash of color on the picture that hung behind the couch, pieces of brain spread like bits of ground sausage on the hardwood, but there wasn't. There was a hole exactly .45 inches wide in the wall just to the right of where Gerald's head had risen.

We held there silent as prayer when Daddy walked into the kitchen. None of us moved an inch while Daddy turned up a bottle of bourbon and breathed through bubbles. He set the bottle down calmly on the kitchen table and ran his forearm across his mouth to dry what spilt. Daddy pulled a crumpled soft pack of smokes from the pocket of his sweatpants and flipped a Winston into his lips. He lit the cigarette and returned.

"Now I'm done with the bullshit." That animal look about him had sobered and Daddy was back to that crazy sort of calmness I knew well, a part of him that I honestly feared more than rage. "Y'all are family. Y'all are all I've got in this world. But I want y'all to understand one thing. Nobody says another goddamn word until I'm finished talking. You got that?"

No one nodded. No one moved. No one said a fucking word.

"We've already been talking, Jacob, but I reckon I'm going to have to back up a bit to get you up to speed."

Daddy walked over to the record player, lifted the arm, and set the needle into a line that never stopped spinning. He started the record over and the first notes of "For the Sake of the Song" started crackling and popping through the speakers. Daddy cranked the volume knob a little higher and Townes's melancholic voice rose.

"You see, there was this family, Jacob, and this family had a dog that had a tendency to go crazy on a scent. The family had got this old hound from one of those shelters, I guess, a stray that must've never done much good running bear. Now, this dog still had the hunt bred into him. Wasn't ever much of a family kind of dog. Anyhow, this dog caught a smell that suited him and those fucking eyes lit up and before anybody in the house could even know to holler, 'Sit,' that dog was off. And so here this stupid-ass dog goes trampling off in the woods and hunting down a smell that took him miles from that yard.

"Well, a little while later the family gets to missing that old dog pretty bad, and they go to calling and calling but never hear a yelp. It's sometime early morning and the wife gets to nagging at the husband that he better go looking for the dog, and as husbands are prone to do, that dumb motherfucker listened.

"Now, there's a dog still trampling off through the woods, and there's a man knowing good and well that if he don't find that dog, he's not going to get a lick of pussy anytime soon. That thought never leaves this man's head as he's trudging through the woods, stepping over rattlesnake dens and everything else just for the chance that he might get some ass if he can track down that dog. That thought just kept eating at him and eating at him and driving him further and further from home until all of a sudden he gets to this clearing, a big ol' sloping hill scattered with rocks the size of Volkswagens, and he hears a single bark cut across open air.

"I bet his dick got hard just as soon as that bark tickled his eardrums, so he tore up that hill ready to grab that fucking hound by the collar and drag his ass back miles through thick woods just for a chance at pussy his wife would probably end up teasing him with anyways. Well, as this man gets up the hill he finds that old hound nestled up next to a half-naked man wrapped tight around one of those rocks. There's a smell about that body after a few days and the man thinks he just might get sick, but he leans down there anyhow and gets to looking past all those burns and all that blood and he hears something. You know what he hears, Jacob? He hears him breathing."

Daddy took the gun and scratched at an itch on his temple with the holey end. He took a real deep breath, rocked his head back, and closed his eyes for a second or two before they settled into me. "He was fucking breathing, Jacob."

A heaviness clinched down around my whole body, a heaviness like I was in a vacuum, and as the magnitude of what my father had said set in, I was choking again. I tried to breathe but couldn't, only Daddy's hands were still right there hanging by his sides. I felt like I was going to be sick, and then, out of nowhere, this numbness came over me and it was as if my body was still sitting in that chair, but my eyes had floated off for a better view. I could see the whole room, the Cabe brothers and me sitting there while Daddy stood over us with the pistol. I was floating even higher now, and it was a calming sort of feeling the further I got away. As I rose, the rubber band started stretching thin the further I went, until there was no more give to be given and that rubber band snapped and I shot back into myself, all of that reality driven home that at barely eighteen years old, I was as good as dead, and I threw up all over my lap.

Daddy looked down at me with a disgusted sneer wiped across his face.

"Now, I don't have to tell any of you how serious this is. I don't have to tell you that the fact a man who was supposed to be buried two goddamn days ago is alive and breathing in a hospital bed tonight is a problem. Every single one of you knows that this is a big fucking problem. This is the type of mess that can't be cleaned up, and there ain't a goddamn thing any of us can do but sit back and wait for the story to unfold.

"So there's two things that could happen. Right now as we speak, that cranked-out son of a bitch is laid up in a hospital bed unconscious with breathing machines doing most of the work to keep him tied to this world. Any minute that son of a bitch could flatline, and aside from a few John Laws trying to figure out what the fuck happened, we'd be in the clear. That's one thing that could happen.

"The other thing that could happen is that those doctors could keep him alive for days, weeks, months even, and one day in a split second that son of a bitch could wake up and when the words finally settle in his mouth and get to tasting good, he might just have a story to tell. It's that story that presents the problem. It's that goddamn story that gets every single one of us locked up for the rest of our fucking lives. At my age and where I'm at in life, that's the kind of thing that I just couldn't let happen." Daddy stopped for a second and stared at that pistol as he turned it back and forth in the light. "At my age, I reckon I'd just blow my fucking brains out in the trees somewhere and let the crows have a taste. But for y'all's sake, let's hope it doesn't come to that. For y'all's sake, let's hope that son of a bitch keels over."

Daddy walked into the kitchen and sat down at the table. He laid the pistol on the tabletop and slid the bottle of bourbon into his chest. His dark hair was slicked and wetted with sweat, and his jaw seemed to flex with every beat of his heart. He pulled the cork and took a long swig, washed that rotgut around in his mouth for a moment, and swallowed. There wasn't another word spoken. "Don't You Take It Too Bad" bled into "Colorado Girl" on the Townes album, and when the song finished out, someone would have to turn to Side B.

Daddy was staring into the bottle and scratching away at the tabletop with the tip of the pistol when the Cabe brothers eased from the couch and snuck for the door. There still wasn't a word said, and the final refrain sounded from the speakers as the screen door creaked closed. The final crackles and pops of blank album slid away under the needle and the arm rose, pushed off to the side, and fell into the cradle. Silence.

Daddy stood and walked calmly into his bedroom. After a few seconds, he came back out carrying a .22 pistol he used to put down hogs on days when a knife proved too much work. Daddy slid the long bull barrel down into the back of his sweatpants and headed out the front door.

I sat right there and didn't move until I heard two short snaps like a cap gun echo from the yard. I got up and peered out of the window then. Daddy was walking back from the Cabe brothers' pickup and the moonlight lit his bare chest blue in places where Irish skin still shone. The Walkers spread as he came through the yard, every hound moving as far back on its lead as it could to get away from him. The bullet hole and splash of color I'd been sure would spread wide open just a few short minutes before was certainly spread now. There was a mess that would need cleaning soon.

13.

In a perfect world we could've waited for a new moon to shroud us in secrecy. In a perfect world we could've buried those bodies in a place where we could dig them back up and move them when the time came. But it wasn't a perfect world.

The blood had dried in the hours since those two shots of rimfire came across the lawn, but Daddy had wanted to wait. If it'd been me, I'd have moved those bodies before souls had time to flee. Then again, if it had been me, I don't reckon I'd have pulled the trigger.

Jeremy always drove the pickup, so he sat in the driver's side, his body fallen over, arms tucked under him, and his head facedown in his brother's lap. Gerald's head was rocked back on the seat where a headrest should have been, but wasn't, so his head just lay there, throat angled toward sagging ceiling fabric and that cap nearly falling off backward. His eyes were open, his mouth too, and his nose was the color of a plum where Daddy'd smashed it with the pistol. The entry hole had caught him right above his left eyebrow and there wasn't an exit, just that one hole and a thick line of dried blood wavering on his cheek. That was why Daddy had changed guns, to keep it as clean as possible, to just let that lead go to rattling around against bone until everything inside was pudding.

Hanging halfway out of the left side pocket of Jeremy's jeans was a small pocket Bible like might've been found in the bedside drawer of a motel room. Until I saw it there in Jeremy's pocket with my own two eyes, I'd always thought the stories were lies, just tales told to add to the mythology of my father. I'd overheard it a dozen times since I was a kid, folks telling stories about Daddy laying a pocket Bible on the chest of every man he killed. The boys who told the tales all gave different reasons for it, none of those reasons really adding up to anything I knew of my father. Come to find out, though, it was a story that held water. I looked across the cab and pressed against Gerald's chest by his suspenders was a second Bible just the same.

I had my guesses for why he did it. I figured it had something to do with his father, my Papaw, a man whom Daddy had loved. You wouldn't have known it anymore, but we came from a long line of God-fearing people, good Baptists who never missed a Sunday. When I was a kid, Papaw used to take me to church with him and make me sit through fiery sermons. It was always the Old Testament. That's all Baptists seemed to have any use for. During those Sunday mornings of my childhood, I learned those verses just like everybody else, learned them until they were memorized. Even now, years since I'd been in the sanctuary, I could quote them. The difference between Daddy and me was that after Papaw died, I didn't have to go to church anymore. For Daddy, it was different. Daddy never missed a day of church until he was out from under his father's roof. I reckon there was something buried down deep in him that no one knew about, something buried so deep that only he knew he carried it. Daddy had put those Bibles there as part of some ritual of his, and I would never ask why. Even if he'd offered it up, I didn't want to know. That type of evil was something best left alone.

He waited until three a.m. to move the bodies. It had to be done by morning, and with night patrols running from six p.m. to six a.m., it was generally about nine hours into the shift when Charlies and Davids started letting their eyes hang low. So that's when we left.

A few phone calls and there were friends of the family stationed on both sides of The Creek, cars parked in muddy pull-offs with eyes hidden in darkness looking for any sign of patrols. Another phone call had woken the barge operator, a man employed to take summer folks to and from their houses on Buck Knob Island in the middle of Lake Glenville. Rich folks could afford those luxuries. They could afford to build their houses in a place that no one without a fortune could get to, so they did. Oscar Buchanan earned his living taking those people back and forth, and dropping off groceries when they just didn't want to head the half mile to land to mingle with us lower forms of life. But in winter the pay was low, so Oscar took his cut like so many others, and in return, Daddy kept a spare key to the barge and the landing.

"You're going to drive their truck, Jacob, and I'm going to follow you."

"What about the bodies?"

"What about the fucking bodies, Jacob, they're there, aren't
they? You can't drive with them there, can you? So fucking move
them."

I knew there wasn't a chance in hell of me moving Gerald, but
seeing as he was propped there like a mannequin on the passenger side, I figured he was fine to ride just how he sat. Jeremy
would have to be moved. I opened the driver-side door and the
key alarm went to buzzing as keys just seconds away from ignition a few hours before still rested in the switch. Half of Jeremy's
body was already on the passenger side and luckily it was the
messy end. I yanked up on the back of Jeremy's baby-blue T-shirt,
tried to budge his head from his brother's lap and into the floorboard. Deadweight proved a task for two hands, but once his head
crested the edge of the seat, gravity took over, and he rolled face-
first onto the mat. From the waist down he was still on the driver
side, but the legs were easy lifting, just a matter of balancing him
into a headstand with his feet over Gerald's shoulders.

Daddy already had his Jeep pulled up behind the Cabe brothers'
truck by the time I got the bodies situated. As he pulled on a cigarette, the glow lit his face and I could see his scowling eyes
watching me. There was a part of me hopeful that soon as that
truck made it onto the barge he'd put one into me as well, send
me to the bottom of the lake with the Cabes. But there was a bigger part of me, a fearful part of me that said no matter what, I was
his son, and there wouldn't be any getting out of this mess that
easy. In just a few short minutes, dying had become simple. It was
the living part I feared.

———

THE PRIVATE LANDING was fenced off just a couple miles down the road, and as I drove, Daddy followed closely. A bump in the road rocked Gerald's head to the side and those wide eyes and gaping mouth opened toward me. I couldn't keep from staring. I was already a nervous wreck, and now those empty eyes set dumbfounded on me. I drifted off the shoulder and overcorrected a bit to right myself, bald tires screeching against pavement as I straightened out. Daddy never let off, just drove bumper to bumper till we hit the gated landing down a short gravel road.

He unlocked the gate and swung the heavy steel arm back. "Pull the truck onto the barge," he said as he passed the open window, never even stopping to look me square.

The rusted iron ramp creaked and banged as tires rolled over the threshold and onto the platform. I parked it dead center on a barge built big enough for a school bus, cut the ignition, and stepped out of the truck. Daddy walked across the gravel lot after locking the gate and concealing the Jeep from the road behind a line of trees. He jumped on the barge and threw a lever to get the hydraulic ramp humming, moved fast as if it were something he'd done a time or two before. He didn't say a word, just crossed the barge and climbed onto the pontoon towboat. The hydraulic ramp had just finished peaking out when Daddy gassed the Evinrude and the engine boiled water. The barge slowly backed away from land as the pontoon pulled in reverse, and once we'd hit open water, Daddy shifted into drive and began to push the barge further from shore.

I walked back and climbed onto the pontoon, took my spot beside him on the deck. "Where are we going?"

"Dumping grounds." Daddy kept his eyes fixed ahead, those acne scars on his face holding shadows with such little light. He still wore the sweatpants, but had wrapped a jacket over his chest, that jacket and his hair both blowing wildly as wind came across the water.

"Whereabouts?"

"River channel by the dam. Water tops one twenty there."

"What about—"

"Shut the fuck up, Jacob! Just shut the fuck up and get back on the barge. If it wasn't for you, we wouldn't be doing this. Wasn't for you, one cocksucker would be buried and these two dipshits would still be doing oil changes. Just get back on the goddamn barge!"

His words couldn't sting me now. I was well past numb. But the summer air was crisp on the water where the wind had a chance to ride unrestrained between the mountains. The moon was already starting to descend behind the ridgeline, with stars that much brighter in its absence. Just a few short hours till daylight now. The boat putted toward the dam, but it would be twenty or thirty minutes before we made it there. I leaned against the front bumper of the Cabes' truck and kept my eyes fixed on the sky.

THE PONTOON IDLED on flat water when we finally made it within rock-skipping distance of the riprap. Daddy crossed over onto the barge and knocked the hydraulic switch to lower the ramp toward water. When the ramp flattened out and clanked locked, he walked over and peered into the truck. He looked around in there as if to scan for anything worth taking, but didn't spot anything.

"Get in there and roll both of those windows till they're just about a finger's length open."

"Want me to get the back glass too?"

"Did I ask you to get the goddamn back glass, Jacob? For fuck's sake, boy, just do what you're told."

I climbed into the driver side and stretched out over the bodies to get my hand on the window knob. I rolled the window down till it seemed about right and looked back over my shoulder for Daddy to give me the okay. He walked to the open door and reached back behind him. "Just a little bit more," he said. As I turned away from him, that was when I thought it would come, that was when I thought he'd send a bullet rattling around my head too. But he didn't. Instead, he rolled up the driver-side window till it was just right, and dropped the truck down into neutral.

I crawled out and shut the door behind me. "Want me to get their wallets and the paperwork out of the glove box?"

"What the fuck for, Jacob?"

"So that if that truck ever does come back up, they won't know who they are."

"What about the goddamn VIN numbers and plates? You don't think they could run those fucking VIN numbers or plates and get their names? In this little shithole of a town, you don't think an old Ford Ranger, maroon and white, with two bodies piled in it is going to put John Law onto something? You don't think they'll recognize that fucking vehicle, that they won't think, 'Aw hell, the Cabe boys have been missing awhile,' and put two and two together?"

I just looked at him blankly, that numbness holding me there on that creaky barge.

"All right then, well, shut the fuck up. There's a whole god-damn car lot down where this truck is headed, and if it ever did come up I reckon there'd be a lot more to worry about than fuck-ing wallets." Daddy brushed past me, got in front of the truck, and put his hands on the hood. "Now, quit being a pussy and help me push?"

I didn't say a word, just put my hands on the rusted hood of that truck and heaved. The pickup rolled slowly until it got mov-ing and dropped ass end first into the lake. Once the water topped the tailgate and filled the bed, Lake Glenville turned the Cabe brothers' Ford Ranger on end like a slip bobber and gurgled wildly until all of the air was pushed out of the cab. When those last bub-bles popped, the lake was flat again, not a ripple across the sheet. The Cabe brothers sank down deeper and deeper in the silence. All I could think was how I wished I were riding shotgun.

14.

Sunlight and darkness became the only testament to time. The way those shadows rose and fell along the walls was the only proof hours had passed at all over the next few days. A low yellow shone through the blinds each morning until white light spread across the room, then the blues settled on evening until it all went black again. I studied all of that movement and light in a drug-fueled delirium. The morning after watery graves, I spent half the cash I had on a quarter bag and twenty white ladders. Those white Xaney bars brought a dreamless sleep and I was thankful.

Those days alone were the first time I ever remember praying, and that's the thing about folks who aren't used to offering words to God. Praying's easiest when you need something, selfish kinds of prayers, and that's the type I prayed. I prayed that Robbie Douglas wouldn't wake up. I prayed that no one would miss the Cabe brothers. I prayed that I could get the hell out of this town. And I prayed that I could sleep without nightmares. That last prayer was the only one answered, but it wasn't God. It was pills.

God never answered a McNeely prayer.

Daddy and I hadn't spoken since the night on the barge, and after what we'd done, I wasn't so sure there were any words left between us.

"About time your pussy ass decided to face the world," Daddy said, only glancing at me for a second before turning his attention back to a skillet full of livermush. "But believe me, I understand. A man needs a little time to himself to let things settle."

"I don't know if I'd call it settled."

"That's just the bitch in you. It'll all settle with time. One way or another, that's just how it works." He had on an old pair of blue jeans dotted with grease stains. A navy blue button-up shirt like the one Jeremy Cabe had worn the night at the camp held loosely around Daddy's shoulders. His hair was still slick and wet from the shower and lines from a comb shone where he'd raked his hair to the side.

I opened the refrigerator to find something to drink, but both the orange juice and milk shook empty. Only the beer shelf held anything fit for drinking, so I popped a top on a Budweiser and took a seat at the table.

"What the fuck are you doing?"

"There's nothing left to drink."

"I been meaning to tell that bitch to run by the store, but hell, she won't even crawl out of bed this morning."

"Josephine?"

"Naw, Jacob, your fucking mother. Why, hell yes, Josie. She's sprawled out in there covered in peter tracks. Useless I say. Ain't good for shit."

"Then why in the hell you keep her around?"

"Because a man's got to have him one outlet, Jacob, and I reckon that's about what a woman's fit for. Stress management."

With the type of women he was referring to, he was right. With the type of woman I was after, he'd never understand. So like always, I just kept my thoughts on the matter to myself.

"You're going to come down and work around the shop for the next few weeks until I can track down some new help."

"New help?"

"Well, fuck yeah, son. I don't know if you realized it or not, but my workforce has just upped and disappeared." Daddy turned away from the skillet and looked me square for the first time since that truck sank beneath flat water. "Got to keep things moving forward, Jacob. Got to keep this ship sailing."

"I ain't too good around engines. Transmissions never made a lick of sense to me."

"I'm not asking you to build me a fucking race car, Jacob. Simple shit. Tire rotations, oil changes, simple shit till I can find some help."

"And when did you want me to start?"

"Soon as we eat."

"What's today?"

"Monday, Jacob, goddamn." Daddy looked back over his shoulder and smirked at me. He flipped thin slices of livermush over in the skillet and that gray meat popped and sizzled against the cast iron. "The day of rest was yesterday for fuck's sake."

15.

The three-bay garage smelled of burnt oil and transmission fluid, and the banging and grinding of an impact wrench covered any sound of summer birds chirping outside. Daddy had an International Scout on the lift and was taking off the last tire when a patrol car pulled into the front lot.

"Roll over those tires and wheels from over there in the corner." Daddy only stopped the impact wrench from busting lugs long enough to speak and ash his cigarette.

"Dad!"

The clatter of torque hammering away at rust-locked lugs kept him from hearing.

"Dad!"

The words caught him just as one nut came free and he dropped the wrench to his side like he was holstering a pistol. "Goddamn it, what?"

"A deputy just pulled up." I kept my eyes fixed on the patrol car.

"About fucking time. Thought I was going to have to wait around all day."

A middle-aged deputy stepped out of the vehicle and flipped open a pair of sunglasses before slipping the shades over his eyes. He resituated his belt, slammed the car door, and headed toward the first open bay. The raised Scout partly concealed Daddy and I from view.

"Over here," Daddy hollered, and the deputy caught himself mid-stride, changed directions on a pivot like he was marching in the Marine Corps.

"McNeely?" the deputy asked, as he rounded the back bumper on the Scout and first made eye contact.

"Yes, sir. Charles McNeely. Nice to meet you." Daddy smeared the grease from his palms down his jeans and held out his hand to shake, but the deputy never offered his hand.

"Dispatch said you wanted to file a missing-persons report?"

"That's right."

"And who might this missing person be?"

"Well, it's actually two missing. Both my mechanics, two brothers, you see, ain't been around since last Thursday. Now, it's not like these two to go missing, and I haven't been able to get them on the phone. Hell, I even stopped by their house on Satur-day and Sunday, and it's like those two just vanished. Seeing as they don't have any family left, I kind of figure them for my own."

I couldn't believe what I was hearing. I couldn't believe that he was going so far as filing missing-persons reports on two boys we sent to the bottom of the reservoir. But I kept my mouth shut and listened for his reason.

"These brothers have names?"

"Cabe. Jeremy and Gerald Cabe."

"How old are they?" The deputy had a notebook out now and was jotting down the bullshit my daddy was feeding him. I'd never seen that fat-ass deputy before, but I knew he wasn't any friend of the family. His hair was speckled gray on the sides, and the thick mustache over his lips held that same speckling. The tan button-down and black slacks he wore looked pressed like he had his uniform dry-cleaned to look real official. His fat face never showed any signs of emotion, just pudgy and hanging there, sunglasses hiding his eyes so that we couldn't see if he was looking us square or sleeping.

"I reckon Jeremy's about thirty or so, and, well, Gerald would have to be a good three or four years older, so I'd figure him for thirty-three or thirty-four. Got their birth dates back there on their paperwork if you want me to run and check."

"That'd be proper."

Daddy wiped his hands down his jeans again and headed toward the office at the front bay. Just me and the bull now, and I wasn't sure what kind of guilt or innocence I had spread across my face.

"How you doing today, son?"

"I'm doing." I tried to keep it short and leaned around the Scout to see if Daddy was headed back.

"Helping your old man out today?"

"Yes, sir. Just till he gets his help back."

"That's good. That's good." The deputy held one hand to his face and spread his mustache with his index finger and thumb.

"You know, I've heard a lot of stories about this place." He kept spreading that mustache over and over. "A lot of stories about your father too."

"That right?"

"Yeah. But you know I got to say, he keeps this place looking pretty official."

"It's a nice shop."

"That ain't what I meant, son."

Just as the line of questioning was venturing into briary country, Daddy came around the corner carrying two file folders splotched with greasy fingerprints. "Let's see." Daddy thumbed through the top folder. "Now, Jeremy, it says right here, was born on April twentieth of 19 and 78, so I reckon that would put him at thirty-one years." Daddy slid the paperwork back into the folder and thumbed through the next. "And Gerald, well, it says he was born on September third of 19 and 75, so that'd put him at thirty-three, no, thirty-four this fall. That sound about right?"

"I guess."

"I'm not too good at ciphering." Daddy chuckled and slid the papers back into Gerald's file.

"And you say these boys have been missing since Thursday?"

"Well, they were here all day Thursday right up till closing, but I haven't seen them since. They were supposed to be in on Friday and then again on Saturday, but like I say, I haven't seen hide nor hair of them, not even at their house."

"Whereabouts they live?"

"You know the fire station up there on Yellow Mountain?"

"Yeah."

"They're the next drive on the right. Big chunk of land, but just a little old single-wide tucked there at the back of the property."

"You got an address?"

"No. No, don't reckon I do. But like I said, it's just over there on Yellow Mountain Road, next right after you pass the firehouse."

"Now, they didn't happen to tell you they were planning a trip or going to see somebody, whereabouts they might have been headed, did they?"

"Well, I reckon if they had, I wouldn't have had much fucking reason to call, would I?"

The deputy pulled his glasses away from his face and slid one of the sunglasses' arms into his front pocket so they'd stay fixed there. Bright blue eyes squinted a little bit and focused hard on my father. Those blue eyes, big creepy blue eyes, were just a few hues from white. "No, sir. I don't reckon you would've."

"So, is there anything else?"

"Not sure." The deputy opened his eyes wide as if to question whether what he'd been told was the whole story. "Is that all you can tell me?"

"To be honest, the only other thing I can really remember is that last Thursday afternoon we were talking about how they found that Douglas boy over there in Macon County. The two of them seemed awfully skittish when I told them how those deputies had found that Douglas boy alive over there near Ellijay. The shape he was in and that he was still alive, you know?"

"You saying you think the Cabe brothers had something to do with what happened to that Douglas boy, Mr. McNeely?"

"No, now, I ain't saying that at all. I'm just saying that's the last thing I remember us talking about. Probably wasn't even worth mentioning."

"But you did."

"Yeah, I don't know. I reckon I was just trying to think back on it and see if I could think of anything else that might've been help-ful." Daddy leaned down and picked up the impact wrench from the concrete floor. He held the wrench in one hand and grabbed the nut from where he'd set it in the rim he was working loose. "Sorry I can't help you more, but I sure would hate if something were to have happened to those boys. Damn good mechanics. Damn good guys, for that matter."

The deputy closed his notepad and slid it into his front pocket. He pulled the sunglasses free from his shirt, pressed them back over his eyes, and spread that mustache two or three more times before he spoke. "Guess I'll run over there to Yellow Mountain and see if I can see anything, but you let me know if you hear from them. All right?"

"Sounds good, Deputy. And you do the same."

"I'll be in touch either way."

"Sounds good." Daddy nodded at him and smiled, and as the bull turned away, Daddy focused his attention back on the Scout.

I couldn't keep my eyes off the deputy, though. I watched him walk stiffly from the garage and situate his belt again before climbing into his patrol car. I watched him in his car fiddling with the computer and rearranging something that I couldn't see in the passenger seat. The deputy sat there for a long time just star-ing forward, no way to know which way he was looking with those sunglasses covering his eyes. After a few minutes, he pulled out of the front lot, and I heard the V8 barrel through first as he mashed the gas up the highway.

"What in the world you do that for?"

"What in the fuck are you talking about?"

"Telling him all that shit."

"For fuck's sake, boy, somebody was going to realize those

Cabe brothers were missing sooner or later, and it's always better if you can have your hand in the deck. Best if you're the one dealing out those cards." Daddy pressed the tire of the raised Scout up onto his shoulder and slid it off of the lugs. He grunted when it came free and all that weight was balancing on him, but he didn't ask for help and dropped the tire to let it bounce a few times before settling on the floor.

"Why'd you mention Robbie?"

Daddy smacked me hard against the side of the head and stared deep into me. "I told you not to ever speak his fucking name, Jacob. Don't you ever mention his fucking name again." Daddy looked at me for a moment, then rolled the last tire off the Scout to where he'd piled the others. "Bottom line is if they ever go to connecting those dots and tying those Cabe brothers to what happened there that night, that little seed will have been planted. Dead men tell no tales, Jacob. The ones left to living are the ones who write the history."

Daddy pulled his soft pack of Winstons out of his shirt pocket and flicked a cigarette up into his lips. He struck a match against the running rails on the Scout, lit the cigarette, and passed it to me. I took it and pulled a long drag as Daddy flicked another cigarette out of the pack and lit it just as the match was burning down into his thumb.

"Now go get me those new tires and wheels from over there in the corner, Jacob."

I did what I was told.

16.

A hand in the deck was one thing. Waltzing into Robbie Douglas's trailer was another. Taking Robbie's belongings and raking them out thick as manure in the Cabe brothers' place was damn near crazy, but that's what I decided to do. "Best if you're the one dealing out those cards," Daddy'd said, and the way I figured, it was my turn to shuffle. If that burnt-up son of a bitch ever did wake up, he wouldn't have to mutter more than a few words for me to be skinned. I imagine a few of those first words might be "Jacob McNeely." I couldn't leave it up to that kind of chance. Better to just water that seed Daddy'd planted in the deputy's mind and let that story grow.

Robbie Douglas lived way back in a damp holler that had

rusted that old tin box just as soon as the tractor unhitched and pulled away. From where I crouched in the laurel, it looked like rust colored everything in the yard burnt red: an old push mower, the pull cord rotted in two and dangling; a children's tricycle, chrome pitted, plastic handlebar streamers bleached pink; a wheelbarrow that had a grate thrown over the bucket for grilling, a hole burnt slap through the bottom. The whole lot was in dire need of a tetanus shot.

I'd parked the pickup on a four-wheeler trail cut high on the hillside above his property and hiked down to that small nest in the laurel thicket to play lookout for a while. Nothing stirred at the trailer, only a murder of crows that swooped down low over the property and cut up into a tulip poplar across the way. The crows cawed and cackled back and forth between limbs. Still I knelt there and scouted. I wanted to make damn certain no one was around. The story that was unfolding with Robbie Douglas was one that no soul would want to be tied to, so I took my time and gave myself plenty of room to run.

The coast clear and daylight burning, I made my way through the snagged curls of laurel and trotted down a steep bank that flattened at the front steps. Algae slimed the wood green, slicked those steps like creek stone, and the planks mushed and warped under my weight. A blue tarp had been tacked from the roof of the trailer and held in a droopy bend over a small deck by a pair of sawn two-by-fours. Brown-tinged water fattened the place where the tarp sagged, and from underneath I could make out leaves and twigs, pine needles and a crescent wrench stagnant in that water and illuminated by daylight. The front door didn't sit square, but rather at an angle like might have been found in a fun house or a maze of mirrors, a shape my geometry teacher had called a parallelogram way back in my learning. I never knew why I remembered shit like that, but those funny words a man never had use for were the only thing that stuck from all that schooling.

The door wasn't locked but still required jimmying to break loose from the frame. The thin door bowed under pressure and slapped against the wall behind when it finally budged. The smell hit me first, the smell of clothes soiled wet and dried and soiled again, a sour stench that clung like armpit stains. Whatever storm had come through that holler had skipped the yard altogether and manifested right there inside. It had slung everything Robbie owned into an ankle-deep pile that had to be waded.

I slipped a pair of leather work gloves onto my hands, the thick, rough kind never meant for anything delicate, but the only thing I had to hide my prints. I first filled the black garbage bag I'd brought for toting with tangled wads of clothes, but realized about the time that bag started to bulge lumpy on the sides that those clothes could've belonged to anyone. It wasn't like Robbie Douglas had scribbled his name on the tags of his underwear with permanent marker. It wasn't like the Cabe brothers were doing his laundry either. So I dumped the clothes back onto the floor, T-shirts and shorts piling into a little knoll of an island in that sea of trash and filth. I did keep a flannel shirt, one of those bricked-off red flannel shirts that held a few hairs off Robbie's head from the last time he wore it. I figured the law could run those hairs and get about as much guarantee of Robbie Douglas as an ID card, and that was the type of shit that needed collecting.

The main living space of the trailer led right into the bedroom, only a side door to the john acting as a hallway between the two rooms. The mattress sat cockeyed on box springs and thin cotton sheets were ripped away from the elbows of the mattress, the sheets crinkled wavy where it bunched. The mess from that front room bled over the threshold into the bedroom, but fanned out and stopped like a high-water mark near the bed. A tall stack of mail, bills left unpaid, teetered on a side table, and I checked the little plastic windows on the fronts of envelopes for his name. All of the envelopes held that certainty, so I shoved them down into the bag.

Sticking out from under the bedsheets was the edge of a leather-bound book, the corners worn round and shabby. I pulled the book from under the pile, HOLY BIBLE pressed in all caps and gold leaf across the front. The book was old and tattered, thin pages transparent and yellowed. The front page had been scribbled like a ledger, all different kinds of names and dates in all different kinds of handwriting and ink. Only one thing held similarity down the page: every name, no matter the front, ended in Douglas. A folded photograph had been shoved about two-thirds through the book to serve as a marker. It was a picture of Robbie smiling and holding that Bible when he was twelve or thirteen. His folks stood proudly at his sides. It must have been taken at some sort of confirmation or religious dunking at the Baptist church, his hair seeming wetted and slicked in the photo.

I looked that picture over and seeing him brought on the same paranoia that shook me from dream each night. I could feel the sweat beading on my temples and my palms going clammy. I shut the photograph back in the book and chucked the Bible into the bag, but that image of him stayed taped up on the backs of my eyelids. My mind warped that still image and melted away at his face, melted it just how I'd seen, and the screaming rang back deep in my memory. I wanted it gone, but it was all so fresh. I could still smell his skin burning, see the way that skin peeled and held to the tarp as we drug him through the woods. Those types of things don't just fade away. They are the worms of the living and eat at a man for as long as he's breathing. I reckon I deserved what burrowed in me just as Daddy deserved his.

17.

The road back into The Creek bent and curved for what seemed forever, split off one way toward Walnut Gap and cut off another toward Yellow Mountain. That forever is part of what gave the place its lore. Folks that far removed had seldom associated law and justice with badges. The old-time stories told tales riddled with bootleggers and murder, stories of copper stills on the fingers and branches of cold mountain streams, heads bashed in and buried before the blood had time to cool. I reckon it was a fitting place as any for men like the Cabes to eke out an existence.

I parked the pickup at the fire station, a four-bay aluminum garage that seldom saw firemen aside from the occasional chimney fire. A muddied rag I used for checking oil was thrown behind the seat, and I rolled that rag up into the driver-side window to make my pickup look like nothing more than a breakdown to anyone who cared. It was a short hike up the road, but what I'd packed into that black garbage bag wasn't anything I wanted to be questioned about should a bull pull up and offer a lift. So I didn't take the road. Instead, I hiked through a tangled briar thicket fit for rabbits and sparrows, but little else. Besides keeping me hidden, that thicket could offer a damn good excuse should the law pass: "Hunting blackberries," I'd say, and those bulls would take me at my word rather than risk the thorns and chiggers.

Briars scratched my arms and left red lines that itched more than stung. Walking was slow. I had to pinch vines between my fingers so as not to press into prickers, and then move those vines out of the way to pass, but I was hidden. Tunnels were cut through the low sections as I bent down and crawled under a thick tangle, tunnels that had been cut by cottontails that knew the ins and outs of that thicket in a way that only small creatures could. I wasn't so small and the briars hung in my britches and ripped a long hole in the plastic bag I carried. Robbie's flannel shirt poked out of the tear, plugged that hole so nothing else could leak, and before long I was out of the thicket without too much blood to show for it.

A tall hillside stretched up to the Cabe brothers' trailer, a hillside not so steep as to scare a man on foot but steep enough to frighten hell out of a man on a tractor. The bush hog had mangled the hillside just a few weeks prior, the grass and brush trimmed low except uneven lines left between passes. I was in the open now and exposed, and none of that sat easy with me. I didn't see any patrol cars parked at the top by the trailer, though, and anyone making their way up the drive would have to come up the gravel along that thicket before the field opened up and they could spot me. I knew I would hear gravel crunching under tires and low gears revving high if someone came, so I tried not to worry too much. Still I walked fast, made it up that hill and to the trailer in no time flat.

Bobtail, mitten-paw strays that folks kept for barn cats, were as common as crows, and the Cabe brothers had kept a whole mess of them around their trailer. Every cat I could see held the same gray tabby coat and stood taller than average housecats. A few lay on the grass, basked in the sun, and inspected me as I came close. One of the two didn't seem to care, blinked slowly in the sunlight, and bathed itself with long strokes of its tongue. The other proved skittish and fired off into the woods when I neared.

Another cat seemed a statue on the wooden steps of the front porch, the lines of its coat camouflaging it against the grayed wood. A pair of yellow eyes peered from a dark opening cut in the skirt around the trailer, and those eyes never let off, never came into the light. There were five I counted from where I stood, the fifth a stringy, young cat wrestling a chipmunk that could barely crawl a few inches before claws stabbed again. I didn't know what in the world would drive someone to keep after all those cats, but the Cabe brothers must've kept them all fed for so many to stick around.

The cat on the front steps stretched in a tall arch when I got close. Purring wildly, the cat rammed its face into my britches leg and ran the length of its body against my shin. The cat's face pressed so hard into my leg that its lips turned back along teeth and the purring grew louder. I crouched to pet that old tabby, sure that those last few days had proven awfully lonely with no kibble to fatten its gut. As my hand neared, its ears lowered, hairs raised, and the cat hissed and clawed till I got my boot into its flank and kicked it from the porch. That's why I'd always hated those sneaky fucking animals.

The front door was locked and I peered through a clouded window beside the door to get a view inside. No lights were on, just rectangles of sunlight through the windows on the far wall. A box fan was propped in an open window on the back side of the trailer, the fan blades still and dusty. That was where I'd enter.

The Cabe brothers' trailer was a good bit longer than that rusted sardine can Robbie Douglas called home. Though it wasn't really anything to which a man might attach a word like nice, the paint was still fairly fresh on the aluminum and red mud hadn't dirtied the skirt too awful much. Around back the hillside jutted up fast and ragged-barked locusts towered above. The hillside was steep enough that, reaching just right, I had no need for a bucket to stand on in order to touch that window and slide the box fan to the ground. With those leather gloves fitted over my hands, I yanked once, the box fan came loose, and as it did, the window slammed down hard on the seal a few seconds shy of broken fingers. A short section of two-by-four was on the ground. Stood on end, it held the window propped enough for me to shimmy my way inside belly first onto stained carpet.

The sun hung low behind the locusts now and the only light to be had shone through clouded windowpanes. That hazy light wasn't fit for seeing, so I pulled the bead-chain cord of a table lamp that rested beside the open window to take a look around. The main living space was broken like most single-wides with a larger section meant for a living room running into a tight kitchen area, only the shift from ratty carpet to peeling laminate marking the divide. A leather sectional sofa and matching chair that might have been nice when it was new overfilled the living room. The leather had started off black but had been shredded in every place that held cushion, and the tears that proved too big to leave had been patched with shoddy X's of duct tape. There was no question they'd salvaged that fine suite from the rusted bins at the recycling center. Those were always treasured finds greeted with shit-eating grins for folks like the Cabes.

A bedroom capped each end of the trailer, and I took the one nearest me to nose through first. I dropped the black plastic bag by the window and tromped into the bedroom, even light footsteps thudding loud on a floor stretched thin as hide on a bass drum.

The room was kept tidy for the most part, even the window being cleaner than any other in the trailer, clear enough to let evening light the room golden. Only a deep rut in the mattress gave any clue to which brother it belonged. It'd take a man Gerald's size to rub that kind of waller into a mattress. Planting Robbie's belongings was something I planned to do in the main room, but a bedroom left this neat didn't suit a man who'd shot off on the lam. A man in a hurry would've roughed the place up a bit to speed things along, so that's what I'd do.

I drew the drawers loose from a dresser by the door and spread the clothes over the bed and floor in a layered mess that looked rushed. I split the folding doors on the closet and lifted one heap of shirts on hangers from the rod, spread that armful out across the bed like a hand of cards. A lack of anything dressy meant Gerald kept a long line of empty hangers, and I tossed those hangers every which way to make it look like they'd held something and what they'd held had been taken. As I stepped back into the narrow closet, my boot crackled against something on the floor. It was too dark to make out what lay bunched at my feet, but I nudged it with the tip of my boot until a corner flipped into yellow sunlight.

The second I saw that blue tarp, my mind shot back to the night I stood with the Cabe brothers on the edge of the bluff and how Robbie Douglas had rolled with arms and legs flailing till he found that place on the rock. I remembered how Gerald had folded the tarp we used to drag the body so carefully, bending and tucking that tarp just so like he was folding a flag. Couldn't be, I thought. That son of a bitch couldn't be so dumb as to save it.

I tugged the leather gloves tightly against my hands and pulled the crumpled tarp out into the room. The tarp had a smell about it, a smell that usually reserved itself for things on the roadside, bodies that swelled in the heat and shrunk back with the coolness night brought, that rising and falling bringing life to something long since dead. I unfolded the tarp and was startled by the stains, the places where blood had dried dark brown. Skin still held from where it had peeled off of Robbie's face, that skin thin and yellowed, flaking like fish slime dried on a rag. Near those scabs of skin the tarp was warped and burnt from the acid, and that smell caught me again. Only a fear of leaving anything of myself behind kept me from spilling over onto the floor. He couldn't have been that stupid, I thought. But it wasn't really about being stupid or smart. A man who'd save something like that did so out of pure meanness. That meanness was what I lacked, and that lacking was why I'd never be able to do the types of things men like the Cabe brothers or my father could do. I was soft in Daddy's eyes. I'd always been a pussy. But if this was what it took to be hard, then that type of hardness was something I would never know. I dragged the tarp out into the living room and left it unfolded and sagging off the edge of the couch.

Jeremy's bedroom was what I expected to find: a living, breathing mess that seemed to crawl across the floor. The metal walls were dented in places, four knuckles distinctly nudging just a little bit deeper in each one of the impressions. The marks were a testament to his quick temper, an alcohol-fueled rage that used to boil him over out of nowhere. A game trail was cut to the bed. No sheets were on the mattress, only the rose patterns printed across polyester ticking and a broad brown stain that looked like it had been wiped and spread many times without lightening in color. An alarm clock set on top of a closed trunk flashed red numbers beside the bed. Jeremy's two best friends in the world, Jack and Ginger, made residence alongside the alarm. The fifth of Jack Daniel's still held a few strong slugs, though the top wasn't screwed on and fruit flies buzzed about the mouth. A two-liter of Canada Dry was all but gone, the bottle squashed and creased in the middle, held in that angle since the top had been screwed tight.

I squatted down to pull clothes pressed flat by footsteps from underneath the pile, and that's when I saw the bottle beneath the window. It was a glass jug shaped like a jimmy-john that might have been used to hold cider or moonshine, with a large white-and-black sticker wrapping around the belly. "DANGER! CORROSIVE!" it read, with an image of liquid pouring from a test tube, squiggly lines rising from the hand where it fell. "SULFURIC ACID (H_2SO_4)." I picked up the jug and swashed the clear liquid around like I was proofing beads on a gallon of corn whiskey. The oily fluid swirled, hung to the sides of the glass, and dripped down slow. The jug was still nearly full with only a pint or two missing, a pint or two that I'd seen splash and fizz.

If I had known, I wouldn't have come. Those Cabe brothers had their necks wrung and feathers plucked before I ever climbed through the window of their trailer. I reckon if they'd still been alive it wouldn't have mattered too much. They could've hid it all when the time came. But the fact they were fish now, and all that was left to tell their story was spread out across that trailer thick as cow pies, left little wondering. A name like Robbie Douglas tasted sour in a man's mouth. Soon as Daddy planted that name in the deputy's mind, it was left there to fester. All that was left was to bring that festering to a head, so I set the jimmy-john of acid by the recliner, spread Robbie's shirt right next to the tarp, and placed the bills and Douglas family Bible on the coffee table like tabloids.

I was just about to make my exit through the window when I heard tires spinning gravel into a crackly racket up the drive. Through the front window I could barely see through the clouded glass, but there wasn't any mistaking the blue light bar running across the top of the car. I stood still as stone till the patrol car parked where the gravel ended and sparse grass began. A glare on the window kept me from making out who was inside, but the deputy kept the car running and didn't step out. The cats circled the patrol car and I backed away from the window long enough to ease my escape route closed and cut the only lamp giving light. There was no way out now aside from the front door, but I couldn't have that bull notice a window left open, couldn't have him catching whiff of anything awry.

Back at the glass, I saw the deputy step out of the car. It was the bull who'd taken the report, that pepper-haired, no-nonsense bull that liked to keep which way he looked hidden behind sunglasses. He wore those shades now, though the sunlight was all but gone, night bugs already starting to chatter from the woods. The glaring of cats spiraled around his ankles and he made the same mistake I had. The cocky bull took all that purring and rubbing as a sign of civility, like some other living, breathing thing might have loved him, until he leaned down and jerked back, hand slit where claws sliced.

My first fears were relieved by the lack of papers in his hands and the lack of backup for inventory. I'd seen my fair share of searches in eighteen years as the son of Charles McNeely, and two things always rang true: there were always at least two badges, and one of them always carried papers. My second fear, though, was standing right there in front of me. A deputy was at the trailer, and I was inside.

The bull copied something back to county through the radio on his chest before resituating his belt and walking toward the door. I didn't see what came next. By the time his first foot took a step, I was lying flat behind the leather couch. I heard the boards creak under his weight as he came onto the porch. Then the first knocks pounded *boom-boom-boom* in a thunderous manner that almost took the locked door off its hinges. "Sheriff's Department," he shouted. Then another *boom-boom-boom* just as hard as the first.

I was certain one more boom would send that door to booming and flying and then all that would be left was to turn into a rabbit and shoot right past him before he knew what flushed. "The man who looks back gets caught," Daddy'd always said, and as I lay there, my heart pattering in a frenzy, even shallow breaths seeming to sound out of wind, all I could think was when that time comes, don't look back.

The porch planks shifted under him as he moved, and I stayed still. I prayed to a God that I had no use for outside of these types of situations. I prayed that if He were real, He'd puppeteer that bull to leave. But that old truth held true once more: God doesn't answer McNeely prayers. A broad shadow, darker than inside, rose on the far wall as the deputy moved in front of the window. Then a wide, hazy circle of yellow light ran the room from top to bottom and side to side. I pulled back my feet a hair, and watched the flashlight illuminate the carpet just past my toes. The light clicked off and the boards creaked as the bull made his way off the porch.

Loud bangs sounded against the outside of the trailer, bangs that nearly sent me out of my skin. Each bang hammered a little further along the trailer, the deputy racking his metal flashlight against the aluminum walls as he walked. From the sound of it, the bull cut the corner and banged against the far wall of Jeremy's bedroom, then cut the corner again to the back of the trailer. From the window where I'd climbed in, he'd spot me with one swoop of that flashlight, so I rolled onto my stomach and wriggled like a worm till I made it to the far side of the sectional couch. I lay right where the ratty carpet ended and peeling tile began as the rapping on the outside of the trailer walked its way along past me and closer to the window.

The banging on the trailer stopped and instead a different kind of banging echoed from outside. It was more of a clanking than banging. The racket sounded like the bull was kicking at the box fan on the ground where I'd dropped it, the fan blades and motor rattling against the plastic frame each time his boot hit. That's when the last noise I ever wanted to hear at that moment sounded loud and squeaky inside. The window I'd come in through rose, the frame shrieking against unoiled guide rails. The window opened and then slapped closed, came up again as the bull got his footing and lifted a second time.

I could hear him huffing now, hear that fat boy breathing like a schoolkid running suicides. He'll never fit through that window, I told myself, but running like a rabbit through the front door and never looking back didn't leave my mind for a second. The flashlight ran from corner to corner, made light of every square inch of the walls till nothing was left that hadn't been seen. I was sure he saw the tarp there, that red flannel shirt on the couch, the stack of papers and Bible on the coffee table, the jug of acid by the chair. The light kept running and those breaths kept huffing and my heart kept pounding, and I was certain, I was absolutely certain, that I was caught. Soon as that tubby got his belly onto the windowsill, his body half in and dangling on both sides, I was going to burst up and hit that door wide open. Don't look back, I told myself, just don't look back. But the window slapped closed and the flashlight banged its way back toward the far side of the trailer and I lay there till I heard the patrol car crank and tires crunching gravel as they spun.

Sometimes a rabbit doesn't have to run.

18.

There was never a moment in my life when I bought into the idea of light at the end of the tunnel. That old adage rests entirely on the direction being traveled. Out of darkness toward the light, folks might find some sort of hope in moving forward, some sort of anticipation for what awaits them. But my entire life I'd been traveling in the opposite direction, and for those who move further into darkness, the light becomes a thing onto which we can only look back. Looking back slows you down. Looking back destroys focus. Looking back can get you killed. And that's why I hadn't spoken with Maggie since the morning in Panthertown. There was already too much on my plate.

Monday night she called. I was cleaning the dirt from under my fingernails with the sheepsfoot blade of an old Case Stockman when the phone rang.

"I don't think I understand you at all, Jacob McNeely."

"Maggie?"

"Will you tell me something, and I want you to be absolutely square with me, because I don't think I could take it again, Jacob. I'm not going to take it again."

"What are you talking about?"

"You came looking for me and told me that you're still in love with me, and even after the way it ended last time, I put my guard down and I kissed you and then I don't hear from you in almost a week. I just don't understand you."

I wanted to tell her everything. I wanted to tell her about being arrested, about what my father had made me do, about the nightmares that kept me from sleeping. But more than that, I wanted to tell her how I felt about her. I wanted to tell her everything she needed to hear to ensure I would never hurt her again, but the *man* part of me wouldn't bring myself to tell her. No, I bottled all of that shit up the way I always had. "I've just been busy. I've been swamped helping my dad. But more than that is what I've always told you. I don't want to hold you back, and that's exactly what I'd be doing."

"I'm not a little girl now, Jacob. I'm a grown woman, and if I were to let you hold me back, that would be just as much my fault as yours. So why don't you let me worry about that. For once, let me worry about whether or not you're holding me back."

I didn't say anything. I didn't know what to say.

"Is that fair?"

"What?"

"Is that fair that you let me worry about whether or not you're holding me back?"

"Yeah, that's fair."

"Then the only thing I need from you is for you to be honest with me. The only thing I need from you is for you to let me in."

"Let you in?"

"I'm not asking you to spill every secret you've ever had."

"Then what are you asking for?"

"I'm asking you to trust me. I'm asking you to trust *me* and to trust *us*. If you're not willing to do that, then it can't work."

I'd never had anyone ask me to let them in. Inside was a place most folks wouldn't have ever wanted to glimpse, much less be a part of, but Maggie had always been banging on the door. Maggie had always been trying her damnedest to take part of the weight off of me, and I'd never let her. I couldn't let her then, and I wasn't sure that I could let her now, but the one thing that was for certain was that I'd carried that weight for too long. I'd carried it until I was almost broken, and the only thing that had ever come along and offered to fix any of it, whether she held that power or not, was her.

"I'll try."

"I'm serious about this, Jacob."

"I know you are."

"Then promise me."

"I promise."

"That's your word." For the first time in our conversation her voice seemed to ease.

I wasn't quite sure what to say. She'd opened herself up to me again and was standing in front of me with open arms and I didn't have a clue how to get to her. I picked up a pack of Winstons from the table, lit a smoke, and let those next words ride out along the first drag. "How do we do that?"

"You could start by just talking to me."

"About what?"

"You said you've been busy helping your dad, so what've you been helping him with?"

"Just helping him at the shop."

"You don't mince words, do you?"

"What's that supposed to mean?"

"It means getting you to talk is like pulling teeth. It always has been."

"I don't know what you want me to tell you."

"What does he have you doing?"

"Oil changes."

"What else?"

"Changing brakes and shit."

"So do you like it?"

"Shit, Mags. This is pointless as hell. We're talking, but we aren't saying a goddamn thing."

The phone line was filled with laughter. She knew how much I hated small talk and she'd led me along until I was riled just so she could listen to me snap. The men I grew up around were men of few words. She'd always picked on me about things like that, ragging me until I broke just for a laugh. "I'm just messing with you."

"I know."

"So don't get your panties in a wad, okay?"

"Shut the hell up."

"Hey, now!" Maggie laughed.

We'd always gone back and forth at each other and until that moment I hadn't realized how much I missed it. The playfulness and lightness of it was something nonexistent in every other part of my life. It was a good sort of feeling. There was a long pause on the phone, and I didn't want to be the one to break it. That feeling inside of me was an itch that needed scratching, and it was itching and itching, but that *man* part still wouldn't let me tell her how much I'd missed her, how long I'd waited to kiss her again, how many times I thought I'd blow Avery Hooper's brains out for the chance. Luckily she spoke first.

"Look, I'm not asking you to be an open book."

"I know."

"I'm asking you to make a spot for me in your life with all the other bullshit aside. When you left before, you had shut me out. Long before you left, you had shut me out, and looking back on it, I should've seen it coming. I don't want it to be like that again."

"I told you I'm sorry."

"It's not about that. I'm not ragging on you, Jacob. I'm not saying this to try and get pity or to try and make you feel bad." There was warmth and kindness and compassion in her voice. "I'm telling you that I want to be with you and if I'm going to be with you then this is how it has to work."

"I get it, Mags."

There was time that passed between us then that seemed to make everything okay. All of that anger and hatred she'd built for me after what I'd done was gone, and as it lifted, so did my regret and shame. That was one less thing for me to carry, and she'd taken it off my back.

I asked to take her out Wednesday, and she said yes. I didn't have a clue where we would go, but it didn't matter right then. What mattered was that she wanted me back. What mattered was that there was excitement in her voice. It's funny how it only takes one person taking the time to show you they care for all that bad shit to not seem so bad for a moment. It's not like the demons go anywhere. What haunts you is still right there when you go back under, but that one gesture from one person can bring you to the surface for a second or two. And for a very long time, all I'd really needed was to come up for air.

I told her I'd pick her up at six, and when I heard her click off the phone, I found myself reared up in my seat with no clue how I'd gotten there. My feet tingled, my palms were sweaty as hell, and that cigarette I'd lit during our conversation had all but burnt out between my fingers. I lit a fresh smoke and sank into the couch to let the blood flow back into places needed for reasoning. I tried to replay that conversation, hoping I hadn't sounded like a complete asshole. Then that nervousness settled into excitement, and for the first time in a long time, I was happy. I could feel a smile spreading across my face, and I just sat there awhile floating without a care in the world for where I was, who I was, or what I'd done. Maggie had always been the type of girl that could make a man forget all those things, or at least glaze it over awhile until it had a chance to settle. It was that forgetting and that settling that I needed more than anything in the world, and with her back beside me, it all felt within reach.

I WAS SITTING PRETTY and had even popped the top on one of Daddy's Budweisers to celebrate when the cordless phone rang on my lap, and I caught it before it had a chance to ring again.

"Hello."

"Charlie?"

"No, this is Jacob."

"You sound just like your daddy, boy. He around?"

"No, he must've headed off somewhere. I haven't seen him in a couple hours."

"Well, that's all right. Listen, this is Lieutenant Rogers."

"Lieutenant Rogers?" Knowing I was talking to a bull, any bull, even a bull that I was supposed to be able to trust, put an uneasy feeling in my stomach like I had to answer everything he asked just right.

"Yeah, just had a message that I needed to get to him, but you can pass it along. Thing is, I just wanted to let him know that your mama's been turned loose."

"She's home?"

"I reckon. They held her on a seventy-two-hour hold, but once that sleep eased things, there wasn't a whole lot left that they wanted any part of. You know how that shit goes. If a person doesn't have money, those doctors aren't going to *give* them a bed, you know?"

"Yeah, I guess."

"Just pass that along to him. All right?"

The phone call ended, and any high I was riding from Maggie was gone. There for a while I got caught up in dreaming, and dreaming's an awfully good thing when you don't have to wake up. But staring back at the light only to stumble further into darkness hurts worse than never dreaming at all. That phone call from Rogers brought me out of my dream and showed me what was real. I sat on that lonely couch in Daddy's house and sipped on a beer that had gone warm. I drank it not to celebrate, but to fog that wicked world into something a little easier to swallow.

There was no escaping who I was or where I'd come from. I was shat out of a crank-head mother who'd just been cut loose from the loony bin. I was born to a father who'd slip a knife in my throat while I slept if the mood hit him right. Blood's thicker than water, and I was drowning in it. I was sinking down in that blood, and once I hit bottom, no one would find me.

Some souls aren't worth saving, I thought.

There're some souls that even the devil wants no part of.

19.

By midday Tuesday, my arms hung loose as broken fan belts and my hands felt tight in places unfit for grease guns. Daddy had me taking off the exhaust on an old Chevy Nova, a car that looked meaner than hell even stripped down and primered. The Nova was a project car Daddy kept around the shop and tinkered with off and on when business slowed. Those times rarely came, so that car had been sitting for years without ever being restored.

I hadn't told him about the phone call. Didn't think I would. For the life of me I just couldn't put my finger on why Lieutenant Rogers had felt the need to call and tell Daddy that Mama was home. Only thing it could have been was that she'd blabbed on that night the crystal drove her crazier than a shithouse rat. And if that was why he was calling, Daddy must've had plans to set things right. So that phone call and the fact she was home was something I kept to myself. Sure, he'd find out sooner or later, but every minute I kept quiet was a minute she had for breathing. Truth was I'd never hated her like he did. I'd never blamed her for what she was.

Bologna sandwiches in a lunch bucket were the noontime staple of Daddy's workday and always had been. But me, I took my lunch break as just that, a break, and left him sitting there in the office smacking white bread against the roof of his mouth. I didn't like being around him any more than I had to, and two days into working side by side, I was already certain that I hated him more now than ever. I drove the few miles down Highway 107 to Mama's house and pulled back into that dark cut just as the sun was peaking so straight overhead that shadows vanished.

The front door was propped open like always, though the rotten chinking between pine planks would have offered just as much for cross ventilation. There wasn't a sound coming from inside, but the house held a noise all its own: creaking planks and the unrelenting chirps of spring peepers living out hot summer days in the cool damp mud beneath the porch. I walked up to the door and peeked inside. Mama was lying across the couch, her back pressed against the far armrest, and bare legs running the length of cushions. She was staring at the wall and didn't seem to notice me standing there.

"Mama?"

Her stare pulled back from a picture that hung on the wall, a bright-colored picture of an Indian on the back of a horse, the type of artwork that's sold in dirty filling stations and flea markets. She fixed her eyes on me, her stare brightened, and she smiled a bit, not full-on happiness but an I-ain't-completely-alone-anymore kind of smile. "Jacob?"

"What you doing?"

"Oh, you know, just sitting here thinking, that's all." She pulled her legs up into her chest and tugged a loose-fitting T-shirt over them so that her whole body fit inside that shirt. She patted on the cushion next to her and gestured for me to sit down beside her. I could tell that she was sober, and I could tell that those few days off the shit had left her mind someplace else.

"What were you thinking about?"

"Oh, I don't know. Just where he might've been headed, I guess."

"Who?"

Mama turned back to the picture and nodded.

"The Indian?"

"Yeah, I guess I was just wondering where he was headed off to all dressed up like that. Might have been going to fetch him some lady or something. Might have been going off to die."

"Might have been, I guess." What she was saying didn't make a whole lot of sense, but then again, I'd never heard her say much worth remembering. Regardless, she had more sense about her after a few days of sobriety than I was used to. Those times rarely came, but I'm pretty sure those times were also why I couldn't hate her.

"Don't really matter where he was headed just so much as he was going there, I guess. I think I'd kind of like to be headed with him, you know?"

"Yeah."

"Yeah." Mama kept those big bulbous eyes focused on that Indian and squinted a little to suck it all back inside of her and not let it out. She ran her tongue along the front of her teeth with closed lips, and that movement seemed to exaggerate her cheekbones and how her skin sunk in on her skull. Neither of us spoke for a minute or two. We just sat there, her staring at that Indian and me staring at her. I pulled a cigarette from a soft pack in my jeans and lit one of Daddy's Winstons. That movement and that sound brought her back and she looked at me and smiled. "So, what are you doing?"

"Been helping Daddy over at the shop."

"What in the world for? Got more business than those Cabe boys can handle?"

"No, they haven't been around for a week or so."

"What do you mean, they haven't been around?"

"I mean they haven't been around. Went missing."

Mama cut her eyes hard at me. I don't know if it was what I said or how I said it, or if it was just the fact that she knew how things worked, but she looked into me like she could see straight through me. She looked at me like she could go back behind those words and grab ahold of the truth no matter whether I was willing to say it or not. "Well, I guess it's good you're helping him. I'm sure he appreciates it."

"Oh, yeah, he's a real appreciative son of a bitch all right."

Mama laughed a scratchy, wet-sounding laugh until the phlegm caught in her throat. She pushed her hair back out of her face. Her dark hair didn't seem so stringy and greasy as before, like maybe they'd washed it while she was in the hospital, and that seemed to make all the difference in the world. She looked better than I'd seen her in a long time.

"I'm sure he appreciates the hell out of it," I said.

"Well, what's new with you?"

"What do you mean?"

"I don't know. I just don't ever get the chance to really talk to you, you know?"

"There's a reason for that."

"Goddamn it, I know. I know there's a reason for it." Mama reached out and took the cigarette from my hand, put it to her mouth and took a long drag, her cheeks sucking into dark shadowy depressions. "I'm about as clearheaded as I remember being in a long time, and I guess I just want to use it."

"You could just stay that way."

Mama took another drag off of the Winston and held it back out to me. She looked up at that Indian picture again and stared way back into it like she was thinking about what I said, thinking about where that Indian might have been headed and how she might get there. Then she turned to me and grinned with teeth half eaten by dope. "But what are the odds of that, right?"

I wasn't really sure what to say, but I knew she was giving me the closest thing to truth that she had for giving. She had a fate she was trapped to just the same as I did, just the same as Daddy. Wasn't any use in sugarcoating that type of shit.

"So, what's new?"

"I don't know. Not a whole lot. I do have a date with Maggie Jennings tomorrow night."

"Maggie Jennings? I don't know her, do I?"

"You ought to. Me and her dated for a few years, and, hell, she grew up right by the house."

"That little girl that used to live right down the road, the one you used to play with so much when you were little?"

"Yeah."

"Oh, Jacob. She's cute." Mama smiled at me and wriggled her legs beneath that T-shirt. The thought seemed to make her happy. "At least she used to be really cute from what I remember."

"She's fucking hot now."

Mama laughed. "You sound like your daddy."

That "sound like your daddy" didn't sit too well with me. "Well, she turned out really pretty. A really good girl too, you know?"

"That's good, Jacob. That's good." Mama pushed her bony legs out from under the T-shirt and stood up from the couch. "Well, listen. I'm going to get in there and try to scrounge up something to eat, and I know you've got to be headed back to the shop soon anyhow, but why don't you stop by later in the week and tell me how that date went, all right?"

"You still going to be worth talking to?"

Mama smiled really big, and for a minute, I could almost picture her how she'd been in those old-time photos before some of those teeth got missing and those holes checkered her smile. "Aw, I'm always worth talking to, Jacob." She stretched her arms back behind her and popped a few cricks out of her spine. "Besides, I ain't got no money."

It was the closest thing to a normal conversation I'd ever had with her. It was the closest thing to a mother she'd ever been. And if we'd have been normal, I reckon that would have been the time we'd have hugged each other and she'd have kissed me on top of my head. I reckon that would have been the time that we looked each other square and said we loved each other. But we were a far cry from normal. There never had been any room for that sappy shit. There was a part of me that was happy for that, a part of me that thought the hardness that came with it helped to protect us from all the other bad that was in this world. But there was a part of me that knew the downfall. There was a part of me that understood that with that hardness came an inability to ever let anyone worth having get close enough to love.

20.

When I caught sight of Maggie walking down Breedlove Road in a white sundress that hung to mid-thigh and clung tight in the bodice, I knew I was underdressed. Then again, a girl like her with a guy like me, I couldn't have pulled it off in a Jos. A. Bank's. She had her hair down, blond curls draping her shoulders and leaving just enough of her collarbones exposed to hold my eyes. Tan skin seemed to glisten in that golden hour of early evening, but it was her eyes that always had me.

I pulled up beside her in my ratty pickup, stepped out of the truck, and walked around to get the door for her, her pursed lips widening into a smile as she came toward me. Those big silver eyes had a way of taking my breath, wouldn't let any words out, like I was drowning in them or something.

"Well, aren't you a gentleman," Maggie said as she got into the truck.

I watched that sundress slide up her thigh as she climbed onto the seat, me thinking all along that she couldn't be more wrong, but knowing I'd never tell her. For a life with her I could be all sorts of things. "What time you have to be home?"

"It doesn't really matter."

"What do you mean?"

"I mean they were in the middle of fighting about money. They never even saw me leave."

"I might just keep you then." I looked over to Maggie and smiled. She grinned back, but there was uneasiness in her smile, an uneasiness in how she spoke of her parents. "Shit, Mags, we don't have to go anywhere if you're not feeling up to it."

"No. It's not that. I needed to get out of there. You're the highlight of my day."

"Then what is it?"

"I just don't want to talk about my parents right now. You understand?"

"If there's one thing I understand, it's that."

Maggie scooted toward me on the seat and rested her hand on my thigh. I looked over at her and she forced a smile. Her smile was genuine, and it was clear that her frustration was not with me, but there was sadness in her eyes that I couldn't explain. All I could do was change the subject.

"I think you'll like where I'm taking you."

"Where's that?"

"Up on the Parkway."

"Where?" Maggie's eyes lit up with excitement and if her smile told me anything it was that I'd actually managed to come up with something that might please her. "Max Patch?"

"Not unless you want to spend the night."

"Then where?"

"Kind of in between Cherokee and Maggie Valley. The Thomas Divide."

"I've never heard of it." Maggie reached into her pocketbook and pulled out a tube of the sweetest-smelling lotion I'd ever caught whiff of, some foreign kind of fruit smell like something that might grow on an island. She spread the lotion up her arms until it was all worked in. "What's at the Thomas Divide?"

I barely heard the question, my mind wandering. "The spirit lights."

"Spirit lights?"

"It's this place where lights come out over the mountains, but there's no reason for the lights to be there."

"You're so full of shit." Maggie laughed.

"No, seriously. My dad used to take me out there sometimes when I was a kid."

"And you've seen these lights with your own eyes?"

"Ain't seen them with anyone else's."

Maggie leaned over and slapped me in the shoulder. She shot those silver-dollar eyes at me and I was sure I'd run off the road. Winding around Cabbage Curve, headed north along a highway that bent serpentine, I was certain I better keep my eyes on my driving. But the way that sunlight reflected against her thighs, any lick of sense that had ever made residence in that pea head of mine was useless as tits on a boar hog at the sight of her.

We stopped at the Coffee Shop in downtown Sylva for supper, a place that'd been feeding locals for a lot further back than my lifetime. The little family-owned dive had kept the prices low and the plates piled high since sometime back in the 1920s, and had never had any use for going touristy like other places in town. Not all that long before Maggie and I broke up, I'd turned sixteen, gotten my license and a truck, and taken her there for one of the first real dates we ever had. I wouldn't call it our restaurant or some pussy shit like that, but it was a spot we'd shared when the world seemed slower, a place that seemed to hold an energy similar to that spot in the creek where we stood as wide-eyed children with spring lizards squirming in our hands. In the two years that had passed, both of our lives seemed to have lost that simplicity. Both of us carried things now that we hadn't carried before. But being there, being there with her beside me, seemed to bring back all that old feeling. When we were together it seemed like everything else, all the bad shit that surrounded us, stopped and we were all right for a moment or two. It was never a thing that felt like forever, but sometimes all a person needs is a chance to catch their breath.

THE SUN had already sunk behind the ridgeline by the time we made it to the pull-off, and I threw the pickup in park as that late June fire began to burn down into embers behind the mountains. I reached under the seat and grabbed a couple beers I'd smuggled out of the fridge, the cans sweaty from the long drive in warm air. I handed one to Maggie and she hesitantly cracked the top. She barely sipped enough to taste, but I gulped hell out of mine in a face-wrenching swallow and tried to chug past the foam.

"Sorry it's not colder."

"No worries." Maggie took another sip of beer and scooted over on the bench seat till her legs pressed up against mine.

I sucked half that can down on the next swallow in a prayer that the alcohol would hide my nervousness. The last bits of orange melted over Big Cove, and it wouldn't be long before blue faded to black and all that was left for light was moon and stars. "Kind of pretty, ain't it?"

"I'm not putting out that easy, Jacob." Maggie pulled away and scowled in a fashion that sent my heart up into my throat. I could feel my face flushing and palms getting clammy when she widened those eyes and smiled. "I wish you could see your face right now. Priceless."

"I hate you."

"No you don't." Maggie nuzzled up against my shoulder, and I wrapped my arm around her, held her close enough to feel her breathing on my chest. I didn't talk much until that first beer was down, and I cracked the top on another.

"What was bothering you earlier?"

"What are you talking about?"

"When I picked you up. You looked like you were about to cry."

The shrill of field crickets and spring peepers resonated through open windows, and it took Maggie a while to respond. "I really don't want to talk about it."

I'd never been able to leave well enough alone. I knew she would have drug it out of me, so I did the same. "That shit's not right. You tell me you want me to open up, but you won't talk. That doesn't make any sense."

Maggie pushed up from my chest and looked me square. Anger

grew inside of her, a fire building in her eyes. "I don't really know how to say it other than just to say it. I'm not going to college."

"What are you talking about?"

"I mean I can't go. I'm not getting out of here."

"That's crazy, Maggie. You were always top of the fucking class."

"It's not about grades."

"Then what is it?"

"Money. It's about money, Jacob."

"I don't understand."

"That's what my parents were fighting about tonight and that's what they've been fighting about for months. For months they've been at each other's throats."

"But why?"

"Mom hates Dad because he blew my college fund, and he hates her because she didn't get the paperwork mailed off. And what both of them don't seem to get, what both of them can't fucking understand, is that I'm the one who's stuck here."

"When did you find out?"

"A couple months ago, but it's been building and building since then. First we found out I didn't get the loan. Mom missed the deadline and by the time they got to me they could only offer part of what I need. But rather than taking any of the blame, she's mad at my dad for spending what little bit of a college fund I had back when I was a kid. It's just a fucked-up situation, Jacob. It's just fucked-up."

"How much did you need?"

"I don't know. Three or four thousand dollars, but it doesn't matter. It wouldn't matter if it was a few thousand or a million, we don't have it."

"Three or four thousand dollars is nothing, Maggie."

"It is when you don't have it. And it is when you have to pay it every semester."

The two of us sat there for a while, neither saying a word, Maggie shifting stiffly as if she sat in a rocking chair with her hands tucked under her thighs. I could tell that she was broken, but I wasn't sure how to make it all right. I was slowly coming to terms with my fate, and while there was a part of me that desperately wanted to get out, there was a much bigger part of me that knew I never would and accepted it. I knew it had to be different for all of that weight to come suddenly, to hammer someone all at once. There was nothing but darkness outside now. A sliver of moon hung low in the sky and though the stars shone brightly, there was a flickering in their brightness, a flickering that insisted at any minute they could all burn out.

I scooted toward her and pulled her into my side. Maggie looked up at me, her eyes glassy with tears, and buried her face into my chest. I held her tightly curled in one arm and ran my free hand through thick blond curls, traced the tips of my fingers in circles against the back of her head. She didn't move, and I didn't either. Even when my arm went numb and I caught an itch at the base of my back, I didn't move. She needed something solid.

After a long spell, that tightness she carried seemed to lift and she felt weightless in my arms. Only then did I speak.

"What if you were able to come up with the money?"

"I've already told you. We don't have it."

"I mean if you were able to come up with the money is there still time?"

"School starts in a month and a half, but maybe."

"What would you have to do?"

"Just get the paperwork in."

Maggie was still motionless against my chest. I finished my beer and tossed the empty into the floorboard, stared out of the windshield to where ridgeline met sky.

"I could get you the money."

"What are you talking about?" Maggie pushed up from me, her hands pressed against my chest, and looked at me with squinted eyes.

"I mean I've got money."

"Don't joke about this, Jacob."

"I'm not joking. I've been getting paid my entire life, Maggie, and I've never spent a goddamn dime of it. Everything I've ever made is sitting in my daddy's bank account and it's as simple as me telling him I need some of it."

"I couldn't let you do that."

"Why?"

"Because it wouldn't be right, Jacob. I mean it's sweet for you to say, but it wouldn't be right."

"Well, my offer stands."

Maggie stared at me. There were all types of things that seemed to be running around inside of her that went unspoken. Some thoughts can't be put into words. She took both of my hands in hers and rubbed her thumbs across my knuckles. She stared at my hands the way she'd done on the couch that afternoon and then she sent those silver-dollar eyes back inside of me again.

"I'll get there eventually, Jacob. And I'll get there on my own."

"I know you will."

"It just won't be this fall."

"But it could be."

"No, it won't. But I'm all right with that." Maggie stared off into the darkness with a calm certainty in the words she said. "You know, you could come with me."

"Where?"

"To college."

"I didn't even finish high school."

"You wouldn't have to go to school. You could just move down there and get a job. I mean, at least it wouldn't be here."

"Where?"

"Wilmington."

"Fuck, Maggie. That's all the way across the state."

"And what's wrong with that?"

"Ain't it on the beach?"

"Yeah."

"I've never even seen the ocean."

"All the more reason to go."

"And what the hell would I do in Wilmington?"

"You could work as a mechanic. I mean, you're already doing that here."

"Not really. I'm not a mechanic by any stretch of the imagination."

"But you could be."

"I guess I *could be*. I *could be* all sorts of shit."

"Then why won't you?"

"I might."

"You will or you might?" Maggie nuzzled her head against my chest and I could smell the sweetness of her hair, and it was almost enough to confuse me into promises I wasn't sure I could keep.

"I might."

There were things that Maggie could never understand, and part of the reason was that she'd always been just passing through.

The life I was born into seemed set in stone from the moment my last name was scribbled across my birth certificate. But in a lot of ways I'd come to terms with it. There comes a time when you're so worn that you can't fight that type of shit any longer and so you just surrender. There's a peacefulness that comes with surrender. Slowly but surely it seemed that I was finding peace.

"I love you, Maggie." I kissed the top of her head and cracked open the last beer I had.

Maggie turned and looked up at me, and in that moment it seemed like she felt the same way that I did. I don't know what she saw in me. Maybe it was the fact that I didn't gloss over everything. Maybe it was the fact that I called the world's bluff. She pushed up and kissed me, and I held on to her bottom lip until it pulled away and glistened. Her eyes were squinted and looked deep into me. Then she settled back against my chest, rested one hand on my stomach.

Maggie rubbed her hand against my stomach like she was trying to massage all of the bad shit I carried away, but her eyes stayed fixed on the distance. She didn't say anything, and the two of us just sat there, the bugs and frogs offering the only sounds. I was honored that she asked me to go, and there was a part of me that desperately wanted to follow her. There was a part of me that wanted to burn what had been my life up until then. But trusting her entirely was still too uncertain. Hope and faith are loaded guns.

Everything I'd ever been taught told me things that were too good to be true usually are. It was a silly thought to think that I could ever get out of these hills. It was a silly thought to think that the life I was born into was something that could be so easily left behind. Some were destined for bigger things, far-off places, and such. But some of us were glued to this place and would live out what little bit of life we were given until we were just another body buried on uneven ground.

A small, yellow orb of light rose over the peaks in the distance and bent up and to the left slowly before changing directions mid-air and falling down into the valley. It danced down there in the gorge, then dropped further and out of sight. Maggie sat up from my chest and pointed out to where the light had gone. "Did you see that, Jacob? Did you see that light?"

I wanted to tell her I did, but I took a deep breath and another long swig of beer. "No," I said. "I didn't see a thing."

21.

A small Tupperware bowl that sat by the office was slap overrun with keys come Thursday morning when I showed up at the shop. Big sales somewhere off the mountain meant Daddy had to keep the work orders piled high if he ever wanted to shimmy that cash into respectable places. So, that's what he did.

Daddy kept a long line of easy fixes—oil changes, turning rotors, and such—so I could help him move small chunks of change into the bank. But the bigger fixes, heavily overpriced work like transmission replacements that really padded the deposits with zeros, had to be done by him until he could find good enough mechanics to do the work and keep their mouths sealed.

Sinking those Cabe brothers down into Lake Glenville had really thrown a monkey wrench into the whole operation. But dead men tell no tales, as Daddy said, and I guess he figured he could suck it up till then.

Those bologna sandwiches were surely ripe in Daddy's lunch bucket by the time he realized we'd worked straight through lunch. It was mid-afternoon, and aside from him telling me what to work on first that morning, we hadn't shared a word. A light drizzle had sprinkled all day, never did turn to nothing more than a piss trickle, just that hazy kind of misty rain. I was thankful for it nonetheless, as it kept the early-summer heat from melting us, made the job a little more bearable.

A loud buzzing came over the garage, a shrill mechanical buzzing that sounded like an amplified tattoo gun. The buzzer served as a doorbell by the office, so folks working in the garage would know when someone was amongst them.

"Jacob!" Daddy hollered from the next bay over. His head never popped out from under the hood of an old, ragged Cutlass. "Go see who that is!"

The oil was draining out of the ride I had on the lift and there wasn't anything left to do till the draining petered off, so I wiped my hands on a rag draped across a mechanic's chair and headed toward the noise. Standing by the office door was that wide-bodied deputy from a few days before, the one with salt-and-pepper hair who'd taken the missing-persons reports, the one who'd been almost close enough to hear me breathe when I lay flat on my back in the Cabe brothers' trailer. Being this close to him again brought that rabbit feeling back, my hands jittery, my legs just a thought from running. He had his back to me. His shoulders shrugged up around his neck and his head was cocked back like he was trying to stretch some sort of stiffness brought on by catnaps in patrol cars.

"Can I help you?"

The deputy turned around, no sunglasses today, just those creepy-ass blue eyes. "Josh, ain't it?"

"No. Jacob."

"Yeah, that's right. Jacob." The deputy began spreading his mustache with his fingers. "Got a nephew named Jacob. That should've been easy enough to remember."

"Well, what do you want?"

"No reason to be short." The rain had his speckled gray hair slicked along the sides, kind of hid that gray amidst the hairs that still held color.

"We're swamped today. That's all. So, I don't have a lot of free time."

"I needed to have a sit-down with your father, if that's all right with you. He around?"

"Yeah, he's over there."

"You reckon I might have a word with him?"

Rather than offer an answer to another half-assed question, I just hollered for Daddy.

"What is it?" Daddy yelled from across the garage.

"That deputy's back. Says he needs to have a word with you."

"Give me a minute." You could hear the irritation in Daddy's voice, hear him cussing under his breath, but in my mind he'd brought that irritation on himself with the tales he told. I heard the hood slam on the Cutlass and could make out Daddy shuffling across Oil-Dri. "Take him in the office and get him some coffee."

I opened the office door and led the deputy inside. A twelve-cup coffeemaker still held half the pot from that morning, the coffee brewed down thick as stew now. I still poured a cup for myself, needing something to take the edge off, and offered a cup to the bull.

"I'm fine," the deputy said as he walked a circle around the small office and shuffled through piles of paperwork with his eyes. The .38 revolver Daddy'd loaned me the night all went to hell was sitting on top of a stack of work-order receipts on the desk. The deputy eyed that gun for a minute, then took a seat in Daddy's chair, a tall, leather spinning chair, the only one worth sitting on in the whole room. The bull toed the chair across the laminate and bellied up to the desk. He grabbed the revolver handle between two fingers like he was picking up evidence, turned it in the light to check all sides. "Nice gun."

"That's just an old beater Daddy keeps around." I walked over and stood directly behind the deputy as he held the gun I'd waved that night. I took a sip of coffee, that thick burnt taste holding to my tongue. "Has to keep a gun around. You know how people are."

The deputy swung open the cylinder and shook out the shells into his palm. He set the empty revolver on his lap and picked up one of the bullets, turned it and looked at it head-on. I stared at that bullet and thought how the slit hollow point could mushroom out inside of his brain. He set the bullet back down in his palm with the others and looked up at me with those blue eyes. "Yeah, I know how people are." Daddy walked in just as the deputy dropped the last bullet back into the cylinder and slapped it closed. The deputy slid the revolver back on top of the stack of papers and turned to my father. "I was just telling your boy, that's a pretty nice gun."

"Can't beat those old Smiths," Daddy said. "A lot of those new autos, well, like that one on your belt for instance, will hang up when it gets to rolling. But those old revolvers, those old revolvers'll fire come hell or high water."

The deputy didn't answer.

Daddy walked over to the coffeepot and poured himself a cup of thick brew. The pot stunk of burnt coffee, but he never was one for wasting. "My boy offer you a cup of coffee?"

"Yeah, he offered."

Daddy sat down in a stiff chair next to the desk. He made it seem like it was all right, but I could tell that it was eating at him that the deputy had taken his seat. He could keep it hidden, but the fact that he gave up any bit of power to that son of a bitch was flat out eating him alive. He scooted the chair, and it grunted against the laminate, skirted against the floor, and left a black mark scribbled like crayon. "Leave us be, Jacob."

"Sure you don't need me for nothing?" I wanted desperately to stay, to hear the next line of lies he'd tell, but he wouldn't have it.

"What did I say, Jacob?" Daddy scowled. "Just fucking listen. Finish up what you're working on and get the hell out of here, all right?"

"All right."

The deputy turned and looked at me, squinted those pale blue eyes the same way he'd done days before, and I nodded to him. He didn't nod back, didn't even twitch his mustache, just kept his eyes drilling into the back of my skull till I was all the way out of the room. I shut the door behind me and heard music start playing inside as Daddy cranked the knob on a little radio. Like always, he didn't want outsiders listening in, and this time, it just so happened that I was the one on the outside.

22.

Lightning bugs flickered across the yard, and for a second or two, I found myself remembering a time when I was small, filling a mason jar with bugs to keep as a night-light. Come morning the whole room stunk sour, and Daddy tanned my hide. I'd never much cared for those bugs after that, but in the hazy blue fog that held around Mama's house that night, the drizzle all but gone, it was kind of beautiful.

I'd never seen her front door closed in summer. Open screen doors and bare feet had always been a part of her routine once temps rose into the eighties. All the lights in the house were on and that yellow light glowed through busted screens and dangling plastic. There was music playing inside from a small stereo she kept in the living room. I didn't bother knocking, just walked on in.

The living room was empty and New Age country rocked from the small stereo set beneath the picture of that Indian man on the horse. I called for her, but didn't get an answer, didn't hear her shuffling around either. I shut the stereo off and called again. I poked my head into the kitchen, but she wasn't around.

In her bedroom is where I found her, and I'm pretty sure that at that first sight of her my heart stopped beating. I'm pretty sure I didn't breathe until the screams.

She lay in the bed, her bottom half underneath thin cotton sheets and her top half flopped sideways in the direction the bullet had taken her. Blood flared out wider on the wall the further it moved away from her head in the same way a flashlight's beam widens further from its source. That blood was thick on the wall near her, thick enough to drip down in long zigzagged lines as it moved over planks, settled into cracks, pooled, and ran again. It washed over the baseboards into puddles alongside the bed. Further away, higher up the wall, the blood was thinner, more of a spray that had settled onto the planks. It was thicker and meatier there on the bedsheets, running out of the backside of her head somewhere behind the ear that lay flat. Where the bullet had entered the blood was smooth, not nearly as explosive as how it exited. That was all I could stare at those first few moments as I stood in the doorway screaming. The blood was the only thing I could see. It took a long while before that screaming settled and I could really look at her.

Mama's eyes were open and dried into a matte stare, all of that light that had been in them gone and glazed. She peered toward the doorway where I stood and when I blinked I found myself wondering if she had too, if maybe we were blinking at the same time, that maybe she was still alive. I crept inside her bedroom and stood at the foot of the bed, her stare never flinching from the doorway. Her mouth hung open and nostrils held flared, like in one last huff of life, time had upped and stopped right there on her face.

That was when the tears came, and I collapsed beside the bed, knelt eye level with the dead and looked her square. Tears poured until I couldn't see, and I welcomed that not seeing. Blindness was easier. I heaved for breath between loud, choking whimpers that started heavy and faded like echoes until all of the air was gone. That's how I stayed for a long time, not moving, unable to move, except the shakes that walked hand in hand with that wailing.

When there were no tears left to fall, I pressed up onto the bed, my hands pushing down into blood spilled. A loose T-shirt hung around her chest, bare breasts fallen along her ribs and showing through the shirt. One arm dangled off the side of the bed beside me, the other lay flat, palm open cradling the gun she'd used to do it. When my eyes first found that pistol, I couldn't really believe it. I couldn't really accept that it was there.

The Commander-sized 1911 Daddy had waved around in my face that night, the .45 auto he whipped across both Cabe brothers' faces and blew a hole in the living room wall with, was what rested in her hand. She had no way of getting ahold of it. Mama never had been much on guns, even in the types of shady places she was known to put herself into. There was no doubt in my mind that he'd given it to her. There was no doubt in my mind that he'd told her what to do. I don't know what he must've said to make her do it, but she had, and it was done. It was long since done, and there wasn't any coming back from that type of doing.

Then I saw it on the bedside table: a small pocket Bible just like the one Daddy'd shoved in Jeremy Cabe's pocket, identical to the one slid under Gerald's suspenders. The Bible was crisp and flat, never having been opened or read, the dimpled cover still shiny black and the edges of pages gilded gold.

My crying turned to rage, and I just sat there on the edge of the bed, her sprawled out beside me, and examined that pistol in her hand. Untreated steel rusted along the slide where Daddy had kept that gun for years in the damp floorboard of his jeep. The rubberized grips were worn and cracked, nearly dry-rotted from all that time heating and cooling from day to night, freezing in winter and cooking till it was too hot to touch in summer. Her little hand was barely big enough to hold it. Her frail hand, thin fingers little more than bone, spread open around that gun now. Those hands would never do another thing. And whether those hands would've done something worthwhile or not I hadn't the foggiest, but the fact that they would never do another thing ate at me. The hammer was cocked ready to bring life to another round, but I didn't touch it. I didn't want any questions asked when the law came.

I turned to the Bible on the bedside table, and more than anything else, it made me question how I was his son. Someone with that kind of wickedness had that shit running through his veins, and if it ran through his, then it ran through mine. With that type of shit inside of me, it was only a matter of time before the darkness showed itself. Having that type of certainty about what I was made me want to take that gun and follow in my mother's footsteps.

It was harder and harder to look at her. There was a queasiness pushing down deep in my gut, and if I stayed there any longer, I was certain it would come out of me. So when I couldn't look anymore, when I couldn't sit there beside her body for another second, I stood up from the bed, walked out of that room, and left her where she lay.

WHEN THE HEADLIGHTS and strobes came through the front windows of the house, I was standing there in front of that Indian. I didn't look away. No, I kept staring right at him and to where he was looking as those headlights ran a line up the picture and wall and settled on the ceiling above me, the room flicking blue.

He must've been one of those out-west Indians, the kind John Wayne used to get into run-ins with in old westerns, with the big headdresses that hang feathers damn near the ground. Nothing like the Indians from around my parts; Cherokee never seemed to have much use for those fancy feathers. The Indian looked like some kind of chief or something, and he sat tall on the back of one of those spotted Appaloosa horses. That horse had stopped right at the edge of a ravine and that old Indian was just staring out into open plains, someplace far off that would've been hell to get to. There was no telling what a man might've found once he got there, but for folks like me and Mama, I doubt it would've been much different. I really doubt it would've been that much better.

The deputy didn't bother knocking, just marched into the house, the screen door slapping hard against the frame behind him. That slapping and being that close to a lawman on one side and a body down the hall shook hell out of the trance I was in, and I must've been looking at him wide-eyed as an animal when he unsnapped his pistol. I stared right through him for a while, knowing he was there but not really seeing him at all. But when that dilating brought him into focus, I was rattled by who stood there.

"Now, keep your hands where I can see them," the bull said. He yanked up one side of his belt with one hand, and drove the handle of that pistol and the holster downward with the other, bringing a cockeyed slant to that belt and his stance. I didn't move a lick, but that didn't seem to bring him any comfort. "Dispatch said there's a body in the house. Is that right?"

I tried to say yes, but the words couldn't come out. I started breaking again and all I could muster was a rattled, crackly "Mama."

"I'm going to need you to show me where the body's at, boy." The deputy kept his hand on that pistol, but lifted it up and down in the holster, never enough to bring it fully into light, but just enough to ensure he could draw it in a hurry if the need arose. "Slowly," he said.

The young deputy with that high-and-tight do, that eat-shit-and-die expression smeared across him, seemed eager to get me back into cuffs, settle a grudge that surfaced after I spent no more than a few hours locked up after he'd taken me in. But any bit of fight I had was gone, any smart-ass line I might've thrown his way any other time was muted by a hurt and a pain that kept me from saying something as simple as "yes."

"You got any weapons on you, boy?"

I shook my head no, but he patted me down anyways. His patting was hard and determined, and I was so noodly that his hands rocked me back and forth on wobbly legs like he was pushing around one of those children's bop bags. He motioned with his hand for me to lead him, so I did, down the hallway and to the doorway of the bedroom. I didn't look inside. I just held there by the open door as the deputy eased past.

"Yep, I'd say she's dead all right. DRT: Dead Right There." The deputy's words left a sour taste in my mouth, and I was certain I could take him from behind, but I let it slide and kept my eyes on him as he neared the bed. The deputy pulled a pair of latex gloves from his chest pocket and stretched the rubber back over his hand till his fingers fanned inside like a cock's comb. He popped the rubber around his wrists as the gloves grew tight, and that popping sound startled me. I couldn't handle any kind of noise. Just silence. The deputy secured the weapon out of Mama's hand, dropped the magazine from the gun onto the bed beside her body, racked the slide to empty the chamber, and eased the hammer back down onto the firing pin. "Awfully big gun for such a skinny woman. Awfully *skinny* woman. That's what that shit'll do to you, ain't it, boy?"

The deputy turned and looked me up and down in the doorway. He knew that she was my mother. He knew that his words were gnawing me near in two. But more than anything, he knew there wasn't a fucking thing I could do about it. So there I stood.

The bull bent down and swiped the round that had flown from the slide, set that loaded shell alongside the magazine on the bed. Then he looked around for a minute, found where the empty casing had ejected, and slid an ink pen down inside the brass. He dropped the empty casing into a small bag that he'd kept tucked in his other chest pocket.

The deputy ran his eyes along the wall, squinted at how the blood widened into spray. He looked down at Mama lying there, at her gaping mouth and dried eyes, at where that bullet had entered along the left side of her brow. "Yep, deader than wood," he said.

He strutted up to the doorway where I stood, and motioned for me to lead him down the hall. I held there for a minute and looked deep into his eyes, brown eyes with that baby kind of glint still holding off any kind of hardness he hoped would overcome him. He was a pussy, and I knew it. Somewhere deep down he knew it too. When he was alone, I reckon it came to him, and he stewed on it awhile. A man can't hide that type of softness about himself no matter how hard he tries. Sometime or another, it's going to eat at him.

We headed into the living room, and he told me to follow him onto the porch to wait for the others. On the porch, moths were batting their wings hard to stay in flight, their fat bodies circling and falling around the porch light, the walls of the porch blinking blue from the patrol car's strobe. The lightning bugs had headed back into the trees and flickered from perches held high on wetted leaves and limbs. I slouched to the edge of rotted planks, scooted my butt onto the porch, and dangled my boots toward a puddle of water that had overflowed filled gutters and gathered along the foundation.

The deputy sauntered over and puffed his chest out. He took out a small notepad and the pen he'd used to pick up the casing. "So she's your mother, you say?"

"Yeah, that's what I said."

The bull breathed in deeply until there was a bucket full of air in his chest. He puffed that heavy breath toward the sky and situated his belt with his free hand. Then he jotted a couple of things in his notepad and looked me up and down. "Makes a lot of sense, I reckon."

"What's that?"

"You being her son and all."

"How's that?" I looked up from the puddle and set my eyes on him square. I could see in him that he knew he'd struck a nerve, but that cockiness in him couldn't let it alone. No, he had to push it just a little bit further to see if I'd snap or cower.

"I mean it makes perfect sense you being her son and all." The bull dropped his hand back down to the handle of his gun and left his other hand down around his gut, clenching that notepad and pen. "Folks like y'all have that shit in your blood. Outlaws, I reckon." He took another deep breath and huffed into the sky like a bull elk. "Shame she had to go and blow her brains out. Always heard she'd fight like a man."

Every word out of his mouth was chewing, and any minute now I was likely to turn wild. Just one more fucking word.

"Makes sense, though." The deputy slid the buckle over his firearm and snapped it closed. "Ain't been out of the nuthouse but a couple of days. Makes perfect sense she'd blow her brains out."

There was no thought to think, no thinking to stop it, only action. I'd come off that porch in a forceful spread eagle and wrapped around him before he had time to move. I was on top of him. His back pressed into mud. My knees straddled his rib cage and dug down through sparse grass into red clay. I hammered that first fist into his forehead hard as I could, and it dazed him senseless, the blue strobe flashing and seeming to quicken the melee. I pressed one thumb deep into his eye and cracked another line of knuckles across his chin, and that one set him straight. His good eye widened and he knew he was in for it, his hands grasping at his belt for something to stop me. He came out with a shank, one of those bent-handled shivs the cops fancy, and slit it plumb lengthways across my right bicep, but I clenched his wrist and started beating that hand against one of the concrete stepping-stones that made a path up to the house. About the fourth or fifth time his hand rammed the concrete, the knife came loose, and I pushed it out of reach, hit him with an elbow along the edge of his brow. That one knocked him loopy and I had him. Bloodied his nose with the next hammer fist. There was nothing coming to mind to stop me. My mind was blank as I chiseled away at all of that rage I had for him, I had for my father, I had for my fucking life. There was no coming to this time around. I was going to beat him until it was all mush or until my arms gave out. One way or another it wasn't ending till it was done. His eyes started to roll back, and I was just about to swing away when I got knocked from the side, a big hefty brute on top of me now.

It had all happened so fast that I never saw the other deputy drive up, but he had me up and my arms cranked behind me. He wrenched upward until I was certain my elbows would snap. I yanked to see who had hold of me, but couldn't get turned, and that rookie deputy on the ground lifted himself and drew his Taser from the front of his belt. The laser beamed a red dot on my belly and that deputy was just seconds away from firing probes into me, when a voice yelled from behind.

"Goddamn it, goddamn it! Put that fucking thing away, Deputy! Put that fucking Taser away, now!"

The bull could barely stand and looked baffled for a minute, the scowl scrunching his face and blood into a beaten row of dark red furrows. Then the fire died back out of his stare and he holstered the Taser along his belt.

When I gave in and relaxed, the bull holding me let my arms down to my sides, but he wrapped one arm around the front of me, hugged my chest and kept me there. He motioned for the rookie to go to his patrol car. The young bull tried to brush off mud, but it only soiled deeper into his slacks, and he headed toward the Crown Vic. The deputy never took his eyes off me while he stomped away, leaned up against the front fender of his car, and wiped the blood from his nose along the sleeve of his shirt.

The bull behind spun me around then, held me at arm's length with his hands clamping my shoulders. "What in the fuck has gotten into you, Jacob?"

I could see him now, Lieutenant Rogers standing there with a confused look on his face. He was a big man, more round than tall, but handled himself well. I'd heard stories, so I knew he'd taken it easy on me when he tackled me and hemmed me up. He was bald on top, but the shape of his head wore it well. He wore the same uniform as before, just khakis and a polo shirt, the sheriff department insignia embroidered over the left pocket of his shirt.

"Tell me what the hell happened?"

I knew I could trust him with anything I said, but right then words failed me. Instead I was going to cry. There was no holding it back or hiding. No, it came out of me like a deluge through floodgates, and I fell into his chest, crying my eyes out into him. Rogers wrapped his arms around me tightly and held me there. He pressed the back of my head into him harder, clenched me tight enough that I didn't even have to stand. I couldn't remember anyone ever holding me like that, and I thought at that moment that it had to be what love felt like. If that feeling and that comfort wasn't what love felt like, then love never existed.

Rogers didn't say a word until my heavy breathing slowed, and all of the tears I'd carried had soaked into him. When that weight was gone, Rogers pushed me back to arm's length. "Let's go talk in my truck," he said. He led me over to the unmarked Expedition he drove and to the passenger side with his hand never leaving my shoulder. He opened the door for me, and I climbed inside.

Sitting there was the first time I really noticed my arm bleeding where the bull had cut me. It was the first time I felt it stinging. The blood seeped into the sleeve of my T-shirt mostly, but some of it dribbled down to my elbow and dripped onto my britches. I pulled my sleeve down over the cut and pressed it hard to make it clot.

Through the windshield I watched Rogers walk up to the other deputy. The young bull packed a tin of tobacco in his hand and loaded his lip full of long cut. The deputy slid that wad of tobacco along his gums with his tongue till his cheek pushed out like a boil. They talked back and forth for a minute, and about the time the deputy's first line of spit bounced off the ground, Rogers let into him with an intensity that had me believing words could strangle the life out of a man. I couldn't hear the words he screamed, only the fierceness in his tone, and that wildness lighting in the electric blue strobe. The deputy tried to say something, but Rogers chewed his ass and the deputy's stare fell to the ground. He wouldn't look up again. He just stood there and took it like the bitch that he was.

Not long afterward, the deputy climbed into his patrol car and shrank inside, his silhouette flickering each time the blue lights flashed. Rogers marched back to the Expedition with his anger holding his shoulders high and stiff as he came. My blood was spread across the front of his shirt where he'd held me, but he never paid it any mind. He climbed onto the driver's seat and turned his eyes on the patrol car in front of him, then shot his look to me.

"Now, what happened in there, Jacob?"

"Mama shot herself."

"I know that. That's how the call was paged, but I mean, did you see her do it? Did you just walk in on her like that?"

"Yeah, I found her like that."

"I'm sorry to hear that, son." Rogers leaned back in his seat and yanked at his britches legs to loosen them around his thighs. He breathed deeply, blowing his cheeks out until the air hissed from his lips. "There's nobody needs to see something like that, especially nobody your age, and especially not their own mama."

"I'll be all right."

"I'm sure you will be, son, but a lot of folks ain't. For a whole lot of folks seeing something like that changes them, and that's all right too." Rogers leaned over and settled his hand onto my shoulder.

"Really, I'll be all right." The crying had turned into numbness now, that same kind of numbness that came after leaving Robbie Douglas wrapped around a rock and that same kind of numbness that came as I drove the Cabe brothers to water. Just as it had then, it was the numbness that scared the shit out of me. Feeling things like pain and fear seemed natural. But feeling nothing at all made me question what I'd become.

Rogers slipped two cigarettes from a pack of Lucky Strikes and passed one of the smokes over to me. He ran the Zippo down his britches and lit the wick aflame with a tall jumping fire. He ran the fire to his first, bit that cigarette between his teeth like he always did, and then passed the flame over. I took a long drag and let it settle deep until it burned at my lungs, that first shot of nicotine rendering me woozy the longer I held my breath. I welcomed any feeling at all.

"You know what was strange in there?" I took another puff from the cigarette and slouched against the seat.

"What's that, son?"

"The gun that was in there." I turned and looked Rogers square.

"The gun that was in there, the gun that Mama used to do it, that was Daddy's gun."

"What are you talking about?"

"That was his .45." I pressed my head back against the headrest and aimed my stare at the ceiling. "And you know what else? He left a Bible in there beside of her."

A confused look came over Rogers, and he shifted uncomfortably in his seat. "A Bible? What the fuck are you talking about, a Bible?"

"One of those little Bibles like will fit in your pocket. He left one in there on her nightstand." I took another puff of smoke and blew a cloud against the ceiling where I stared. "Always heard he left those Bibles, but never put much stock in it till I seen it."

"Best not to say things like that." Rogers pulled away and propped against the door. He clamped the cigarette hard between his teeth, the smoke rolling up around his face and shrouding his eyes from me. "Best to just keep things like that to yourself."

I didn't say another word about it. It made sense for Rogers to say that, seeing as he was the one who called the house to tell Daddy the very moment Mama was cut loose. The thing about it, I wasn't mad at Rogers for lying. The way I saw it, Rogers was on the payroll and the pay had a way of outweighing morality. Rogers took home rolls of money to keep his mouth shut and Lord knows his family needed that cash. He got paid shit to wear that badge, and he had mouths to feed. Who I was mad at, who I had just enough anger inside of me to kill, was the one who gave her the gun, my own flesh and blood, my own fucking father. That was the son of a bitch that fueled the fire growing inside of me. That was the son of a bitch that held it all.

23.

The fixed-blade skinning knife was my first thought. Push that thick drop point down into his throat and listen to him gurgle. But that would've been too messy, might've even given him a chance to fight back for a second or two. So I settled on the .22 pistol, same as he did. Seemed awfully fitting to put that son of a bitch down in the same way he did the rest of the animals. One shot and done.

When I was younger and Daddy used to keep a passel of hogs, he would slop the pigs when it came time to butcher. He'd pick one out and toss a whole bucket full of feed and wait till that hog got to chomping, and the hog never even saw him put the barrel to the back of its ear, never heard the shot. Killing a man wasn't so simple. Men had a way of not getting so fixed on one thing, and men like Daddy always had an eye out for the world to fall off-kilter. So I did it while he slept.

The clouds had cleared, and the moon had come out by then and lit his bedroom a funny kind of blue through the window. Everything was cast in blue: the dresser top where he kept his wallet and spare change; the side table where the lamp hovered over a .40 S&W auto he used as bedside protection; the white cotton sheets he slept beneath. A sapphire kind of shade draped everything, even skin. Daddy always slept on his back like a corpse, his arms folded around his stomach, toes pointing straight up under sheer sheets. With his head rocked back on a down pillow, Daddy sawed logs in a sleep deep as hibernation. But it wasn't him I was so worried about waking. It was her.

Josephine was curled up in a tight ball beside of him, her head nuzzled up against his chest, blond hair feathered across his arm. She was naked underneath those sheets, and the fabric had drawn down to her rib cage, one tit glowing blue and round. She was pretty except for the talking, so she was always sexiest when she slept. How she managed a wink of shut-eye with all of that rasping and grunting, wheezing and snoring, was beyond me, but that's where she lay most nights. She slept heavy too, but often woke up in the middle of the night for a swallow of water and a trip to the john. Her eyes twitched the way one's do in a dream, so I didn't think she'd wake, not in the time it would take to do it.

The plan was to do it how he'd done. One round for each of them, load them up in his jeep, and sink them down in that wet graveyard with the Cabe brothers and God knows who else. I'd feed the deputies the same lines: got to talking an awful lot about Robbie Douglas, started acting awful funny, and then poof. He vanished. Make those bulls think he was on the lam or something.

I'd taken my shoes off to soften my footsteps and neither had stirred when I entered. I'd been standing over the two of them for what felt like days, but according to the alarm clock on the side table was precisely three minutes. 2:42 a.m. The bottoms of my bare feet were getting sticky with sweat and seemed to glue me to the hardwood floor. But I was as close as I needed to do it.

The long bull-barrel Ruger hung by my side. Like all guns, this one Daddy kept loaded with one in the hole, racking that first bullet into the chamber and refilling the clip so he was always one over capacity. "Ten ain't near as good as eleven," he'd say, but I only needed two. I was thankful I didn't have to chamber a round, just one less noise to worry about waking them.

It took more than once for my brain to tell my arm to raise, and those first couple of times my arm was flaccid and unresponsive. But then my arm rose stiff as a pipe, settled when that front fiber optic glowed red over his face. "Just the front sight you have to worry with," Daddy'd said when I was young, and he first taught me to shoot. He'd been right, and the Harrington and Richardson ripped apart every clay he threw. That was one of the few times he'd been proud of me. I could count those times on one hand even if I had lost two or three fingers in a sawmill. Thinking of that fact brought on the anger, and I needed that anger more now than ever. I needed it to fuel me. The second I saw that gun in Mama's hand, I knew what it would take to make things right, and I needed that anger to ensure the deed got done.

The front sight quivered right and left across his face and I took a deep breath to still my hand. I was counting down in my head, backward from a hundred, and when the numbers ran out I'd do it. Pull the trigger on the exhale. About 75 the doubt set in, but by 50, I was good. Each breath came and went. The numbers fell. 30. Breathing became less and less about keeping me standing and more and more about steadying my aim. 15. The breathing quickened during that last set of ten and it was all I could do to hold it there, my hand gripped bloodless, knuckles pressed white. Zero came and I pulled, swung the pistol to Josephine right after that first crisp trigger break.

Only when Daddy moved did I realize there hadn't been a bang, just a loud click as the firing pin hammered away on nothing. I moved fast then, yanked back those bolt ears to eject a misfired round, but the bolt held on an empty chamber. Daddy's eyes were open and out of the grog he came, rising so fast that it sent Josephine rolling out of the bed, just a naked top of woman parts spinning wildly on the floor. Both hands had ahold of my wrist and ran me back into the wall, the pistol falling out of my grip as Daddy rammed my hand through the windowpane. He lifted me up and flipped me in midair, body-slammed me, my shoulder hitting first, then my neck and head cranking against the base of the dresser. By the time I rolled over, my back holding me up against the wall, he was overtop of me, having already grabbed his pistol from the bedside table. Josephine screamed and yanked the sheet off of the bed to wrap herself up. She sprinted out of the bedroom, her feet catching in all of that cloth as she hit the door, and tripped face-first into the hallway.

"*Don't you fucking move!*" he screamed. Daddy shuffled for the light switch, never taking that gun or his eyes off me. Josephine's screams moved further and further away, her footsteps banging across the floor, the screen door slapping hard behind her, and those Walkers baying and snarling just as soon as she stepped foot outside. Her screams turned to a high-pitched cry as one of the hounds got ahold of her, but she must've wrestled free, since the next thing I heard was her car crank and tires spin gravel down the drive.

That first flash of light blinded me, my eyes having long since settled to the darkness. When my eyes unknotted, the white light brought color to the room. Daddy stood over me. His tattooed chest heaved. The gun never wavered from my head.

"Jacob!" Daddy hollered. "Jacob! What the fuck are you doing?"

I could barely move my arm. My shoulder felt dislocated and my neck near broken. But I sat up as much as I could, and scowled with rage that had not waned. "You killed her!" I screamed. "You fucking killed her!"

"Who the fuck are you talking about?"

"Mama. I found her there and you killed her! You killed her, you son of a bitch!" I pushed up off the floor with my good arm and rammed toward him, but a swift blow pounded me in the top of the head as Daddy smashed the pistol and hammered me back onto the floor.

"What the fuck are you talking about?"

"I found her there and she'd blown her fucking brains out! She'd blown her fucking brains out with the gun you gave her! And then you left one of those fucking Bibles there beside of her, you sick fuck!"

"I don't know what you're talking about, Jacob, but what in the fuck were you doing standing over me with that gun?" Daddy never took that pistol off aim. The hammer was back and it was a sure bet that he wasn't sitting on empty.

"I was going to kill you, you son of a bitch! I was going to blow your fucking head off and make shit right!" I came off of the floor again, got about the same distance that second run, but when the steel found its mark, my vision spiraled like the end of a Looney Tunes cartoon until all that was left was black.

WHEN I CAME TO, Daddy sat on the edge of the bed, sweatpants rolled up to his knees, bare chest graffitied with tattoos, one hand resting the pistol on his lap, the other hand holding an apple up to his mouth as he took another bite. I slumped against the wall as it all came into focus, and noticed he'd wrapped my hand up in a shirt to stop the bleeding from where he put it through the window. I stared at him and didn't really know what to say. My anger was stupefied and weak. Daddy picked the pistol up from his lap and gestured like he was about to say something as he chewed on the apple.

"You ready to talk now?" Jagged bits of apple peel and mashed fruit cut somersaults along his sentence. He spoke so matter-of-factly that there was a part of me wondered if any of what I remembered really took place, but there was that pain running from my shoulder to my neck, that bloody hand wrapped in a shirt to remind me. I kept quiet and didn't answer, not exactly sure what to say. "Well, all right then, I guess I'll do the talking. Seems you think I had something to do with your mama dying, is that right?" I nodded and he continued. "And seems you think that gun that she used might have been something that I gave to her, is that right?" Again, I nodded. "Well, you're goddamn right I gave her the gun, and you're goddamn right I told her to do it. You fucking piece of shit, you ought to be thanking me."

"Thanking you?"

"Yeah, Jacob. That woman was a fine piece of work, a fine

fucking piece of work, I tell you. Want to know how fine a piece
of work she was? Fine enough that she stole from her own husband, fucked every friend I ever thought I had, and left you, you,
Jacob, her own fucking son, like a bloody fucking tampon. That's
what kind of woman your mama was."

"And that was cause for what you did?"

"No, I don't reckon it was. I reckon if that'd been cause, I
would've shot that sloppy bitch a long fucking time ago. I'd have
done it my fucking self." Daddy took another bite of apple,
scratched at an itch with the end of that pistol, an itch that hit him
right where a bunch of spiderweb was inked on his chest. "No, I
guess what I did was just show her the error of her ways. I guess I
just explained to her how much hurt she'd caused and how much
hurt she was still causing, and then I gave her an out. The out I
gave her was that gun you saw, and just like she should've, that
fucking bitch took it."

"I don't think that's how it happened."

"*Then why don't you tell me how the fuck it happened, Jacob?*"
Daddy was screaming. He'd jumped from the bed, thrown that
apple to the floor, and spit like a seed spreader as he yelled in my
face. His eyes bulged, and his face sizzled red. He pressed the barrel flush against my temple, but I didn't flinch. No, I prayed he'd
do it. "Tell me what the fuck you think happened since you're so
goddamn smart!"

"You want to know what I think happened, then I'll tell you."
My words were calm, and I kept my eyes fixed on the wall in front
of me, never bothered glancing his way. "I think you got it in your
head that she'd ratted you out the night Lieutenant Rogers came
up to the house. Then I think, no, I know, he gave you a heads-up
when she got home. I think you got it in your mind that she was

too much of a threat, so you went over there and told her she had two choices. Either you could take her out of this world and take your damn precious time doing it, or she could do it herself. And then you gave her the gun to do it."

"You don't know nothing!" Daddy slapped me across the face repeatedly with a hand that seemed big enough to palm a beach ball, and I didn't move. His strikes came numb at first but then grew into stinging like frozen skin washed under scalding water. "You ain't got a goddamn clue!" He slapped me back and forth across the face until his chest heaved again, all of those tattoos swelling and shrinking with every breath he took. He fell back onto the edge of the bed and buried his head in his hands. I was rooted against the wall, my whole face afire. And that's when I saw him do something that he'd never done. My daddy, that hard-as-nails piece of shit, sobbed like a child. He wailed down into his hands and let out one of the god-awfulest roars I ever heard.

He hadn't cried when he had to lay lead to his best hound, a dog he loved more than me. He hadn't cried when his daddy was eat up with cancer so bad that he spent that last winter coughing on blood and choking on his own spit, nor when he buried Papaw on that slanted ground in Hamburg Baptist Cemetery. And he'd certainly never shed a tear that I'd seen for any life he'd taken. But whatever this was, whatever worms were digging into his gut right that second, shattered every bit of man he thought he was. I think there was a place deep in him where he held something heavier than any other weight that he carried, a part of him that still loved her.

"Goddamn it!" he screamed, with his wetted face aimed straight toward the ceiling. "Goddamn that worthless cunt!" He glared toward the light and blinked his eyes fast to try and clear them.

"Bury her," I said.

Daddy turned his attention to me, a confused look lowering his brow, his eyes red, and his face sheened with tears. "What the fuck did you say, boy?"

"I said bury her."

"What the fuck are you talking about?"

"You pay to have a preacher do his prayers over her, and you pay to put her in the ground." For the first time since that rage, I was looking him square. "That's the closest you can come to setting this right."

"She ruined my life." Daddy started to break again, but he didn't hide it behind his hands. He sat there and let me see it. "She ruined my fucking life!"

"And she's paid for it." I looked deep into him and tried to pick at that one piece of humanity that I'd never seen. "All you can hope is to set this right."

"I won't spend a goddamn dime on that bitch! I don't owe her a fucking thing!"

For a minute I stewed on all of that hate in his heart. Those moments of silence that passed between us felt like days. Then words finally came to me and I spoke. "Then set it right with me."

Daddy stared at me as if he were really rolling it around in his head, milling that thought up till nothing remained but absolute fact. "Truth of it is, I don't owe you a fucking thing either, Jacob. Truth of it is, you're grown. You can fend for yourself." The anger came back over him, and his eyes hardened till there wasn't a bit of light left in them, nothing alive in him anymore.

"What about my share? What about all those numbers you've been adding up and subtracting ever since I can remember?"

"That's all just a bunch of shit, boy. Like I said, I don't owe you a fucking thing."

I picked myself up from the wall, my body beaten near limp, only pride holding me there. I limped to the edge of the bed and stood over him. I looked him dead in his eyes, eyes that had been sucked dry a long time ago, eyes that should have held something in them but didn't, the way a dead man stares. All living things I'd ever seen held that light, but those bulbs had burned out on him a long time ago. "Bury her, and we'll call it square."

Daddy looked up at me, all of that pain flushing his face, his eyes like wetted stone. "I'm going to bury her, boy, but it ain't got a goddamn thing to do with you."

24.

It was already daylight when I hobbled out of the house for the last time. I would've felt better leaving if I'd have doused the whole place in gasoline, poured a trail up the drive, and lit that mother-fucker up like a pile of dead Christmas trees, but I didn't. No, I just gathered my shit and left. There was a few hundred dollars stashed in a hide in the hardwood floor by my bed, a place where a single plank lifted and revealed joists and insulation. I'd always hidden things there. When I was a kid, I hid packs of stolen ciga-rettes, a porno mag or two at times, and never told a soul other than Maggie. But aside from the money, packing was just a mat-ter of piling clothes in the pickup, swallowing the last two Xaney bars I had, and driving away.

I spent that first night parked way back on a dirt road where hippie kids from the university liked to camp and burn empty bottles of Aristocrat vodka and Barbarossa spiced rum. The camp-fires they lit left dark ovals up and down both sides of riverbank. A long ways back, a man by the name of Aiken owned all of that land, and Daddy had told me once while we were fishing that Aiken blew the whole front end off a kayak when a couple of tree huggers demanded access to the gorge through his property. According to those stories, old man Aiken had already made his stance quite clear, and when those water rats decided to take their chances, Aiken hammered off a shot from a .30-30 high up on the ridgeline just as soon as the paddle made its first cut into water. That was back when mountain ways still mattered, back when men were men, and the neighbors were too scared to call the law.

Nowadays it was all game lands overseen by the Forest Service, though it was seldom patrolled by the dark green pickups the rangers drove and that's why I'd come. The rangers with fancy college degrees, who wore golden badges and government-issued logging boots with kilties rolled back over the laces, spent most of their time cutting fire lines.

I had parked at the end of a rutted trail down to the river where water purred and whispered over smooth stone. It was a good quarter mile from the main road, a main road that was loose gravel and only wide enough for one car. During the day, the road saw lots of drivers, the dust never seeming to settle back out of the air. After sunset, though, the fly fishermen and paddlers headed out, and the road was traveled only by drunks looking to cross the mountain without the hassle of saying their ABCs backward, standing on one leg, or touching their noses with their eyes closed. I sat on the tailgate and struggled to roll a loose cigarette out of a bag of Bugler with my good hand, no more money for name-brand smokes and no Winstons to steal. Stale tobacco burned with a dusty smell and puckered a bitter taste in my mouth with every puff.

The woods already smelled like rain, though the clouds hadn't arrived just yet. A summertime thunder-boomer echoed over a set of peaks just to the south, and the sky flashed with light a few seconds before each wave of sound arrived. I knew it wouldn't be long before summer rain pushed the river over its banks and washed the shoreline clean.

I didn't know what to think of Daddy agreeing to pay for my mother's funeral. I'd never really expected he would. I'd never really seen anything close to compassion in his heart. I hated him for what he'd done. I hated him for what he'd raised me to become. But there was a tiny bit of respect that came the night before, when he told me to head to his lawyer's office to work out the details of my mother's burial. In the morning I would visit Queen, and in a few short days I'd put Mama in the ground. I had Daddy to thank for that, and being thankful toward him was about as confusing a thing as I'd ever felt. Mama wasn't the only thing that needed burying. I wanted to shovel dirt on those feelings too, bury them deeper than six feet.

The first drop of rain fell through an opening in the jack pines. It smacked me in the top of the head and burned at the place where Daddy had cold-cocked me with the butt of his pistol. Somehow or another the blows he hammered hadn't split my scalp, but a tender knot had risen on my skull and that's exactly where that first drop of rain struck. Another drop fell and thumped the pickup, then another and another, and within seconds the rain came. I snatched my cell phone and the pouch of Bugler off the tailgate and threw the things not suited for water into the cab. But I wanted the rain on my skin. I wanted that coldness on my muscles, and I climbed back into the bed to lie there and let the world wash over me. My shoulder hurt and my neck was whiplashed stiff. Raindrops stung the places where skin had yet to heal, but it was a soothing kind of pain that I welcomed. The water was cold and the air warm, chills raising goose bumps on my arms, and all that rain seemed to wake me up out of a nightmare that had held for too long. For the first time in a long time, I felt alive.

Lightning screamed sideways across the sky, and beneath a tall stand of pines was a place most wouldn't have found comfort, but it was the closest I'd ever been to baptism. My mind cleared and that clearheadedness brought on a dream of setting the world right. It wasn't vengeful or fueled by hatred, but rather a settling of debt owed, a righting of the world that had needed righting for a long, long time. Daddy had been dead-on about two things: I was grown, and I could fend for myself. But that was all he had right.

He was wrong about those numbers he'd ciphered in that book all of my working life. Those numbers weren't *shit* like he'd said. No, he'd been wrong about that. The money was something I'd earned, a small payment for the burden he fixed to my back when I was young. Seeing as he'd piled on a weight that would stay with me as far into the future as I could imagine, probably hanging around my neck and weighing me down till the day I died, Daddy owed me that. And it wasn't just me who needed that money now. It was Maggie. I was certain I could talk her into taking the money, and I was absolutely certain that I wanted her to have it. I knew my father kept enough in the safe at the shop to cover most of what I'd earned. I wasn't sure how I'd manage to get in and out of there quite yet, but the one thing I understood was that the time for cashing out had come.

I spent hours texting Maggie that night to convince her to take the money. I lied about where it came from, but it was a lie that I knew had to be told. She loved me, but she never loved the life I led. She respected me, but she never respected how I made my money. I knew she wouldn't have taken it any other way. So I told her it was my inheritance from when my grandfather died. I told her it was a loan rather than a gift, and that she'd have to pay it back. And after a whole lot of telling, a whole lot of convincing that it wasn't me giving her anything, she finally agreed. She'd mail the paperwork in and she'd be out of here come fall. The minute she made that promise, I felt happy, truly happy, and that happiness grew from the fact that Maggie would never have to surrender to anything. Maybe I wouldn't either.

The rain poured, all the while those thoughts becoming a little clearer and a little more certain. When it was done, I'd never be able to come back, but that fact didn't frighten me. There had never been anything here for me anyways. No, it was staying that frightened me. Staying was something that I just couldn't figure. I knew right then that there are things in this world far worse than dying, things that'll push a man to greet death like an old friend when he comes. Staying was one of those things. Staying meant that I'd become just like him in time.

25.

Irving Queen kept his office in a two-story house just a block or two off Main Street in downtown Sylva. White paint chipped from the wooden siding, but the black shutters were fresh and shiny, giving a mascara outline to every window on the house. The windowpanes were that old kind of glass that had a wavy look about it when the sunlight hit it just right, but the sun wasn't out that day. Up close, bubbles were visible in the glass, little pockets of century-old air frozen inside the panes. A rocking chair swayed back and forth as I walked across the porch, and the warped porch planks squeaked against rusted nails.

I turned the tarnished brass doorknob that fit loose in its socket and walked into the front room of the office. Box fans were placed

obtusely throughout the room, and the breezes blew in every direction, an indoor dust devil whirling about that place. A middle-
aged woman behind a cluttered desk slapped a glass paperweight
down on a stack of papers just before the top pages caught wind,
the cross breeze generated when I opened the door proving too
much.

I'd never met her, but I'd heard the stories when Daddy drank.
Queen was married to his high school sweetheart, a woman who
put on the weight not long after vows and aged poorly in the years
to come. Whether he was just too chickenshit to leave or stuck
around for appearances, Queen never divorced. But like most
men, he'd started sleeping around a few weeks after the honey-
moon. Being one of the few lawyers around, he'd always done
well, and that type of money dazzled the eyes of girls who'd been
raised on mayonnaise sandwiches in the holler. When he was still
young he was able to keep a whole mess of girls around, but those
chances faded once his hair thinned and gut bulged. Now all he
had was this one mistress who worked as his secretary. Daddy
had always called her Franken-slut after all the nose jobs and tit
jobs Queen had paid for to keep her looking young.

"Ought to have somebody tighten the screws on that doorknob," I said as I walked toward her. "Felt like it was going to
come off in my hand."

"Haven't noticed." The secretary pushed a pair of narrow reading glasses to the tip of her nose and ran her eyes from my boots
up to my face and back down to where my hand was wrapped in
an old shirt. The hand Daddy rammed through his bedroom window was cut to bits, and I'd wrapped it as best I could. She sized
me up, and the disgusted look on her face seemed to say she didn't

figure me for the type who could pay. "And who exactly did you say you were?"

"I didn't say, but it's Jacob. Jacob McNeely, and Mr. Queen ought to be expecting me. We have a meeting at noon."

She flicked a loose-fitting wristwatch up onto her hand and turned the face of it till cheap crystals sparkled in the light. The time must've suited her, because she went straight into flipping pages behind the leather cover of her appointment log. "There you are, dear." For the first time she smiled at me, finally figuring I wasn't delinquent. "Let me just go see if he's ready for you."

The secretary stood up and walked to a closed door at the far end of the main room, her high heels knocking and knocking across the floor. A tall slit rose in the back of her skirt and she rocked her hips as if she walked a catwalk for some imaginary crowd. Across the room she pecked at the closed door, turned to me and smiled. A voice I couldn't make out over the fans must've told her to come in, because she did and disappeared into the room for a second or two before she strutted my way.

She looked like she might've been pretty at some point earlier in life, but instead of riding that natural beauty out gracefully, she'd opted to hitch her wagon to Queen and let doctors pinch and poke and stretch and prod till wasn't anything left that duct tape could fix. Her face looked as if wires pulled all of the skin back behind her ears. A low-cut white dress shirt was unbuttoned far enough to expose her breastbone, a breastbone that wouldn't have looked near so bony and rippled if the skin that once covered it hadn't relocated onto the sides of implants two sizes too big. Doctors had worked long and hard to counteract gravity on her body and failed miserably.

"He'll be just a minute, dear," the secretary said as she returned to the desk. Her blond hair was pulled up, feathering at the top, just how porn stars playing secretaries wore it in the movies. Those hackles that sprigged off the top of her head blew around in the breeze of box fans. She settled into her desk and smiled at me, overly white teeth beaming against the orange glow of spray tan. "You just go ahead and have a seat right there, dear. You can keep me company."

Her smile put me off, and I wasn't quite sure what to say. I was more focused on deciphering the riddle of surgeries that pieced her together than conversation. "At least it's nice outside." It wasn't. I knew it was stupid as soon as I said it. The storm from the night before had spread till there wasn't a bit of sunshine to be had, just gray clouds and drizzle. The secretary glared past me and through the bubbled windows to see if she'd missed something, but she hadn't. Her eyes squinted as if to ask, "Are you dumb or something?" but before either of us had time to answer, the door slammed at the other end of the room and Mr. Queen shuffled across the floor.

Now, if Humpty Dumpty hadn't fallen off that wall, and if all the king's horses and all the king's men hadn't tried so damn hard and failed, I would've sworn old Humpty slipped on a Jos. A. Bank's, moved to Sylva, and changed his name to Irving. That pudgy little bald-headed devil was a walking, talking hard-boiled egg.

"Jacob, my boy, how the hell are you?" Mr. Queen slithered up beside where I sat, smiled at me with nubby, yellowed teeth. Cheap whiskey and gas station cigars fogged his breath. He wrapped his hands around my shoulders and gave as tight a squeeze as he could muster.

"Ain't worth a damn, Irv, but I reckon you knew that."

Mr. Queen pulled up on one sleeve of my T-shirt, and I stood out of the chair. He pressed at the base of my back and opened out his other hand to gesture toward his office. "Good, good. Glad to hear," he said, smiling and nodding at the secretary as he ushered me across the room. It wasn't until we were in his office and the door was closed that his smile straightened and his eyes narrowed.

The wall behind his desk was lined with framed papers with cursive writing, fancy gold leaf seals, and wide-arced signatures. One of the bubbly glass windows on the sidewall looked out onto a pin oak in the front yard. Mr. Queen sat down at a chair behind an executive desk, reached into a drawer, pulled out a pint bottle of whiskey, and took a long, bubbly slug. He leaned back in the chair till I was certain it'd tip, propped his feet up on the dark wood desk, and rested the bottle on his belly where lapels flared away. I took a seat across from him, the leather inlaid desktop all that stretched between us.

"We'll get straight to business. I'm a busy man with little time to fool with such piddly affairs. But seeing as your father has managed to keep hundred-dollar bills falling out of my pockets for all these years, I'm obliged to do what he asks. Just know that my obligation lies with him and him alone, and that is the only reason I've agreed to take any part in this. These types of things are generally the responsibility of the family, not an established attorney such as myself. So go ahead and tell me what you're after, keeping in mind that I've got other things to tend." Mr. Queen lowered his head and goggled at me with wide, impatient eyes. Tilting his head pressed what little neck he had flat, just a fat face spreading into a thick roll where his neck overlapped his collar.

"I don't really know what you're looking for."

"Details, Jacob, I need to know details: what you want, where you want it. Do you want a preacher, or do you not? Do you want it in a church, or do you want it in a funeral home? Flowers, songs, what? Details, Jacob, and hurry along with it."

"Well, I reckon I haven't given it that much thought."

"Then what in the fuck are you doing here, boy? Wasting my time? Is that it?" Mr. Queen slapped the chair back flat and bellied up to the desk. He slammed the bottle of whiskey down on the desktop and narrowed his eyes onto me.

"In a church, I guess."

"Good, good. Now we're getting somewhere. What church?"

"Hamburg Baptist. That's where she grew up, and I guess that'd be my church too."

"And I take it you'll want a preacher with it being in a church?"

"Yes. I definitely want that."

"And do you have a preacher in mind?"

"Well, Hiram Bumgarner, I reckon."

"Who's this?"

"His name's Hiram, and he's been the reverend there at Hamburg all my life. I guess he still is."

"I'll see if he is and if he'd mind holding the service."

His agitation and the fact I really didn't know what to say had me flustered. I picked at the wooden laminate of his desk along the edge with my thumbnail and stared at the floor. When a clear thought finally came to me, I looked up at him and spoke. "As far as burial, I reckon I'd like the casket to be—"

"Whoa, whoa, now. Burial? Who said anything about burial?"

"Well, I just figured—"

"There's nothing left for burying, my boy. I mean you could

bury the ashes if you want to, but I don't see it justifiable of any dollars being spent."

"Ashes? Did you say ashes?"

"Yes, son. Ashes. What did you think had been done with the body?" Mr. Queen took another glug and screwed the top down on his pint of whiskey. "She's been cremated. I thought you knew that."

"Cremated? Now, who in the hell told them to do that?"

"These things happen quickly, my boy. Your father made the call and it was done."

I could feel the anger boiling my blood up into my face, my cheeks turning hotter than hell by what he said and how he said it. Mr. Queen leaned back in his chair and interlocked his fingers. His two index fingers pushed together and pointed upward like he was building a church and steeple with his hands. He raised his eyebrows as if to ask what else I wanted, so I told him. "Put one of those things in the paper, telling folks what time the service will be."

"You mean an obituary. Well, how do you want it to read?"

"I don't know, Irv, however they're supposed to fucking read. Something about her being in a better place or some shit, I don't know. Just let folks know she's gone."

"One problem, my boy. The papers have already run, both of them weekly, you know. That little rag out of Cashiers ran Wednesday, and *The Sylva Herald* ran two days ago. So if you really want to get it in the paper, we're going to have to hold the whole thing off for a week, which won't be too big of an issue as I see it, with there not being any sort of burial. So, is that what you want to do?"

"No, I want it done."

"So then no obituary?"

"Just scratch the fucking newspapers and get it done. Get it done as quickly as possible, tomorrow if you can. See if the reverend is willing to say a few words and call it done. I don't want to be waiting around for it."

"I understand, boy. Say no more. I'll see what I can do." Mr. Queen jotted a few notes down on a long legal pad, yellow paper scribbled with chicken scratch that only he could read. "So, is there anything else?"

"No, I don't reckon there is." I was seconds away from coming across the table and sinking my hands where a neck should've been. I'd pop the head off that snaky bastard like the old-timers had done, grab him by the rattles and snap him like a bullwhip till his head severed clean off. That's what snakes were fit for.

"Good, good, my boy." Mr. Queen bellied back up to the desk and opened his booze. He took a long sip and let the whiskey roll around in his mouth for a bit before he swallowed. A tiny dribble leaked from the corner of his mouth, and he leaned back in his chair and rested the bottle on his gut. "I trust you can show yourself out," he said as he fanned out one arm, his hand opening as if to direct the way. I was just about through the door when he spoke up from behind the desk. "One last thing, Jacob." He spoke loudly to try and overrun the clatter of box fans. "Seems there's going to be a trial after all for that assault. Just couldn't get Mr. Hooper to go along with it, you know?" Mr. Queen smiled slyly and licked the dribble of whiskey that beaded at the corner of his mouth. "I won't be able to represent you since you and your father have parted ways. Conflict of interest, but you understand."

I turned around and stopped myself just before I rushed him. "Oh, I understand. I've understood most of my life."

"Good, good, my boy." Mr. Queen squirmed in his chair, all of his movements slithering and serpentine. He opened a desk drawer, took out a three-dollar cigar, and sliced the end off with a razor blade against his desk. The cigar angled toward the ceiling as he slobbered it between his lips and squinted. "And if it wouldn't trouble you, how about shutting the door."

26.

I remember the first time I knew I was capable of killing, and I mean really killing, not just rabbits and chickens and such, was when Daddy took me way back in Whiteside Cove after hogs. I'd never gone with him before, and until then all of my hunting had been distant, nothing hands-on, just .22 rimfire, gray squirrels and cottontails.

The Walkers had a hog bayed in a dried creek bed where smoothed river rocks lay like dusty cobble.

"Stick him up under his arm, Jacob," Daddy yelled over squeals and snarls.

I'd never heard anything like that sound, but when Daddy unsheathed the knife and the cutting edge he'd sharpened that morning on whetstone caught sunlight, I knew what I had to do. He handed me the knife, and I clenched the leather-wound handle as tight as I could, my fist squeezed into a knot, and fought my way through the hounds till I could see the blacks of the pig's eyes.

Eyes wide, chomping cutters, and screaming, the pig seemed fueled by some blend of fear and rage, and I felt tears dam up in my eyes as I pulled the butt end of the knife into my stomach and thrust hard until the steel bolster rested flush against coarse hair and tight skin. All seven inches of blade was in him now and the squealing grew louder, and I pulled out and stuck him again and again until the sound was wet, fell silent, and blood pooled onto dried oak leaves. I wiped the tears across my face with my shirtsleeve as if I was swiping snot from my nose so as Daddy wouldn't see, and the hounds were still clenching firm to the hog when I watched the last bit of light go out of his eyes. The muscles tightened up one last time, then fell lifeless and limp.

"You done good," Daddy said as he squeezed my shoulder. That was one of those few times he'd been proud, but I could hardly hear him or feel his touch. My ears rang. My body numbed.

The high-pitched drone that wailed in my ears went away by nightfall, but it was that numbness that stayed with me. It was the fact that the tingling never left that let me know from then on that, when the time came, I could do it again.

For some reason, that was the memory that played out in my mind over and over as I stared at the back of my father's head in the sanctuary of Hamburg Baptist on the day of Mama's funeral. Daddy sat on the opposite side of the church and about five pews ahead of me. Mr. Queen sat beside him, having brought the ashes and urn up the mountain from Sylva. Queen, his bald head gleaming with candlelight, never turned around to look at me, but Daddy did. Daddy fixed his eyes on me and stared for a long time, a solemn look about his face. I tried to hold his eyes, outlast his stare, but like always he wouldn't be proven weak.

A handful of the regular congregation had stayed behind that Sunday to offer support. I imagined the reverend had asked them to stay, and it meant something that he didn't want the place empty. When I was a kid, Papaw brought me here to this pew every Sunday. Just down the hall was where I'd had to memorize all of those verses. A mean old woman named Mrs. Jones beat those verses into our heads and tanned our hides when we didn't remember. She'd managed to hammer those verses so far down into me that even now, after all these years, I remembered. I'd never believed in any of it, though, even as a child. The only reason I'd gone was because it made Papaw happy, and I liked spending time with him, so I never put up a fuss. I guess it was once the cancer ate him up that I quit going. Never was much use for God after that.

I stared at the back of Daddy's head, greasy hair slicked and combed, while the five-member congregation stood and sang the opening hymn, "Be Thou My Vision." I knew those words well, but for some reason, they failed me that afternoon.

Sharp angles of colored light shone through stained glass and glowed where the light touched pews. A dark brass urn holding the ashes of my mother stood atop a tall pedestal at the front of the church with summer wildflowers spread in a vase behind it. The pedestal was nearly the same height as the podium where the reverend stood. He was the reverend that had been there when I was young, though time had started to wash away the picture I held of him. The reverend was old now, his belly fattened, but all that seemed to disappear behind a curtain of fist-pounding, sweat-dripping hallelujahs. Though his God-given name was Hiram Bumgarner, I'd only ever known him as Reverend, and he spoke with fire, a locust kind of heat kindling on every word. He wore no robes, stoles, or clericals. Never had. He always stood in front of his congregation in nothing more than a white, collared button-down and slacks.

Baptist funerals were revivals. There wasn't time for looking back on lives lost when there were souls that still needed saving. Ten minutes into the sermon, spit flew from the reverend's lips. Sweat beaded on his forehead and bled over him. The summer heat was inescapable in that tiny sanctuary, everyone breathed heavy, and the reverend unbuttoned his top two buttons, his yellow-tinged undershirt visibly wet. The five-member congregation, who had already sat through one sermon that morning, fanned themselves with folded bulletins, sweat gathering on them as well, and they glared on at him, never seeing the man, only hearing the words.

I found myself gazing up at the giant cross above the altar in the same way I'd done every Sunday as a child, and waiting for some sign, some light, to shine down and show me God was real. I'd been waiting around all of my life for that light, but so far nothing had ever come. When I was a kid, I expected it would appear like magic, but even then the idea seemed silly. I did wonder what happened when we died, though, and I'd wondered about it for most of my life. Thinking that nothing happened, that there was absolutely nothing following all of this pain, seemed just as silly as magic. No, there had to be something. And if there had to be something, then there had to be God, so in some way or another I was a believer.

The preaching was just a murmur in the room now, white noise that played in the background while my thoughts spoke and held me in a trance. I reckon the closest I'd ever come to understanding an idea as big as God was the light that flickered in the eyes of the living, the light that Daddy never had. I'd seen that light in every living thing from squirrels to elders, and I'd seen that light burn out when it ended. I thought about that hog in Whiteside Cove, and I could see that hog's eyes clear as day, the way those lights had cut out like a switch had been turned when that pig huffed one last bloody breath. Then I thought of Mama, the way her eyes had glimmered that afternoon we spent talking, and the way those lights were long since gone when I found her there, eyes open, mouth gaping, brains blown sideways. There was a place where all light tends to go, and I reckon that was heaven. That lighted place was what that Indian had his eyes fixed on in the picture Mama fancied, and I guess that's why she'd wanted to get there so badly. The place where all that light gathered back and shined was about as close to God as I could imagine.

On the pew where I sat, though, there wasn't a damn bit of light to be had. Light never shined on a man like me and that was certain. In a lot of ways, that made men like Daddy the lucky ones to have only ever known the darkness. Knowing only darkness, a man doesn't have to get his heart broken in search of the light. I envied him for that.

As the first notes of the closing hymn rang from the mouths of that five-member congregation, the five of them and that reverend belting an off-key a cappella rendition of "I Will Sing the Wondrous Story," I shot back out of that dream I'd fallen into. When the last word echoed, Daddy and Mr. Queen made their way to the back of the church and stood by the door to shake hands and swap niceties with the churchgoers who had stayed. I eyed the two of them, everything inside of me wanting to jump up and kill them both right where they stood. Didn't matter to me that it was in a church. If there was a God, He'd understand.

The reverend tucked his Bible under one arm and headed toward the back of the church. The reverend strode as if he'd been beaten, as if every bit of energy that still held inside of him had been laid out on the altar for sacrifice. The three of them waited there by the open door and talked for a minute. When no words were left between them, the reverend patted my father on the shoulder and all three headed outside into the summer heat. I was the only one in the sanctuary now, and I didn't move from that spot for a long time.

I don't really know why it had been so important for a preacher to say something over the remains of my mother. There was a part of me that thought those words washing over her might be enough to lead her to where that Indian looked. In some ways I believe Daddy had always had those same kinds of thoughts. Though he wouldn't have said it, there had to be a reason for those Bibles he left. The two of us both seemed to think we could fool God into letting the wretched slip through the cracks.

There was nothing ornate or fancy about the dark brass urn that held Mama's ashes. Still, it was better than the Folgers can Daddy would've chosen if he'd had his way. I rose from the pew, ambled to the front of the church, and stood facing the white pedestal that displayed her ashes. The urn was too tarnished to reflect what little light shined in the sanctuary, just a dull, hazy glow reflecting golden off the brass. I picked the urn up, turned it around with my bandaged hand against my bare palm until the metal seemed to hum. It was heavier than what I expected, and I lifted the lid to look inside. The urn was nearly full with fine ash that rose into a mound like an anthill near the top. The mound was peppered with whitish-gray fragments of ground bone, and I shook the urn around till that ash evened out. A small cloud puffed from the opening, powder holding on the air for a minute right above the urn. It didn't smell like cigarette ash, nor did it stink with the thick acridness of doused campfires. The scent was something I'd never really smelled before, a dusty kind of odor that didn't really hold much of a smell at all.

Something shimmered in the pile of ash, and I shook the urn to bring it to the surface. Daddy's wedding band, a ring that had sat on his dresser ever since that day he sent her away, shuddered to the top of the pile. I stuck my hand inside and pulled it out, a white-colored ash powdering the tips of my fingers. The ring rested in my palm, and I looked it over for a minute, its presence raising more questions than answers. The short of it was that there were things my daddy would never say, things I couldn't and wouldn't ever understand. There was a reason he'd given her that cabin after all those years of her running around and stealing from him. There was a reason he'd spent the money to have this service, and just as he'd said, it didn't have a goddamn thing to do with me. I was finished thinking about those things, though. There was already too much shit eating at me to worry with making sense out of something like that. I dropped the ring back into the urn and it clinked inside. I shook a couple more times until the wedding band disappeared under the ash. Some things are better off buried and forgotten.

"Jacob," someone said, and I turned to find the reverend standing right behind me. He still had sweat beaded on his forehead, his hair parted slick in lines across, and was out of breath as he wiped his brow with a handkerchief and stuck it back into his pocket. "You remember me, don't you?"

"Yes, sir."

"I was hoping I'd get a chance to talk with you." He held a hand out to me and grabbed hold of mine before I could even reach out to shake. "How are you?"

"I'm getting."

"Well, I heard what happened and was worried about you and your father. Almost drove out to see y'all yesterday, but didn't know how you'd take it."

"I'd have taken it fine, Reverend, but I'm not living there anymore. Besides, you got more to worry with than us."

"Part of my job's to be a shepherd, son, and you're just as much a part of my flock now as you ever were. That's a horrible thing, what happened. A horrible, horrible thing for a boy your age to see." The reverend paused for a second and stared at me blankly while he thought. "You know the Bible tells us, 'Thou wilt light our candle, the Lord our God will enlighten our darkness.' You just have to let Him."

"Psalm eighteen."

"You know the verse?"

"I ain't been here in a long time, Reverend. I don't have much use for church anymore. But you know good and well Mrs. Jones beat those verses into us."

"Well, have you accepted Jesus, Jacob? That's the question. A man can know all the verses in the book, but it's no good if you don't know Jesus."

I could feel my brow scrunching, and I didn't know what to say. I just stood there a few seconds puzzled. "I don't know," I stuttered.

"Well, it's a yes-or-no answer. Simple as that."

"Nothing's simple, Reverend. Especially not something like that." He went to speak, but I wouldn't let him. I pulled the flowers from the vase that still sat on the pedestal: bright orange lilies, black-eyed Susans, the gaps filled white with baby's breath. Long stems dripped water onto the floor. "I've got to get out of here. I've got work that needs done." I didn't even bother looking at him while I spoke. He wanted something I couldn't give, and it wasn't anything a trip to the lake, a quick dunk, and some words about washing sins could fix. I turned from him and headed for the door, those stems dripping a trail of water behind me, and didn't look back at him or say another word.

"Our darkest hour. In our darkest hour, Jacob," the reverend hollered when I was almost out into the daylight, but I was finished listening.

A SHOVEL RESTED in the corner of a rickety toolshed that smelled of mown grass and gasoline. The shed tucked behind the sanctuary by the woods edge was where the church kept the push mower, weed-eater, and other tools needed for keeping up the property. A padlock rusted open had been all that secured the latch and held the shed closed, so it took no breaking to enter. I hadn't asked anyone if I could borrow the shovel, but my reason was one that churchgoing folks would respect.

It was the twenty-eighth of June that Sunday I carried Mama's ashes to bury her. Folks were already piling into town, the highway filled with passing Florida tags, as part-timers came onto the mountain for the July Fourth celebration that next Saturday. Dog days held the sun high at four o'clock, and that heavy summer heat bore down and cast a fumy haze over the asphalt. Long, stringy clouds blew through the sky and cut sunlight as they passed, but the heat never flinched.

The reverend had already gone home, and the church parking lot was empty. I'd waited in the pickup till he drove away, and though I was certain he saw me sitting there, he knew there was no sense trying to reach me. I was long past that and had been for as far back as I could remember.

Hamburg Baptist sat on the side of Highway 107 right where the woods thinned and Lake Glenville came into view. Across the highway, the Hamburg cemetery rose up a steep hill where sometime back in the 1940s workers had spent weeks moving graves from down in the valley when the river was dammed and the water drowned the township. The lake had been built to fuel a power plant down the mountain that was used to turn out aluminum for airplanes during the last world war, but all that lake was good for anymore was pulling tubes loaded with children during the day and sinking carloads of bodies once night fell.

The steep hillside tilted so sharply that gravediggers couldn't dig so much straight down as at an angle that simply cut into the slope. The head of the grave was always a good three or four feet deeper than the foot. There wasn't a flat piece of land on the whole plot, and so the flowers left on graves blew downhill and stacked in the ditch by the road.

I crossed the highway and climbed the hill with the urn and flowers held to my chest with my bad hand and the shovel carried with the other. Mama's family was buried at the top of the hill, a small patch of headstones that all read *Franks*. She'd been the last survivor from that line of Frankses, her mother, father, and baby brother all burning up in a house fire when she was nearly out of high school. Mama had never talked about it, but when I was younger and those types of questions mattered, I used to ask Daddy about her family. He said it was a lightning strike that lit the house up, burned it down before the first fire truck arrived, none of the family hitting downstairs before the smoke and flames consumed them. He said that Mama had been with him when it all happened, and even at a young age, I remember thinking that all that pain probably had something to do with how she turned out.

I found the place where those three were buried, her father, Joseph, on the left, her mother, Cecilia, on the right, and a small headstone with a lamb on the top that stood between them. At the foot of that small grave I dug a hole about as big around as a milk jug a few feet deep, settled that urn down into the hole till it stood just so. I swiped the dirt I'd dug back into the hole, the red clay staining the rag that bandaged my hand, and watched as the last bit of brass disappeared beneath the soil. Digging a hole, burying something inside, and filling it in always left more dirt than had originally stood, a small red mound built up there now. I mashed it as flat as I could with my boots, but it would take a good rain to wash it smooth.

I left the flowers above the hole I'd dug, between that oval of squashed red clay and the headstone with the lamb. There was a part of me that felt something needed to be said, but those kinds of words had never touched my breath. It was done and settled with me, though, and it felt good. There was nothing left for me there.

I was almost down to the highway when I saw her, Maggie Jennings sitting with her legs crossed and swinging off the back of my tailgate. She had on a beautiful garden dress that showed off

the tan of her legs. White fabric was striped with dark blue out-
lines of forget-me-nots, a silken strap wrapped around her waist,
and blond curls bunched behind her head. Even from across the
road, I could see the way afternoon sunlight glinted in her eyes,
light still flickering when a wide smile creased those eyes damn
near shut. I couldn't smile back.

I reached the pickup and propped the shovel against the bed by
the rear tire. Standing in front of her, I felt those eyes of hers reach
way back into me again, and I knew the hurt I carried was something that I hadn't buried with the urn.

"I wanted to be here for the service."

"It's all right, Maggie."

"I don't really know what to say." Maggie reached out with
both of her hands, and I grabbed them. She looked down when
she felt the dressing on my hand. "Jesus, Jacob. What happened?"

"Went through a window and got cut up."

"You need to take better care of yourself."

We stood there holding hands like we were about to dance,
and when I looked into her eyes, I could see everything I ever
wanted but couldn't have. Knowing I couldn't have it, knowing
that everything I'd ever had I'd lost, brought on a sick feeling. I
was alone in this world, even with her there, and I was certain
I'd cry.

"Will you tell me something, Maggie?"

"What, Jacob?"

"What is it you see in me?"

"What do you mean?"

"I mean what is someone like you doing here with a piece of
shit like me?"

Maggie pushed me away and held me at arm's length. She

looked at me with as serious a face as I'd ever seen. "You're not a piece of shit, Jacob. You're strong. Do you hear me?" She shook me. "You're the strongest man I know."

"No, I'm not."

"You are, Jacob. You really are."

"You can't save me, Maggie." I don't even know where those words came from, but when I said them it suddenly felt like the world fell apart.

"I'm not trying to save you, Jacob, and you're right, I couldn't even if I wanted to. All I've ever wanted is for you to try to save yourself."

I pulled her back into my chest and stared up into the sun when the tears came, and even though they were thick and heavy on my eyes, I wouldn't let them fall. I didn't want her to see how much I hurt. I didn't want her to know that kind of pain. She nuzzled her head into my chest and pressed her cheek where my heart pounded. I lowered my head and dug my nose into her hair, a few tears falling from my eyes onto her curls. I squeezed her as hard as I could and she squeezed back, and we just stood there with that June sun beating down on us, both of us lost, but only her having somewhere to go.

27.

It wasn't our first time together, nor had she been my first. In the years since that morning I woke up from my first wet dream, I'd been with my fair share of women. It was part of growing up in the house where I did. There had always been skeezies around willing to put out for a slack bag or a chance to get in good with my father. They never seemed to mind too much how young I was, seemed to take it as a challenge like they might teach me something. They looked at me how they might've looked at a cute little puppy or a baby, but I didn't care. None of them had ever been all that pretty, nothing compared to Maggie, but those moods came on me like they do any man, and I never said no.

I'd fucked a lot of women, but that night in the truck with

Maggie was the first time I can honestly say I made love to one. The pile of clothes made the bench seat lumpy, but she didn't seem to care about all of those clothes pushing into her back. In time, they worked flat. There was little room in the cab, and we banged against the console, our feet kicking at the door, and she knocked her head against the steering wheel as we slid over each other. I cradled the back of her head like I was holding an egg, my forearms pressing down over her shoulders as I pulled into her. She locked her legs tight around my back and her thighs dug into my ribs when she came, her whole body trembling in my arms, and I wasn't long after.

All of that steaminess fogged the windows, and Maggie wiped her hand across the passenger-side glass to look outside. Until those mountains came into view, the lights of houses on the hillside surrounding us like a pack of wolves, I was certain we'd traveled someplace else. I was certain that what we made in the cab of that pickup was another world, a place fit for living where I might want to stay for a while. Seeing those mountains in the distance and knowing that we'd never left brought back the uneasiness. I just wanted the window to fog again, let me go on believing for a minute or two longer. I didn't need forever.

28.

A late-night rain had already fallen and passed, but left behind a thick fog that put all of the mountains in a cloud. Warning lights at the road's edge, put out earlier in the day to slow traffic while the state evened a deep slope in the asphalt, still flashed. Each time the yellow lights flicked, the light hung on the fog, lit the whole world yellow for as far as I could see. I parked the pickup on the backside of the shop, right next to where Daddy kept the Nova concealed beneath a gray tarp.

He had always kept somewhere around a hundred thousand dollars cash in the safe. That was how much he said it would take to start fresh should the need ever arise to run. "All the money in the world won't do you any good in the bank when the law comes.

They can freeze all of that shit," Daddy'd said. "Cash, Jacob, it's got to be cash if you're going to run." When I was a kid, he'd had to explain it to me for when the time came. Never knowing when that day might come, he kept one safe at the shop and a second at the house, both of them holding similar stacks of rubber-banded bills. He'd had to reinforce the floor at the house with six-by-six joists to support the weight of the safe, but the shop was built on a slab, the whole building floored with concrete.

I still didn't know where I was headed, but I was leaning toward following Maggie. The money in the safe was enough to give her what she'd need for those first few years of college, and still get me the fuck out of town. The idea of heading east with her to some sunny place like Wilmington sounded more and more like the best option I had. Maybe when the money ran low I might even do what she said and get a job working in a shop. But staying, staying was just a slow suicide, and if I were going to kill myself, I'd have done it quick and painless like Mama. One shot. Brains blown up the wall.

Inside I hit the switch and the tube lights above flickered and buzzed till they glowed bright white. Two of the bays were empty, but on the far lift a long, low Cadillac floated in the air with tires drooping beneath uncompressed springs. I don't remember ever being in there when it was so quiet before. Everything I did seemed to echo: my footsteps, boot soles scratching against scattered Oil-Dri, blue jeans brushing together, my breathing, my heartbeat. All of those sounds seemed loud, and I was spooked.

Sweat beaded as fast as I could wipe it away, especially on my palms. I'd found a tube of Super Glue in my truck, unwrapped the shoddy bandage from my injured hand that Daddy put through the glass, and used the glue to seal my skin together. But if my hands kept sweating, there was no telling how long those hillbilly stitches would hold. I kept wiping my palms down my pants to try and keep them dry but it didn't help. My eyes were wide and itchy, and I looked my hands over, not so much trembling, but certainly not still. If he caught me, he'd kill me. Whether it was in the act or whether I was headed for the county line, if he caught me, I was dead. I knew that more than I knew anything else in my life. So I moved quickly.

The door to the office was paper thin, one of those cheap doors like might've been used to close off a closet or washroom. Only a turn lock on the doorknob kept the door sealed. I pulled the old Case Stockman I'd carried since I was a kid from my pocket and opened the blued clip blade, carbon steel stained into a dark patina. The door was loose, and the thin blade slid into the crack and popped the latch without a hitch.

The lights were off in the office, and a bright orange glowed from the on-switch of the coffeemaker. The acrid smell of burnt coffee mixed with settled cigarette smoke. I flipped the lights. Daddy's leather desk chair rested in the middle of the room. Stacks of paperwork had been shuffled square and set just so on the desk. The safe stood in the far corner, a shiny green finish scrolled with gold leaf and lettering.

I remembered the day the deliverymen had wheeled that safe off the truck and into Daddy's office. He hadn't had a legitimate business for long at that point, and back then he did most of the work himself. It was the summer after Papaw died, and I was still too young to stay at the house by myself. With school out for the summer, I spent most days playing around the shop and watching my father cuss like mad when something didn't go just right. Daddy'd called me into the office that afternoon when the safe was brought in. He'd shown me the velvet-lined interior, the heavy steel bars, and the large chrome dial. "Going to use the day your Papaw died for the combination," he'd said. "That way it'll be something I won't forget."

Almost ten years since, I still remembered that cold day when Papaw choked on his blood just two weeks before Christmas, December eleventh, 19 and 99. Those first two numbers being so close made spinning the dial just right about as simple as taking apart a master cylinder. 12, 11, 19, 99. Repeat. 12, 11, 19, 99. Repeat. Every time I finished and cranked on the five-spoke handle, there wasn't a bit of give. Left four times, right three times, left two times, right one. Repeat. 12, 11, 19, 99. Repeat.

I was getting agitated. My hands sweated and that dial became more and more slippery each time I turned. I took a break from the safe, plopped down in that big rolling chair of Daddy's, and tried to calm my nerves. A thin metal ashtray on the desk was piled with mashed-out cigarette butts, but in one of the divots along the rim rested a smoke that hadn't been more than lit before it was placed there and burnt out. The Bugler was in the truck, but I wanted a real cigarette. I hadn't had one in days. I picked that cigarette up, put it to my lips, tore a match from a pack that lay by the ashtray, and struck it aflame. I puffed on the Winston to settle my nerves, and when my hands quit shaking, I focused back into the dial.

Left four times, right three times, left two times, right one. 12, 11, 19, 99. Repeat. It took two goes that second time around, but the wheel pack lined up and when I turned the five-spoke handle, the four lock bars rolled back loudly, and the heavy door eased open. I expected to see the long guns, maybe a pistol or two on the top shelf, and those stacks of banded bills layered like bricks on the second shelf. What I saw, though, was the sheen of black velvet, not a single thing inside except a yellow sheet of paper in the bottom.

I knelt on the floor and grabbed the slip of paper from the bottom of the safe. It was an invoice printed on stationery from the Law Offices of Irving L. Queen III. My eyes ran down the list of fees: legal counsel, a payment to the crematorium, $52.34 to In Bloom Flower Shop, $300 to Hamburg Baptist Church. The bill totaled $2,064.72, with the largest chunk going to counsel. In the center of the page, a big red block with ink barely holding in the bottom right corner stamped PAID on the invoice. My hand shook and that thin carbon paper rattled like a dried leaf.

With the paper quivering in my hand, I stood up from the floor, and just as my legs straightened, I felt a stiff forearm hook deep under my throat, the other arm forcing my head down from behind. Trying to breathe proved worthless. There was absolutely nothing there. No air. No breath. I tried to turn my head, twist my body to see who held me, but whoever had me was strong, much stronger than me, and all of that spinning and fighting got me nowhere. Whoever had me cinched my body up onto my tiptoes, just the tips of my boots still making contact with the floor. Even in a moment when time passed slowest, it didn't take long. The curtains went down on my eyes, fell and fell till there was only a sliver left of the floor, then surrender.

DUCT TAPE WRAPPED my wrists and elbows to the arms of Daddy's tall leather desk chair. I couldn't see how my legs were attached, but they were tucked back under the seat of the chair so that I leaned forward, and they were bound tightly. A cigarette dangled from my mouth and had been hanging long enough to have dried to my lips. As I tried to open my mouth, the skin held on the butt of the cigarette and I had to lick at that dry stub to get it to fall free.

I was facing the desk and that yellow invoice from Queen lay on the top of a tall stack of papers, the invoice squared off and even with the rest of the pile. I turned to the corner where the safe stood open. I turned the other direction to where shelves held the black-and-yellow cases of DeWalt tools. My neck couldn't wrench far enough to see the door. Yanking and hopping, I was able to spin the chair an inch at a time, the wheels of the chair smacking the laminate each time I jerked. When I got turned enough to see, the door into the garage was open. There was no one in the room with me.

I screamed wildly and shook in the chair, and as the first scream faded I heard metal clanking against the concrete slab in the garage. I knew the sounds of that place well, and it sounded like a wrench falling onto the floor. Next came the footsteps tromping toward me. Then he appeared in the doorway.

"You truly are your mama's bitch, aren't you? Couldn't raise the pussy out of you." Daddy stood there and wiped grease from his hands onto a ratty red rag. The white T-shirt he wore was smudged with grease stains, those black marks extending past his shirt and onto his jeans. He scrubbed at his forearms with that rag and itched hard at a place where it was hard to say whether oil or ink tattooed his skin. A day unshaved left stubble sprigging from those aged acne scars. A crescent of hair had fallen from his part and cut a sickle across his forehead. He walked over to the radio and turned on the tunes so he could talk.

"What do you want?"

"What do I want?" Daddy smiled and laughed a little under his breath. "You come in to *my* shop, break in to *my* safe to steal *my* fucking money, and have the gall to ask what *I* want?"

"If you're going to kill me, then kill me! But don't waste the time I've got talking a bunch of bullshit!"

"Bullshit?"

"Yeah, bullshit. You know goddamn well you owe me. You know goddamn well the work I've done!"

Daddy looked at me for a while like he knew I was right, but he didn't say it. He didn't say a word.

"How'd you know I'd be here?"

"There're people watching this place all the time, Jacob."

"Well, go ahead and kill me, goddamn it! Quit wasting your fucking time!"

Daddy walked over and picked up the cigarette from where it had fallen into my lap. He held it to his lips and struck a lighter from his pocket, took a few quick drags, and pushed it into my mouth. Smoke rose from the cigarette and wafted into my eyes. He pulled a soft pack of Winstons from the pocket of his jeans and flicked one up into his mouth. He lit it and walked behind me, spun me around in the chair so that I was facing him as he leaned against the desk.

"I'm going to talk now, and you're going to listen." There wasn't a bit of hostility in his voice and hadn't been since he walked into the room. "I'm tired, Jacob. You understand me? I'm goddamn tired." Daddy angled back and blew a long, narrow cloud of smoke over my head. He resituated himself on the desk and glared into me with narrowed eyes. "When you do the type of shit that I've done, you get to worrying that one of these days someone out of your past is going to show up to put a fucking bullet in your skull.

You understand? I'm tired of having to look over my shoulder. I'm tired of not knowing who might be watching. I'm just goddamned tired, Jacob."

Daddy took one last drag from his cigarette and snubbed it out into the ashtray. He took the cigarette from my mouth too, a long, curved piece of ash breaking loose and crumbling on my lap. He stood from the desk and walked over to the safe, shut the door, turned the handle, and the bolts sounded loudly. He spun the dial and looked at me. "Now, I understood a long time ago that you weren't cut out for this shit. It just ain't in you. You're weak, Jacob. As much as it kills me to say it, you're weak." Daddy walked to the desk and shifted the stacks of already evened paper till he'd re-set them all exactly equidistant from one another. He slouched against the desk again and looked me square.

"I'm out of here come winter, Jacob. I'm going to finish fixing up that old Nova out back and drive till I find a place that suits me. That's the plan. But there's something that I need done in order for that to happen. And there's something that you want."

"What is it you think I want?"

"It's not really a question of whether or not you want it. The money, Jacob. That's why you're here, ain't it? So you do this for me, and I'll give it to you." Daddy looked up at the ceiling. "Every last dime you ever earned, and that's my goddamn word. That's all a man has is his word. I'm not a man of much, but I'm a man of my word."

My arms chafed under the duct tape. Sweat beaded on my brow and rolled down my forehead. Though I hated to ask, there was only one way out. "What is it you want?"

"Robbie Douglas." Daddy slapped his hand down on the desk, that loud slap echoing from that room to the far end of the garage and back. He slid the soft pack of Winstons out of his jeans, fired up another cigarette, and offered them to me. "Robbie Douglas is the only fucking thing left alive that could ruin me."

"And how exactly do you expect me to do it? Ain't like I can just waltz into that hospital and put a bullet in him. Folks say the goddamn law's been standing outside his door since he went in there just waiting on him to wake up so he can say who did it."

"That ain't my problem, Jacob." Daddy stood from the desk, the cigarette hanging and smoking from his lips, and peered into me. He pulled a folding knife from his pocket and flipped it open with his thumb, that old sodbuster blade shining under fluorescents. Daddy knelt and swiped the duct tape loose from my feet with the blade, ran the knife clean through the tape on one arm then the other. The thick rolled tape popped when the blade slid through and I was loose, but I didn't move. Daddy walked past me, his footsteps sounding toward the door, and left me in that chair staring at the stack of papers on his desk, Queen's invoice on top of the pile. I listened to him stomp through the garage. The door hinge creaked open then slammed, the latch clicking as it shut. I was left in the room alone now. The only sound came from the radio. But there were no longer words to hide.

29.

A povidone-iodine yellow glow came through closed curtains as I stared from the parking lot at windows lighting checkered patterns along all four stories. The old hospital had been built to last with bricks that still held red even decades after the mortar dried. Lighter sand-colored bricks cut pin stripes on the building where floors divided, and outlined the windows to add a touch of style. But despite the attempt to liven the place up, there was no hiding it. This is where people came to die.

Electric doors slid back and a woof of air from heavy fans overhead blew against my hair when I entered. Doctors and nurses wearing scrubs with silly patterns like wrapping-paper designs walked in and out of hallways carrying notepads and stethoscopes, one younger nurse bearing a drip bag as she hopped onto the elevator and waited for the door to ding. Check-in was to the right at a long countertop where three women all wearing reading glasses and sour faces squinted at computer screens. When someone would approach them at the counter, they'd hand them a notepad and pen or answer a question without ever looking up from the monitors.

A large, brightly lit aquarium with colorful fish and plants that seemed to pulse and breathe separated the room from where doctors hurried and families waited. The left side of the room was lined in chairs, some of them filled with folks holding sleepless, zombie-type expressions with mouths gaped at a television in the corner spreading the drone of nightly news.

Standing there, I caught on very quickly how the place worked. Folks who stood around with confused looks or walked aimlessly rubbernecking around corners and into rooms were asked what they needed, who they were looking for, or how they could be helped. The people who rushed about frantically and never let their eyes fix onto one thing for too long were allowed free range without a question asked. There were black signs with white type over most of the doorways and similar signs with arrows pointing down halls, up staircases, and into elevators. Following those signs, a man could navigate that place pretty easily without having to speak to anyone. I headed past the aquarium and toward the hallway like I owned the place, and out of the corner of my eye, I saw one of the women behind the counter look my way, but my stride never broke and my focus never altered. Intensive Care pointed into the elevator. Intensive Care pointed up the stairs. I took the stairs.

The dimly lit stairwell smelled of chlorine and the concrete floor felt tacky. My boot soles peeled from the stairs like I walked on transparent tape. There was no one else in the stairwell from what I could hear, but outside elevators dinged, phones rang, and fast-paced footsteps drummed through the halls. Up six flights, a sign over the doorway split the fourth floor between the Post-Operative Surgical Unit and Intensive Care. Robbie was in the latter.

I opened the door into an empty hall. The wall in front of me held framed paintings of boldly colored shapes that never seemed to make much of a picture no matter how hard I looked. The narrow hallway opened up at both ends into brighter rooms, well-lit rooms that beamed a sanitized sort of white light. Large black signs hung from the ceiling by chains at the entrance of each: to the left Post-Op, to the right ICU.

Ambling down that empty hall, it was harder to play it off like I was meant to be there, my boots clomping the stillness and silence that seemed to belong in that place. One nurse perched behind a desk where the room opened up. She was a young Cherokee-looking girl with dark skin, black hair pulled into a bun, and plump lips that she pursed and pursed while she read through the latest Hollywood gossip in one of those tabloids found at grocery store checkouts. She marked her spot in the magazine and placed it down on the counter as I walked by.

"Can I help you, sir?"

I turned and met her eyes. Her stare was wide and her eyebrows angled up and that facial expression told me awfully fast that she wasn't into being cutesy. "Came to see my grandma," I said.

She squinted a bit like she was trying to see through a lie. "Visiting hours were from three to six."

"I know, ma'am." I walked closer to the desk and tried my damnedest to look vulnerable. "Thing is I don't get off work till five and it's a haul up the mountain to get here." I braced my elbows on the top of the counter and looked down at her, tried to get a read on whether or not she was buying. "I just wanted to look in on her for a minute. I won't be long, I promise."

"Like I said, visiting hours were from three to six."

I buried my head in my hands like the disappointment just might kill me. "Please, ma'am. I promise I won't be long." When I pulled my head up out of my hands I could see that I had struck something in her. Her eyes had drawn back into some softer place where things like protocol didn't seem to matter so much.

"Just for a minute or two," she said. "But don't make me have to run you off. I need this job, okay?"

"I promise."

The young nurse nodded, and I strolled around the corner to where a long hallway was lined on both sides with doors. There wasn't a deputy anywhere in sight, but the hall continued around the corner, so I kept walking. Some of the machines in the rooms beeped every second or two, but some let out a raspy-sounding breath when plungers pushed down and gave air. An old man in the room on the left was having a horrible time, and he was groaning as loudly as he could, too weak to yell. A doctor in teal-colored scrubs and one of those paper-type hats they wear jogged from around the corner and disappeared into the room where the man lay. I kept walking till I got to the edge of the wall and peeked around the corner.

A young, strong-looking bull sat on a metal folding chair outside of a room three doors down, the last room on the wall before the hallway turned up the other side. He didn't see me right then, but I didn't want him to catch sight of me sneaking around, so I kept ahead and stood at an open doorway that looked in on some old woman. The woman lay there with tubes running every which way. She was pasty-looking and a line of drool ran from the corner of her open mouth. That old woman had her eyes on me, and I would've sworn her dead if it wasn't for the blinks that came every so often. I turned down the hall to where the bull sat, and he was watching me while he moved a plug of tobacco along his gums with his tongue. His arms rested on his knees. I flicked my eyes back to that old woman, but soon as I did I heard that bull's shoes clapping across the terrazzo floor.

When his footsteps stopped, I could feel him next to me, and I tried to stay calm. That old woman still stared at me with her mouth slouched open, and I smiled at her. "They don't think she's got too much longer," I said.

The bull put his hand on the doorframe and leaned real close to me to peer inside of the room. "That your grandma?" His head right beside my shoulder, he twisted up toward me.

"Yeah. They don't think it'll be more than a week or two." I turned and looked at him, took a deep swallow. "I just wish she could've died at home, passed away in her sleep or something, you know?"

"I know what you mean. Lost mine a couple months back. Same type of thing." The deputy patted me on the shoulder hard and looked at me with dark brown eyes. "It's tough."

I stared at the old woman, who still hadn't took her eyes away from me. I was sure she was somebody's grandma, and I was sure they wished all of those things I'd just said. She just wasn't mine.

The deputy patted me on the shoulder again. "Hang in there, man. It'll be all right." He smiled with a black wad of tobacco poking from his gums. "I'm going to go see if I can't talk that nurse up front into letting me take her out sometime."

I grinned at him and nodded, and that deputy strutted down the hallway, slicking his hair down with his hand. I watched him move up to the counter and rest his elbows across the top. He worked his feet back far behind him so his body slanted at an angle toward the counter, and he rested his head where his forearms crossed, cocked his head to the side to flirt with the Cherokee girl. I had a minute or two to do what needed done, and I didn't waste a second. I walked fast in long strides and tried to keep my feet from making any noise against the floor. Noise echoed in those halls and I didn't need that bull coming back.

The last door before the hallway turned up the other side was where Robbie lay. I would have never recognized him if I hadn't been there to witness what Jeremy Cabe had done. His face was healed past the tissuey white burns I'd seen when the acid splashed and lit him afire, but what healed was a warped smooth skin that bent and curved the way oil does on top of water. Only a portion of his face along his left eye and cheek still looked like him. The rest was darker and looked like a mound of pink clay that children had smudged into a face.

A feeding tube jutted out of his throat. Lines with all different-colored fluids running through them wrapped around his arms and chest and slipped under the sheets to someplace I couldn't see. He was hooked to one of those raspy breathing machines, the expandable plunger rising and spreading like an accordion before it pressed down and huffed. There wasn't a lick of movement about him. His chest never rose when the machine filled him with another breath.

"Who are you?" a tired-sounding voice asked from a darkened

corner at my side. I hadn't seen her there until she spoke. "Who are you, boy?" She stood up from a maroon upholstered chair and walked over to me. She couldn't have been all that much older than Mama, but you'd have never known. The way she wore her hair and the way she dressed made her look a good ten years older than she was. Her dark hair was short and permed into curls that had been mashed flat on one side where she'd pressed her head against something for rest. She dressed like a schoolteacher, with pastel-colored slacks ironed into a crease and a loose-fitting cotton shirt that held like a T-shirt but fancier. "Are you a friend of Robbie's?"

"Yeah, I guess you could say that." I looked at her for a second but turned away fast enough that she couldn't quite get a good look at me. "I mean, I've known him a long time."

"When he was a little boy, why, he was the wildest thing anyone had ever seen." She came close and stood by my side, then turned and stared at her son on the gurney. "He was wide open from the moment the doctor laid him in my arms, I tell you. Ain't ever seen the likes of something so wild." Robbie's mother walked over to the bedside and picked up his hand. For a split second I thought of that folded photograph I'd found in his trailer that bookmarked a place in his Bible, a place in his life when his parents stood proudly beside him. His mother did not seem proud anymore, but she would not leave his side. She held his hand gently and stroked back and forth, right beside where an IV line ran into him. She placed his hand back on the white sheets, turned her head and looked at his face. "Now, I knew he was into some trouble. Me and his daddy had known that for a long while, I guess. But this? No, I don't think either of us could have figured it would come to something like this."

I watched her as she leaned over him and brushed his hair with her fingers so that it lay in a part across his head. I couldn't say a word. Seeing her there and knowing what had been done to her son made me feel sick inside. Daddy had thought that type of shit would harden a man, but all it had done to me was poke at all those places where I'd always been soft.

She ran her hand across his face where all of that skin stretched and curled. Then she pulled the sheet up around him and folded it back just a touch like she was tucking in a child. "It'd take an awfully bad man to do this to one of God's children. An awfully bad man." She turned back to me and scowled. "I just hope they're ready for what they've got coming. Whether it's in a courtroom or at the right hand of God, they'll have to answer for what they've done."

I'd stayed calm the entire time I worked my way through that hospital. I'd played everything perfect to get into that room. But looking at him lying there and listening to her talk about her son, I was absolutely terrified. She didn't know it, but I was already answering for what I'd done. I was answering every day of my life, every minute I slept. The things I had seen could not be unseen. The things I saw haunted me.

"I know you, boy." Robbie's mother walked up and stood directly in front of me. She tilted her head and looked up so as to get the best look her old eyes could piece together.

"No, ma'am. I don't think we know each other."

"Yeah." She drug out that word like the last note of a song. "You're Charlie McNeely's boy, ain't you?"

"No, ma'am."

"There's no hiding who you belong to. You're the spitting image of him."

I could hear the bull's footsteps clapping their way back down the hall, and it wouldn't be long before that line of questioning came from both sides, and I didn't have an answer for any of it. I backpedaled away from her and through the doorway, out into the hall where all of those white lights shined so bright.

"Where are you going, boy?" Robbie's mother walked toward the door. "Ain't you going to at least tell me your name?"

The footsteps were getting close to turning the corner, and Robbie's mother wasn't but a step away from coming into the hall. I was tingling all over, and my hands were sweating something horrible. I was feeling like a rabbit again, a rabbit that had done let them get too close and had to run, so I did. "The man who looks back gets caught," Daddy'd said, so I didn't look back. I didn't look back as I tore down that hallway, ran past that counter and that pretty little Cherokee girl, and into that dim hallway where the stairwell came up on the left. I didn't look back when I jumped those first two flights of steps one right after the other, my knees damn near exploding like Black Cat firecrackers when I smacked down out of the air. I didn't look back when I made it into that lobby and ran through all of those doctors and nurses in funny-patterned scrubs and past that aquarium with all of those colorful fish and through that heavy fan and those electric sliding glass doors. Even when the truck was running, and I was mashing the gas and reaching for the headlights, I didn't look back, not for one fucking second. No, I didn't look back in that rearview until I'd crossed into Jackson County, and even then it was hard, expecting sure as shit those blue lights would flash and there I'd be. But they didn't come for me that night. I didn't look back, and I didn't get caught. Daddy'd been right about that.

30.

No one had been hired to clean the blood from the walls after the coroner loaded up Mama and took her off for burning. All of that mess was still just as thick as it had been the day I saw it, and I kept my eyes closed when I pulled the door shut to seal the room off. There was nothing nice about staying there, but it beat sweaty sleep in the cab of my pickup so I'd slept there every night since her funeral. The storm front that blew into the mountains four nights back made it impossible to sleep in the bed of my truck, so I slept in Mama's house on the ratty couch by the front door.

Inside the house smelled of mildew, the smell strengthening with the doors shut. Mold fuzzed from the cracks between pine planks along the walls, and that smell had eaten at my nose each

night. Straight-line winds sent the jack pines in the yard to flapping, and those thin trees cast shadows that moved like fingers
through the house. The walls tended to move with those shadows,
swaying and teetering and the crossbeams creaking loudly like I
was living out my days on some rickety ship. To watch it gave me
motion sickness, so I closed my eyes and listened to heavy rain
pelt the tin roof, the sound of torn plastic ripping a bit further
from the windows each time the wind howled.

I hadn't seen Maggie since the night we fogged the windows of
my pickup, but we talked for at least an hour every night, texted
each other till the tips of our fingers callused. She'd send me pictures of her, dozens and dozens of pictures, and there was never a
moment when I tired from opening the next. She was the one bit
of light I had, and though the light had always been something I
refused to notice, Maggie was slowly becoming the one thing that
kept me moving forward. We were both busy, but both moving
forward. I was trying to take care of my end of the promise, and
she spent most nights filling boxes with things she wanted to take
with her, throwing out the things she didn't. Move-in day was a
month and a half away, and she'd leave this mountain for good.

I'd yet to tell her I planned to go with her, but my mind was
made up. Maggie was the sole reason I'd go through with what
Daddy asked. When he paid me off for doing it, I'd take that cash
and foot the bill for Maggie's first semester, head east with her,
and start building a life together if she'd let me. It'd make it easier
on Robbie's mama too. Maybe she'd be able to sleep when it was
all said and done. At least that's what I told myself.

I'd already talked to Maggie once that night while I ate room-
temperature beans and franks for supper from a dented can I'd
found in Mama's cabinets. Everything was set from Maggie's end.

She'd faxed over the paperwork, committed to Wilmington, registered for classes, and was waiting on her room assignment. Now
the only thing left was to cut a check, and that rested on me. The
check had to clear by July 15 to make sure her schedule held.
When the job was done, I'd give her the cash and have her get a
cashier's check from the bank. If her parents questioned where
the money came from, then fuck them. So far she hadn't mentioned them asking. Either way, it was their fault she didn't have
the money. It was their fault their daughter's future rested in my
hands.

I called her again hoping I might catch her just before she fell
asleep. As the phone rang, I told myself that I'd tell her this time
around. I'd tell her exactly how I felt about her and tell her I'd
follow her east to give us a good go at sticking together and tell
her all of those things that I hoped she wanted to hear, but the
phone rang and rang and she never answered. I texted, "I love
you," but she'd already fallen into dreams.

THE THIN WINDOWPANE rattled against the aluminum frame,
a loud banging outside that woke me out of a nightmare I was
having about being interrogated for the murder of Robbie Douglas. The dream made little sense. I was tied to a chair in the center of a dark room, only a single lit bulb hanging from the ceiling
above me, and a detective, one of those suit-wearing bulls with a
tanned leather shoulder holster and a tie tacked to a dress shirt,
circled me. He yelled out questions, his spit speckling my face,
and just when an answer came to me, just when I found a lie that
might get me off, he'd rack me in the top of the head with a
Maglite. *Bang, bang, bang!* He kept circling and screaming those

questions, and just as the words came to my mouth—*bang, bang, bang!* I was still trying my damnedest to speak when the banging woke me and my eyes began to settle to daylight.

The rain and wind had finally stopped and pale yellow sunlight shone through what foggy mildewed plastic still held to the window. A dark shadow moved on the porch, but it took my eyes a while to adjust and see who stood there. I scrubbed the crusts from the corners of my eyes and sat up on the couch. Lieutenant Rogers leaned over a bit to peek through a section of glass where the plastic had torn away.

"You alive in there?"

I walked to the front door, undid the dead bolt, and swung that rotted table of wood agape on creaky hinges. Rogers opened the screen door, came inside, and let the screen smack closed behind him. I was still in my boxers, but Rogers was dressed for a day in the office. He wore a khaki-colored polo shirt and a loose-fitting pair of dark green cargo pants. His gun was holstered and at his side.

"You must've been sleeping sound in here, son. I've been banging on that window for ten minutes. I'd just about decided to head down the mountain."

I peered outside to where Rogers's Expedition was parked right up to the back bumper of my pickup. The fog left behind by days of rain had yet to burn off. "What time is it?"

"A little late for some, a little early for others," Rogers said as he walked past me and plopped down on the sofa where I'd slept. He glanced up at me, and I leaned back and stretched, yawned till my lungs couldn't hold any more air. "Judging by the way you're looking, I'd say you fall into the latter."

"That still doesn't answer what time it is." I walked toward the kitchen and he answered just before I crossed through the doorway.

"Half past seven."

Mama had little in the refrigerator or cupboard, but she kept two big red cans of coffee, and I'd been drinking it like water. I turned the sink on and waited for the air to push through the lines and clear water to run, held a steel kettle beneath the faucet and filled it to the brim. "Going to make some coffee if you want a cup."

"I'll take it black," Rogers hollered from the living room.

I put the kettle on the stove, turned the knob so the eye burned red, and headed back to the couch where Rogers sat. The bag of Bugler rested against a tarnished brass lamp on the table by the couch. I shook a tangled mess of tobacco from the pouch into a creased 1.5 and twisted up my morning smoke.

"Rolling your own, huh?"

"Ain't got money to buy a pack."

"Here." Rogers reached into the side pocket of his cargo pants and tossed an unopened pack of Lucky Strikes down the couch. "Have those." He pulled a cigarette from an open pack and put it between his teeth.

We smoked those first cigarettes together while the sun rose behind trees and burned the fog from the ground. Rogers hadn't said why he was there, but I imagined he'd seen my truck in the drive and wanted to check on me. He was loyal to my father, but he didn't seem to hold that same meanness in his heart. That blend of toughness and compassion was what I admired. I liked to think of myself in the same way, that my softness wasn't really softness but rather some sort of innate compassion, the type of humanity that Daddy never had. There was a lot more to admire about a man who could handle whatever the world threw with-out flinching and still be standing there to help someone else. In a lot of ways, he felt more like a father than Daddy ever did. Neither of us spoke. We just sat there and watched that morning sun come up.

The kettle whistled from the stovetop, and I went into the kit-chen to finish the coffee. Mama hadn't kept a real coffeemaker, so I just poured the boiling water into a tall mason jar and scooped in a few spoonsful of grounds. I'd done my best to swirl those grounds down into the water with a long wooden spoon, but the cups I carried back still had grains swirling on top of the coffee like fine bits of pepper. Some of the grounds washed up and stuck on the rim where the coffee swashed, but most of it came together in islands that rocked back and forth when I set the cups down on the table.

"Thank you, Jacob." Rogers lifted his cup and blew steam from the surface. It was still piping hot when he held it to his mouth, took a sip, and let out a long sigh.

I smacked the Lucky Strikes against my palm to pack the tobacco down, tore off the cellophane, and lit my second smoke of the day. The coffee was strong and bitter and tasted old, no telling how long it had grown stale in the cupboard.

"Guess you're probably wondering why I stopped by, Jacob."

"A little, I guess."

"Thing is you said something the other night that's been eating at me ever since." Rogers situated himself on the couch so that his body faced me and he could look me square. "You said something about a Bible that I haven't been able to get out of my mind."

"I was just hot-headed." I ashed the cigarette into an empty glass. "Ain't like me to talk."

"No, no, I think you're misunderstanding me. I didn't come here to growl about what you said. I came here to get you to clarify."

"I'm not sure I know what you mean?"

"I mean, I want you to tell me about that Bible you were so fixed on back yonder." Rogers turned and nodded back down the hall toward Mama's bedroom.

"I just said there was one of those Bibles in there, one of those little pocket Bibles that Daddy's known to leave, and that was one of the ways I knew he had something to do with it."

"Yeah, that's what I wanted you to tell me about." Rogers lit another cigarette just as I mashed mine out. "I found that Bible back there just like you said I would, but what exactly did you mean when you said he was known to leave them?" He talked with the cigarette jumping around in his mouth while he rummaged through his pockets for his Zippo.

"Come on now. You've known my father for as far back as I can remember. You mean to tell me you ain't ever heard that?"

"Heard what?"

"You've got to be full of shit, Rogers. There's no fucking way you've never heard those stories."

"Now, I want you to think about something, Jacob. What is it your daddy pays me to do?"

"Keep an eye out, I guess."

"Exactly. We ain't friends, and never have been. I don't know anything more than what he's told me. I keep an ear out for anything in the office, let him know of any type of federal shit that might be coming down the pipe, and try my damnedest to keep eyes off of him. That's it. That's all I do for him. So what about those Bibles?"

"I'd always heard he left them on the bodies."

"No, I hadn't ever heard that, but I don't see why that surprises you. I mean, think about it. How often does your daddy get his hands dirty anymore?"

"Seldom."

"And how often do bodies show up around here?"

"Not often."

"Exactly. Now, I've heard stories about the type of shit he was known to do back in his day, but I ain't ever heard a thing about Bibles. No, I never heard anything like that." Rogers rolled up from the couch and rested his arms over his legs. He smoked on that Lucky Strike and stared to someplace out in the yard like he was really trying to get a good look. He didn't say anything else.

Before Robbie Douglas, there hadn't been anything close to a body being found in a long time. If something did need done, Daddy had folks to do it. Besides that, the stories of what he was capable of kept most people in line. I finished my cup of coffee and took the mug back into the kitchen for a refill. The mason jar still held a cup or two, the dark liquid just warm now, with steam beading back into water on the sides of the glass. "Want another cup?"

"I think I'm good."

When I walked back into the living room, Rogers stood in the open doorway and stared through the screen door out into the crowded lot of jack pines. I seemed to startle him when I came back into the room, and he turned. He looked me up and down like he didn't expect me to be there, like I was a spook or something, and waited for me to sit back on the couch before closing the main door and joining me there.

"You ever know that I had a brother, Jacob?"

"No, I don't reckon I ever knew that about you."

"Well, I did. Had a little brother named Joe, and he was a mean little shit." Rogers blew a short laugh from his nose and squinted his eyes while he remembered. "Even when we were little, he had this air about him like he knew he was tougher than I'd ever thought about being. I was always a good bit bigger than him but that never seemed to matter. He just had that fight in him, you know?"

I nodded and took a long swallow of warm coffee, lit another cigarette, and listened to Rogers tell his story.

"Well, when we got older he got into some pretty rough shit and wasn't a one of us could tell him nothing. Mama'd get a call that he was in jail, I'd go get him out, and we'd settle him down for a week or so, give him a place to stay. I was working at the concrete plant back then and didn't have much time to keep an eye on him. Then one morning we'd wake up and he'd be gone. Never so much as good-bye." Rogers scrunched his eyes until they were almost closed, but what little bit of white showed glassy as quartz. "One morning we got a call that they'd found him outside of Burrell's, that little old honky-tonk that used to sit across the state line, and he'd been stabbed to death. There were cuts all over his hands where he'd fought, but most of it had caught him where it mattered. The law down there never found who did it. It never even seemed like they looked."

Rogers stopped his story there and smoked on the cigarette until there was nothing left but filter. Even then he stared out of the window and said nothing. His body was stiffening, though, and there seemed to be this anger that built up in him, an anger that didn't need any words to say it was there. Then he turned and looked way back into me.

"Not knowing who did that to my brother was something that ate at me for years. It was why I picked up this gun and badge, Jacob. I thought I was going to make shit right. Then one day it all just kind of settled, and I was all right with it. In a lot of ways I guess I came to terms with what'd happened, you know? Hell, it's going on twenty-five years now. I ain't young anymore. Eventually all of that pain and anger just sort of fades away, and all we're left with is growing old and forgetting." Rogers was still looking in my direction, but his eyes weren't set on me. He looked on to someplace else, someplace beyond, and a few silent moments passed before he spoke. "I hadn't really thought about it in a long time till you said that the other night. I hadn't thought about it in years till I walked into that bedroom back there and seen that Bible lying on the table."

"What are you talking about?"

"I'm talking about that goddamn Bible! I'm talking about the fact that the same kind of Bible, same black Bible, same size, same gold on the edges, same everything that was back there in your mama's room, there was one shoved down in the pocket of my brother's britches just like it. That's what I'm talking about, Jacob. That's what the fuck I'm talking about."

The intensity that lit him afire frightened the hell out of me, and I was certain that any minute he was going to take out all of that rage on the closest thing to him. But he didn't.

"So, what does it mean?"

"What it means is that I'm finally going to have my time. I'm finally going to have my chance to get even with the son of a bitch that did that to my brother. That's what it means, Jacob." Rogers seemed to calm down with that thought and his eyes pulled back out of that far-off place and settled onto the pack of Lucky Strikes he'd given me.

I shook two cigarettes from the pack and held one out to him. He took it and when I had mine lit I offered the fire to his. "Why are you telling me?"

"I'm telling you because I know how that shit would eat at you. You might not think it would, but I know different." Rogers looked up toward the ceiling and blew a long line of smoke that hit the wood and spread like milk. "Whether you love your daddy or not, if somebody was to kill him and you never did know who, that shit would eat at you. That shit would eat you up like worms until there wasn't nothing left of you that you ever knew. It would eat you till you couldn't even recognize yourself in the mirror. It ain't the knowing that does that to a man, Jacob. It's the not knowing."

Rogers and I sat there until every bit of misty morning haze had risen into the blue and left behind nothing but an early July heat wave. Though there was a darkness he carried with him just like every man I'd ever known, I respected him. There was kindness in him that shone past all of that hate, a place inside of him still fit for loving, and I trusted Rogers more than anyone else in my life, more than anyone else I'd ever known other than Maggie. He'd shared his darkness with me, so I shared part of mine. I didn't tell him about Robbie Douglas or the Cabe brothers, but I told him how I'd stood over Daddy that night and tried with everything I had to set the world right. I told him about the right smart amount of money Daddy owed me, and how I needed it to get away and start my own life, leave this place and this world behind. I told him where Daddy kept it.

Then Rogers talked. He told me that he was going to do it on Friday, when Daddy got deep into the bottle and that liquor turned him sideways. He told me how the law would handle it, how those bulls would turn the house upside down and seize everything as evidence, everything, including the money in Daddy's bedroom safe. Rogers told me how there wouldn't be but a small window of time where a man might get in there to take what needed taking before the bulls came. And the last thing he told me, the very last thing he said to me before he walked out of the house and left me sitting there on Mama's couch, was only a single word. That word hit me not because of what he said, but because of how he said it and because of what it guaranteed. He knew he'd never see me again, so he told me good-bye.

31.

The Indian sat tall and strong on the back of the spotted horse, a fearless kind of pride resonating from how he sat, his back arched, chest out. There wasn't a thing in the world that scared that Indian. He just sat there at the edge of the ravine and stared far off to where the sun shined brightly. There wasn't the slightest impression of uncertainty. Come hell or high water, that Indian would get to those plains.

I reckon it was the certainty and fearlessness that kept me watching him most times. I sat on the couch and gazed at the picture for hours and hours trying my damnedest to figure how he'd brave the gap. It wasn't here or there that had ever been scary. It was the middle ground, that long desolate space between, that scared the hell out of me. That type of jump from where the Indian sat took faith, and that was something I'd never had. Faith made a man vulnerable and weak. Faith led to letdown and pain and regret and all of that shit that broke a man past saving. There was safety in not believing, and I wasn't sure I was ready to give that up just yet.

Maggie was different, though. There'd always been something in her that seemed to say she and life had an understanding, some sort of deal between them that guaranteed it'd pan out. Even when we were children, back when cold mountain water froze our wobbly legs numb and our biggest worry in the world was whether or not the spring lizards would squirm through our fingers before the other had a chance to look, she'd had her eyes fixed on that far-off place. She was almost there now.

Evening brought little relief from summer heat, and I drove faster than usual to keep the wind whooshing through the cab of my pickup. I didn't tell her I was coming, but I needed to see her. Phone calls and text messages wouldn't suffice for what I had to ask. Tonight Rogers would do what needed done, and in that morning sun would come my time to jump. So I drove.

Breedlove Road cut through hillsides lined with Fraser fir that speckled yellow pasture with dark green cones. Turkeys had always loved wandering through those trees. A rafter of thirty or forty birds strutted between the rows as I passed, three or four gobblers sporting beards that drug the ground as they bobbed. The Dillards owned most of those fields, and they kept the plots trimmed neat even in summer. Last winter, money kept folks from wanting any tree over eight foot, so the Dillards had to cut the older trees short, burned those stumps in a pile as big around as a small house. The dark scar left behind still held in the field by the road, just a big black circle where nothing new had grown.

Pavement dropped into gravel just before a sharp switchback, and Maggie's house rested on the brim of a steep slope that cut off high to the left. I didn't really care if her parents were home, but as I pulled up her drive it was a relief to see that they weren't, an even bigger relief to see Maggie's bedroom window was lit. I sat in the truck and watched her body cut shadows against the curtains. I couldn't tell her what was about to happen. She'd never understand. No one would question why my father had been murdered, and if it all went smoothly, I'd ride out the investigation, bury his body in rocky ground, and walk away with it all. But if it turned sour, the way most things in my life had a tendency of turning, I'd tear off on the lam with the money in the safe and never look back. Either way, Maggie would determine where I wound up. Either way, I needed to know if she wanted me with her.

She answered the door in white shorts and a thin gray sweatshirt that had the neck cut wide so that it hung off of one shoulder, and though she hadn't been expecting me, my standing there on her doorstep brought a smile to her face. "Talk about catching a girl off guard. Jesus, Jacob. I look horrible."

"That's not true." There no longer seemed to be a filter to hold back things I typically wouldn't say. "You're the most beautiful thing I've ever seen."

"That's sweet, but I don't have any makeup on." She stepped across the threshold and took my hand, led me into the front room of her parents' home without questioning why I'd come.

"I didn't mean to just show up like this, but I have to ask you something."

"What is it?"

"Can we go in your room first?"

"Yeah, of course we can, but what is it, Jacob?" Maggie led me down a hallway lined with family pictures, late-evening sun through a tall bay window lighting the hallway through the open door to her mother's office. Maggie's room was the last door on the right. It was the only room in the house with the lights on, the light almost blinding in a house filled with evening shadows. There was music playing, some newfangled poppy shit that passes for country now, some bullshit song I could never name. She turned the volume down on her stereo until it was silent, and we sat beside each other on the edge of her bed. "Tell me what's going on."

Walls that had always been covered with brightly colored posters and paintings, with pictures of family and friends with smiles stretching their faces, were almost bare now. She'd packed most everything except for her clothes, all of it sealed in boxes stacked in the corner by her window. I had to take it all in before any words came to me. That emptiness—the plain white walls, the vacant dresser top, everything—seemed to affirm this was not home anymore.

"When I took you up on the Parkway, you said something, and what you said has been bothering the hell out of me."

"What was it?"

"You said that I could go with you. You said that if I wanted to, I could follow you down to Wilmington and start a life with you, maybe be a mechanic or something."

"Yeah, I remember."

"Well, what if I wanted to do that? I mean, what if I was willing to just pack up and go? I need to know if you really meant it. I need to know if you meant what you said."

Maggie scooted closer to me until there was no space left between us. She rested her hands on top of mine and looked back deep inside of me. "I wouldn't have said it if I didn't mean it."

"Then that's what I want to do, Maggie."

"Are you sure?"

"I haven't ever been sure of anything in my life, but I'm sure of this."

"This is a big decision, Jacob. This is a really huge decision."

"I know it is, and I want to go."

Maggie's face scrunched. She looked like she might cry.

"What is it?"

She just shook her head.

"No, what is it? Do you not want me to—"

She slapped her hands against mine, stopped me mid-sentence. Maggie kept nodding her head, and a smile came across her face as tears fell from the corners of her eyes. It wasn't sadness in her anymore. Her face was flushed. She was happy.

I wrapped my arms around her and held her tightly, her head finding that safe and solid place against my chest again.

"I was scared of leaving, Jacob. I was scared of going there by myself."

"And you're not scared anymore?"

"No."

We fell back onto her bed, lay flat beside each other, and told each other, "I love you." One of my arms was folded under her head, her cheek resting against my bicep. The other arm was wrapped around her, my forearm running across her chest, my fingers tracing that soft place at the base of her neck. We fit together perfectly. Everything about it was perfect, and perfect was something that in all my life I'd never known. That feeling, that type of perfection, is what waited across the plains. Far off where the Indian stared, the sun sank down on forever. It was the promise of forever that would lead a man to jump.

32.

The Walkers snapped and snarled as I tiptoed just out of reach of their leads. Kayla, Daddy's prized bitch, was the meanest of them all and she stretched her collar till there was no more give when I approached. She'd always been staked closest to the house, and on that morning, I managed all thirty-four two-steps and fourteen ball changes without a hitch, but that cunt of a dog caught me in the chassé. She leapt and managed to get a nip at the loose part of my jeans and I stumbled back a bit, tripped over my feet, and collapsed into the dust at the bottom of the front steps. The collar yanked hard into her throat and she hacked, but never let off trying to get close. I crawled to my feet and kicked dirt in her eyes, and that mean-ass dog howled wildly. I hoped she'd starve with Daddy gone.

His jeep and the rickety Cavalier that Josephine drove were parked out front. The front door was cracked, but there was no sound inside. I opened the screen door, eased into the living room, and stopped just by the couch. Nothing stirred. The hounds bayed in the yard, but inside was silent, a deafening kind of silence about that place. In eighteen years under his roof, I'd never felt the house so still.

Nothing looked out of place. The television remote, a Merle Haggard album, and an open pack of Winstons lay on the coffee table equidistant and squared off to one another just the way Daddy left things. He'd always been methodical about having things just right. When I was stoned I used to shift it all just a tad when he wasn't looking just so I could laugh when he came back and fixed it all perfect. He never could stand to have his world even a hair off-kilter, so he kept it all under his thumb.

Dishes and glasses were stacked in one side of the sink, and the other side was filled with clouded water. The few soap bubbles that were left clung to the outer rim. A piece of cube steak rested in congealed brown gravy in the cast iron on the stove, and a pot filled with mashed potatoes that had dried yellow sat on the back burner. I opened the freezer and took a carton of Winstons from the shelf inside the door. Only two packs were gone and I took the next in line, hammered the pack against my hand, shook a smoke free, and lit my first of the morning. Those Winstons tasted a lot better than Lucky Strikes, even more so than Bugler. Winstons had always been our brand.

I was headed to my bedroom to scan it one last time and make sure I hadn't left anything behind, when I damn near tripped over her. Josephine was sprawled facedown in the hallway, a nasty gash beaten into the back of her head. Her blond hair was matted red and dried stiff where the blood had poured, the puddle still thick and wet where her face lay. Her head was cocked to the side, and if it hadn't been for all that blood, she might've been mistaken for passed out from a distance. The slice across her throat told a different tale, though. Only the places the blade had started and stopped were visible from where I stood, but it was that cut that'd finished her. One arm was tucked under her and the other stretched as far as it could reach. She was naked except for panties, a lacy lime-green stretch of fabric cutting through the crack of her ass. Her legs were turned pigeon-toed, bare feet pointed inward.

Seeing her body made me feel as if I moved inside of a dream. The whole house held that thick, fuzzy kind of illusory blur. My movements were slow and I swam in that thickness, all action molasses-like and sluggish as an ant sinking into syrup. But even in that slothful haze, I understood that this was not make-believe. It was real. She was dead. Spilt all over the floor. There was no sense wading in it. I needed to move. Never mind what was left in my room. Rogers said he'd call the bulls come noon, and I wanted to be long gone by then. Four hours was no time. The safe. The money. Daddy kept it in his room and that's where I went.

It was there in Daddy's bedroom where I saw the most grisly scene my eyes ever saw. Blood ran from ceiling to floor on all four walls. Some of the blood had settled like a fine mist breathed onto walls, but in other places it curved in long lines, ran like rivers before it dripped down and dried. There were brushstrokes. Long brushstrokes that painted thick swaths. Short ones tapering like feathers. There were handprints smeared in places like some

kindergartner had been pressing red turkeys onto paper for a
Thanksgiving arts and crafts project, only these weren't little
kids' handprints, these were grown man's handprints, Daddy's
handprints pressed there and there and there. White sheets were
stained red, but no child had been born. It was a different kind of
blood that had settled onto this place. It wasn't the blood of anything new, but the blood of something old dying. And then I saw
him. Only a part of him first. Just a foot angled out from behind
the corner of the bed. I could feel my heart pounding all through
my body and for a while I couldn't find the courage to move. The
sight of his foot held some kind of voodoo that turned me gar-
goyle. I was stone, all stone, with unblinking stone eyes.

I didn't so much walk as drag myself toward him, boots scrap-
ing against the hardwood as they slid. Only the gray sweatpants
he wore made him recognizable. He lay flat on his back, his hands
clenched into fists and resting at his sides. From his waistline up
his stomach, through his chest and into his neck were enough
stab wounds to put down a whole passel of hogs. Wide gashes
angled and gnarled every which way. Stabs thick and deep darkened almost black. Skin folded back like petals. Places left
unscathed were bright red. Dark tattoos shone through like
drawings on a wall that needed another coat or two of paint to
cover. One of the punctures had caught him right beneath the
jaw, slid down his neck till the blade caught bone. But it was his
face that turned me.

His face was smashed pulp. One eye drooped from its socket.
His mouth was torn at the corner. Bottom lip drooping like rolled
clay. My mind pieced together all of that mashed meat, and I could
see my daddy lying there, the daddy who had never been much of
a daddy at all but the only one I'd ever known. There had been

times when I was young when he was perfect, those times we spent in cold mountain streams chasing speckled trout with red wrigglers and wax worms, those times when he genuinely smiled. There'd even been a few times when I was older when there was a glimpse of humanity in him, a reason he'd paid to have the reverend pray over my mother's ashes. He was a horrible man and no one knew that more than me, but he was my father nonetheless. The way that puzzle pieced together wrung me like a dishrag, and I threw up all over his gray sweatpants. All that came was a thick yellow soup that stung the back of my throat and tasted like bile. I bent and twisted until all of that stomach acid was out of me and there was nothing left but dry heaves, huffing for breath each time my belly unclenched. I fell onto the bed and leaned over him. Tears fell onto his chest and pooled, wetted places where blood had dried in the hours since.

Rogers's words echoed. "It ain't the knowing that does that to a man, Jacob. It's the not knowing," he'd said. I couldn't fathom not knowing. I knew who did it before he'd come. I'd let it happen, and in a lot of ways, I was responsible. That shit'll eat a man too, I thought, and it gnawed into me then. It burrowed down deep and clacked its teeth against the hardest part it could find. There was no place deep enough to bury it, no place buried enough to stop that gnawing.

On the floor beside my father lay a Bible, a small pocket Bible, black leather, gold gilded along the edges of pages. The Bible sat on top of the blood, not a single drop on the cover of the book. Rogers had dropped it there afterward.

I hung down and picked the Bible up from the floor, the backside of the book sticky and wet. I fumbled through a book that had never done me much good and tried to find the words the reverend had shouted at me when I carried my mother's ashes. I knew the verse, knew it for Psalms, but it had been a long time since I'd navigated those chapters. "Thou wilt light our candle, the Lord our God will enlighten our darkness." I read it over my father's body like an incantation and waited again for God to show Himself. I read it over and over, louder and louder, until those words were bouncing all over the room, and I waited for God to show Himself. I screamed and waited, begged for Him to come down and save me, save us, but nothing came. Nothing. It was just as it had always been. Only us. There was no verse that could change that. I knelt beside my father and laid that Bible on his chest, situated it square, then brought his clenched hands to rest over that book and hold it just so.

The tears rode on waves. When I thought it settled, another wave. Choking. Gagging. There was a slow groan when I breathed, an uncontrollable groan that wheezed on every breath, and I knew then that the only way to be rid of it was to run. I stood from the bed but my body hung in the air. My knees bent and my top half drooped limp, but I knew I had to go.

The closet doors were open and the shiny green safe identical to the one at the shop stood in the back corner with its heavy door agape. Long guns were piled inside and pistols sat on the shelves, and I knew if it had been open while Daddy was alive there would have been one more body stiff on the floor. But Rogers wasn't there. Rogers had made it out.

Daddy had always kept his bills folded in stacks of a hundred, ten thousand dollars cinched tight under each band. Where there should've been twenty stacks only one remained, one lonely wad of folded bills with the stretched band holding loosely where some had been taken.

Outside the hounds raged, and I walked out of the bedroom, stepped over Josephine's body, and stumbled toward the window above the sink to look outside. At the edge of the yard a procession of patrol cars parked behind my pickup, their lights flashing madly in the early-morning glow. Rogers's Expedition headed the line and he stood by the back bumper of his rig, two bulls with long guns standing one on each side. The three faced the house, while another pair of bulls cleared my truck and rummaged through the cab. It was all a setup and I knew it then. Not only had Rogers taken what was mine, he'd placed me there with blood on my hands. Means, motive, and opportunity, I had them all. The man I respected, the man I had come to trust more than my own father, had given me his word. "That's all a man has is his word," Daddy had said. Rogers's word meant nothing.

I watched Rogers for a long time while the bulls moved around the cars. There were more of them coming up the drive now, all of them jumping out and popping their trunks for long guns. The deputies rushed about, but Rogers didn't budge. He just held there watching the house, his eyes aimed directly where I stood. I wondered if he saw me, if he could see me peering through the window at him. His face was void, just a blank emotionless gaze. He leaned to the side and pulled a pack of Lucky Strikes from the cargo pocket of his britches, lit a cigarette, and made it jump between his teeth. Arms folded, he propped against the Expedition while all of those bulls moved and readied themselves for the moment he gave word.

I'd never killed a man, but for a long time, I'd known I had it in me. If there was one thing my father had given me, it was that. Killing Rogers would make things square, and if there was no getting out, then the best I could hope for was square. Leave

this world just how Daddy fancied. I hurried into Daddy's bedroom and ran my eyes down the rows of long guns in the safe. I
chose the rifle that he would have wanted for such a task, an old
Marlin .30-30 lever-action that Papaw had given him when he was
old enough to hunt on his own. The blued receiver was pitted and
matte, just a dull and dark bluish gray swirling about the metal.
Daddy had marked every animal he ever took with the rifle along
the black walnut stock. Almost all of the wood was marked with
X's and slashes and refinished over so the stain dried dark in the
grooves he'd cut. I held the rifle pointed toward the ceiling and
racked the lever until brass disappeared into the chamber. I took
one last look at Daddy there on the floor with the Bible cradled
under his fists, grabbed the stack of bills from the safe, and left
him there. I had one last chance to honor my word. One last
chance to make him proud.

I stepped over Josephine in the hallway and hurried into my
bedroom. The sheets on the bed were just how I'd left them,
pulled and mangled from the mattress centering the wall, and I
laid the rifle there. On the far side of the bed was the place in the
hardwood where I'd hidden things as a child, a place I was certain
Maggie would remember. I opened it one last time, centered the
stack of hundreds in the hide, and pulled my cell phone from
my pocket to text her. There was no time to call, and her voice
would've broken me. Even thinking those things brought on a
heaviness that I could no longer carry. So I just texted her, turned
off the phone, put it in the hide next to the money, sealed the
floor, and left it all behind.

When I got back into the kitchen and could see through the
window, Rogers hadn't moved from that spot, and the bulls still
rushed around. He took a drag from the cigarette and flicked it

into the yard, blew a long line of smoke that thinned as it rose. Rogers seemed to stare at the window where I stood, but that blank expression never altered. He mustn't have been able to see me there, because if he had he would've known what was coming. I wouldn't break the windowsill. I wouldn't lift the glass. I'd shoot him right through the windowpane. None of them would expect a thing till it was done.

Braced against the windowsill, the muzzle of the barrel held steady as I drew a bead. My left hand sweated, clenching hard on the foregrip, and I pulled the rifle back into me so that the butt of the stock pressed tightly against my shoulder. The hammer was back and my aim was true and I slid my fingertip over the trigger. There was no countdown. No breathing. Only powder burning. Lead sent to air. Glass flew apart when the trigger broke and from the yard screams came loud over the Walkers' howls, but it wasn't Rogers screaming. Rogers just lifted his hands to the bottom of his breastbone where that bullet hit, and the blood seeped from under his fingers, all of that red staining the belly of his khaki shirt. His eyes were wide, and even from that distance, I could see the fear and pain settling into him. He looked down at the place that burned and then back to the window as he fell and slid down the tail of the Expedition. There was a calmness I'd never really felt until then that washed over me while I watched him, a calmness that Daddy had always carried, but that I had never known until right at that moment.

The bulls dropped and scurried behind the cars. Their rifles rested on hoods and roofs and anything they could use to steady themselves. They hollered to one another with words I couldn't understand through all of the ringing. One of them rushed out to get his arms under Rogers and drag him behind the cars. He must've asked for cover because right about then a round came from their side and blew away shards of glass that hung just over my head. Even through the ringing I heard the bullet whiz past like a pissed-off hornet, and I dropped down behind the cabinets and knelt there for a long time listening to them yell, listening to the Walkers bay.

A few more rounds came through the open window and hammered holes into the wall across from me. I could see Josephine's body in the hall from my position, and the way that she slept looked so peaceful that I thought for a second or two of joining her there. That type of peacefulness and stillness was all that mattered anymore.

I crawled over by the refrigerator and opened the cabinet where Daddy kept his liquor. There was a half-filled bottle of Evan Williams that seemed to suit me right then, so I popped the cork and put the bottle to my lips. My mouth was dry and that woody-tasting bourbon hit it just right, so I took another long slug until my thirst was gone and a woozy clarity flushed over me. I crept across the room, sliding my knees and hands and that rifle along the hardwood until I was in the living room and right beside the coffee table. That opened pack of Winstons looked good, so I shook one from the pack and lit it. I hadn't noticed my hands shaking until I held the cigarette between my fingers, but I was trembling. I set the pack of smokes back where Daddy had left them, squared it off between the record album and television remote just so.

The front door was still cracked open and outside the bulls were waiting. I stood from the floor with Daddy's rifle in my hands and opened the door a bit further till it was only the screen and the porch and the stairs and the yard and those dogs that separated us from one another. I was on the edge of that ravine now and peered around the corner to where the sun shined brightly onto cars, a fierce white light blinding all of the bulls who stood out there in wait. It was a light that no matter how hard they tried, they would never understand, and I felt sorry for them. There was such a sad, sad truth in how clueless they were to what shined down all around them. The gap between here and there didn't seem so barren any longer, didn't seem so far and out of reach. The space between here and there was no distance at all, and I readied myself to go where that Indian had never had the courage to go, the place Mama had peered off onto with a beckoning kind of sadness in her eyes. There was no fear or sorrow or repentance any longer, and I ventured out into that middle ground with a fearless pride that held my back arched and chest out. That restful time was near now, and I finally understood that there'd never been any difference between here or there. Only the middle ground of this wicked world mattered, the vast gap that stretched between, and those who were born with enough grit to brave it.

Acknowledgments

I would like to thank my agent, Julia Kenny, and editor, Sara Minnich, for their unwavering encouragement and editorial vision, as well as the entire team at G. P. Putnam's Sons. I would also like to thank two wonderful friends, Greg Hlavaty and Bessie Dietrich Goggins, for their support from the book's infancy.

Where All Light Tends to Go

DAVID JOY

Discussion Guide

BOOK
ENDS

PUTNAM

Discussion Guide

1. According to the author, David Joy, part of the inspiration for the novel was exploring the idea of manhood. He says: "All young men are faced with discerning what exactly it means to be a man, but, for many, what is illuminated, and even glorified, is volatile." Do you agree? What does manhood mean for Jacob McNeely? What about for his father?

2. Though the novel contains much darkness and violence, there are many scenes where humor and tenderness shine through. Which moments in the book did you find the funniest? The most poignant?

3. David Joy brings to the novel a strong sense of place. What role does the setting play in the story?

4. Consider the characters of Jacob's mother and father. What kind of legacy have they left for Jacob? Is either at all sympathetic?

5. Jacob and Maggie have conflicting ideas about the power of personal agency versus the inevitability of fate. Why are their viewpoints so different? Which perspective do you identify with more?

6. Once Maggie and Jacob rekindle their relationship, it takes quite some time for them to be comfortable with each other again and figure out how they want to move forward together. Why, despite all the years they'd known each other and been close, was this process so difficult? What conflicts got in the way?

7. As the violence continues to escalate, why does Jacob make the choices he does? Were there any alternatives he could have pursued?

8. Were you surprised by the ending? Why or why not?

9. In the book's last lines, it says that Jacob "finally understood that there'd never been any difference between here or

there. Only the middle ground of this wicked world mattered, the vast gap that stretched between, and those who were born with enough grit to brave it." What do you think this means?

10. What is the significance of the title?

11. The author describes the novel as "Appalachian noir." Does that description resonate with you? What elements does the book share with classic noir stories? Where does it diverge?

© Alan Rhew

DAVID JOY's stories and creative nonfiction have appeared in *Drafthorse, Smoky Mountain Living, Wilderness House Literary Review, Pisgah Review,* and *Flycatcher,* and he is the author of the memoir *Growing Gills: A Fly Fisherman's Journey.* He lives in Webster, North Carolina. *Where All Light Tends to Go* is his first novel.